"Nothing like a [...] in the middl[...]

As Caleb spoke over the sound of the smoke detector blaring, he looked at Maggie. His eyes were penetrating, piercing as though she were smoke he was trying to see through.

"So tell me, Marg—"

She put her fist to her mouth and coughed in a desperate and hackneyed effort to stop him from asking about her. If he started probing *Margaret's* life, she'd probably tell him the truth about herself.

"Are you okay?" His concern was real and she felt the bite of guilt she always experienced when a subject expressed concern over her faked moments of weakness.

This was no different. In fact, seeing the worry in his blue eyes was worse. *I gotta get out of this job,* she thought. *Caleb Gomez is going to be the last person I trick. The last person I lie to and hurt.*

Dear Reader,

I made a big realization while writing *Undercover Protector.* As a fan of the romance genre, I finally figured out that the stories are all about the hero. And I think I hit a jackpot with Caleb Gomez—part Dr. Gregory House (from the hit TV show *House*), part heart-of-gold hero. I fell in love with him when he came onto the page in *His Best Friend's Baby* and he just got better for me while writing this book.

The inspiration for Caleb's story came to me while watching coverage of the war in Iraq. I remember waiting, like the rest of the world, to hear word of hostages that have been taken during this struggle. No matter where you stand on this political issue, we are a world united in hoping and praying for the safe return of our men and women overseas.

I hope you enjoy reading Caleb's journey.

Molly O'Keefe

UNDERCOVER PROTECTOR
Molly O'Keefe

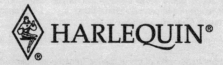

TORONTO • NEW YORK • LONDON
AMSTERDAM • PARIS • SYDNEY • HAMBURG
STOCKHOLM • ATHENS • TOKYO • MILAN • MADRID
PRAGUE • WARSAW • BUDAPEST • AUCKLAND

ISBN-13: 978-0-373-78177-5
ISBN-10:   0-373-78177-6

UNDERCOVER PROTECTOR

ABOUT THE AUTHOR

Molly O'Keefe has been enjoying her new quasi-hermit lifestyle as a mom and writer in Toronto, Canada. In an effort to make sure she isn't as much of a recluse as Caleb Gomez, she does force herself out of the home for lattes and scones. It's a rough life. She loves hearing from readers, so drop her a line at www.molly-okeefe.com.

Books by Molly O'Keefe

HARLEQUIN SUPERROMANCE
1365–FAMILY AT STAKE
1385–HIS BEST FRIEND'S BABY

HARLEQUIN FLIPSIDE
15–PENCIL HIM IN
37–DISHING IT OUT

HARLEQUIN DUETS
62–TOO MANY COOKS
95–COOKING UP TROUBLE
    KISS THE COOK

Don't miss any of our special offers. Write to us at the following address for information on our newest releases.

Harlequin Reader Service
U.S.: 3010 Walden Ave., P.O. Box 1325, Buffalo, NY 14269
Canadian: P.O. Box 609, Fort Erie, Ont. L2A 5X3

For Wanda Ottewell. I can't thank you enough for everything you've taught me.
You're amazing.

PROLOGUE

"JEFE!"

The door to Benny Delgado's office crashed open and ricocheted off the cheap wood paneling on the wall behind it.

Benny's semiautomatic was in his hand, safety off and aimed at the intruder's heart before the walls stopped trembling.

"Jesus," Benny sighed when he realized whom he nearly killed.

His younger brother, Miguel, stood in the doorway like a dog waiting to come in. "Sorry, *jefe,* but—"

"The door was shut, Miguel," Benny said, laying the gun back on the desk.

"I know, but you need—"

"The door was shut." He folded the *Los Angeles Times* crossword puzzle he'd been doing and arched an eyebrow at his little brother.

Miguel twitched and cracked the knuckles on

his right hand, clearly worked up about something, which was odd for Miguel. He was usually too high to get agitated about anything. But whatever was wrong, there was no reason to break the one damn rule Benny insisted on.

When the door was shut, Miguel was supposed to knock.

The rule was put into effect during a particularly nasty period when one of his soldiers was suspected of cooperating with federal agents.

Benny tried to protect his brother from the bloodier aspects of the business.

Finally, Miguel sighed heavily, stepped back and knocked on the open door. "There's something on the news you gotta see."

It was their mother's fault, Benny thought. She'd babied Miguel, allowed too many weaknesses to grow underneath the profile that was so much like her long-dead husband's.

Benny, she always said, looked like a mongrel. Bits and pieces of no one in particular—a fact that had never inspired much maternal devotion.

In the end he was better for it. Stronger than his beautiful brother.

"This better not be an excuse to get the Lakers' score on my TV." Benny reached over to the remote control at his elbow and turned on the giant flat-screen monitor on the other side of the room.

"It's not." Miguel came to stand beside Benny's desk.

"What are you doing watching the news, anyway?" Benny asked, looking at his brother from the corner of his eye. Miguel wore the white tank top and oversize khaki work pants that were the uniform for Chicano street thugs in Los Angeles.

Benny had stopped dressing the part of a petty criminal years ago; looking like a thug raised too many red flags for the cops. And once he stopped being a petty criminal, he could no longer afford the attention.

"Lita was watching it. Turn up the volume, *jefe.* Jesus, you got enough stereo equipment to blow the roof off." Miguel pointed to the flat-screen TV and high-tech stereo equipment that stood out like a shiny technological thumb in the dumpy room. "You could at least listen to it."

Benny could afford better than this crappy house—with its water-stained ceilings and fraying carpet—in Long Beach where his mother grew up, but he liked it here. He had grown up here, was safe here.

"Channel twenty-four," Miguel said. He crossed his arms over his chest and tucked his hands into his armpits. "They been talkin' about it every fifteen minutes."

Benny changed the channel and turned up the volume so he could hear the special report, wondering what *it* was that inspired Miguel to watch the news.

"—the American journalist who was held hostage in Baghdad then rescued in a daring prison break that cost the lives of three American soldiers, is being released from the hospital today," the blond anchorwoman with the great tits said. "Caleb Gomez—"

A photo of a good-looking man with dark skin and blue eyes flashed on the screen and Benny's body went cold.

"See? Isn't that—?"

Benny held up his hand and his brother quieted. Transfixed by the image of the Hispanic man on the screen, Benny stood and walked around his desk.

"Gomez was in a coma for three months following his rescue from the Iraqi prison," the blonde said as pictures of a single-story building the color of sand and surrounded by Iraqi soldiers replaced those of the handsome man. "The tape of his captors holding a knife to his neck demanding the withdrawal of U.S. troops from Iraq circulated the world last spring—"

The picture of the prison was replaced by a far more grainy shot of a soldier holding a long knife to the throat of a bearded, blindfolded man.

Benny had seen the picture a million times, just like the rest of the world. But now, even without seeing the man's eyes, the prisoner seemed familiar. The way he sat, so proud, his lips twisted in what Benny knew was anger. It was so like the man he had befriended a little more than three years ago. The man who, shortly thereafter, had disappeared off the face of the earth.

"Gomez was kidnapped by Iraqi soldiers while covering the war for the *Los Angeles Times*—"

"Benny? That's him…that's Ruben, isn't it?" Miguel asked. "He's been in Iraq? What's this mean?"

Journalist? Benny's brain screamed. *He's a freaking journalist?* All of those conversations. The things Benny had told Ruben, believing he had finally found a thinking man amongst all of the thugs and butchers of his world. The man Benny had trusted with secrets was a *journalist?*

When Ruben had disappeared, Benny had thought for a while that Ruben had been an undercover cop. Or a Fed. But when no harassment or raids had followed he figured him for one of those nameless dead spics found in the mountains.

He'd been wrong.

His hands spasmed into fists, the edges of the remote cut into his palm.

"Gomez won a Pulitzer four years ago for his exposé of the meat-packing industry," the blonde continued. "Many experts say his work from Iraq would have garnered him another award. Gomez was released from the naval hospital in San Diego today. He plans to recover in privacy in New York City."

Benny's brain went cold then hot.

Everything was at stake. All he'd done. It could all be taken away from him if that journalist opened his mouth.

"That's Ruben, isn't it?" Miguel asked. "That journalist. Did you know he was a reporter?"

Benny shook his head. Rage caught fire in his gut—blind and hot and merciless. His chest heaved and he fisted his hands in his hair. He paced between the couch and his desk. He'd been fooled. Him. Benny Delgado.

Benny knew this journalist—this Caleb Gomez—as Ruben Villalobos. Three years ago his sister, Lita, had started bringing her latest boyfriend, Ruben, around the house. Benny had liked Ruben. Respected him. He'd tried to recruit him, but Ruben had resisted and Benny kind of respected that. They'd smoked joints in the backyard and talked about their dead mothers.

"Damn it!" he screamed and shoved over one of the folding chairs in front of his desk. He picked up the other one and hurled it across the room at the TV screen.

Sparks crackled in the dead air.

Gomez knew things about him. Things he had been keeping secret. Things that kept him safe. If that *hibrido* were to write a story about him now…

"The news said he'd be in New York City." Miguel stepped forward and Benny started shaking his head, knowing by the wild hot look in his brother's eyes what he wanted.

"No, Miguel." Benny put up his hand, stopping Miguel's advance.

"Why not?" Miguel asked. "You need to send someone, why can't I go?"

"You want to go do what has to be done?" Benny asked, anger churning hard through his body. "You want to be the man to slit that reporter's throat?"

Miguel's chin went up. "Yes, *jefe*."

Benny looked at his brother and saw only the mistakes. The drug use. The gambling. The soft heart and softer head.

"No way."

"Benny, this guy could screw up the meeting with that ambassador. That Reyes guy. I know—"

Benny worked hard to control his expression, to smother the surprise and outrage. Everyone in his organization knew they were not supposed to tell Miguel these things. Miguel ran some drugs. Kept track of some books. He was not supposed to know about Reyes or the meeting.

"You don't know anything." Benny shook his head.

"I'm your brother, but you don't trust me." Miguel's dark eyes turned liquid, a trick that used to work on Benny the way it worked on their mother.

Not with this. Not ever with this.

"You're my brother," he said instead, clapping a hand on Miguel's neck and squeezing. "I can't risk you. The cops. The Feds. You get caught and it's me who goes to jail."

"Sooner or later, brother, you are going to have to treat me like a man," Miguel said, shrugging away from Benny's hand, like a sullen teenager rather than the man he wanted to be.

Not until you act like one.

"You are a man," he pacified his brother. "But you are my brother first."

"What are you going to do?" Miguel asked. "What if this guy talks? What if—"

"I can fix this," Benny said. The way he fixed that female witness and the cop six months ago.

He had to deal with Ruben— He shook his head. There was no Ruben, never had been. There was only a reporter named Caleb Gomez who had to die, fast, before he had a chance to open his mouth. Before the meeting with Reyes in a month.

First Benny would have a little talk with his sister and then he would send some men to New York.

CHAPTER ONE

"THANKS, GORDON." Maggie Fitzgerald took the cup of coffee from her favorite techie's hand and weighed the pleasure against the pain of taking a sip.

Her doctor said she should cut back on the caffeine if she ever wanted to get rid of her ulcers. But the smell of coffee—even the crappy stuff from the bakery on the corner—was too much to resist. She tore open the small square on the plastic lid and took a sip.

She was so used to her ulcers at this stage, what would be the point of getting rid of them?

Gordon collapsed into the stiff reception chair beside hers and stared at Deputy Walters' closed office door.

"So." Gordon yawned but talked through it. "Why do you suppose we got the royal summons at 6 a.m. on a Saturday?"

"Your guess is as good as mine," Maggie said, watching the steam escape from the coffee cup.

"You're lying." Gordon gestured with his cup and coffee sloshed over onto his brown corduroy pants. "You are totally lying."

Gordon was the best surveillance tech she'd ever worked with and he was—in certain lighting and on special occasions—vaguely loveable. But not so much this early on a Saturday morning.

"What makes you say that?" She took another sip of sugary coffee. She *was* lying. She did have an idea why they were here. But she wasn't about to share that with Gordon.

"'Cause you always know more than you let on." Gordon shrugged and slumped deeper into his chair. "When you're not around the guys in bank robbery call you the freaking Cheshire Cat."

"I think I'll take that as a compliment." It was, after all, better than some of the things she'd been called since entering the hallowed halls of Quantico four years ago.

"You think it's got anything to do with your brother?" Gordon asked.

"No." Her voice was cold, her heart colder. "I don't think it has anything to do with my brother."

"But with Delgado—"

"I don't think it has anything to do with Patrick." She looked at Gordon, feeling the bite of anger and grief that she'd been fighting since the accident six months ago.

She was getting better. Most of the time those emotions only surfaced at night—in disjointed dreams of her brother lost and cold someplace and her unable to find him. But sometimes she was ambushed by her feelings, caught unawares by the terrible reality that Patrick was dead. Gone.

Murdered.

"Okay." Gordon raised his hands in truce. "But I think you're wrong."

Maggie didn't say anything and they drank in stiff, uncomfortable silence.

"Whatever it is I hope I'm being reassigned to the Delgado task force. I've had it about up to here—" he held his hand about a foot over his head "—with bank robberies and celebrity stalkings."

Maggie smiled. They were in L.A., after all. Celebrity stalking, bank robberies and gangs composed about seventy-five percent of the workload.

"How is it over at gang violence?" Gordon asked. "Better?"

"I wouldn't say better. I'd just say less mundane."

He nodded his head. "I like less mundane. But since your brother got killed and that witness—"

"Gordon," she said through tight lips, "shut up."

"Right. Shutting up."

She had the sinking fear that Gordon was right. She was here because of her brother. Maybe she would be removed from the Delgado case because of the media coverage surrounding Patrick's death.

Nothing like a few headlines shouting *Dirty Cop* or, worse, *Dead Cop Linked to Drug Lord* to sully a whole family's name. No matter if they were true or not.

"Hey, did you see the Lakers game yesterday? I swear I keep betting on the wrong team—"

Luckily, Gordon's small talk was cut short by the sudden opening of Deputy Walters' door.

Curtis Johnson, the agent in charge of the Delgado task force and the closest thing she had to a mentor in the Bureau, stood in the doorway like a huge black shadow in an ill-fitting suit.

"Come on in," he said in his deep baritone that sounded like the voice of God in the cartoons Maggie had watched as a kid. Gordon leaped up and Curtis stepped out of the way as Gordon walked past him. Maggie took her time, trying to catch Curtis's eye before going in those doors, but she couldn't discern anything from his locked-down expression.

Her ulcers didn't like this one bit.

"Relax," Curtis whispered as she walked by.

"Easier said than done," she whispered back.

Curtis chuckled and followed her into Deputy Walters's inner sanctum.

Maggie took a deep breath and pulled the loose collar away from her throat. The oak paneling and oil paintings seemed to close in on her with every breath. Her father had this dream of her being the first female assistant deputy director of the West Coast Bureau, but if that meant working in this ever-shrinking room every day, dear old Dad could forget it.

Deputy Walters was a small man who looked far younger than his years and much too young to be the assistant deputy director in charge. He was dwarfed by the large oak desk he sat behind, which Gordon loved to make penis compensation jokes about. But there was no joking about this meeting.

Walters had held his position for five years and in the year since the Bureau had put Delgado on the Ten Most Wanted list, Walters had already gone through two agents in charge. Flores and Smyth hadn't managed to bring down Delgado and were now fielding bomb threats and UFO sightings at their desks.

Curtis had been put in charge a month ago and she'd been angling to get on his team from the start. Two weeks ago, he'd brought her on board. And so far she'd turned up nothing. Trying to get information on Delgado was like running into a brick wall headfirst. No one in the neighborhoods would talk. No one in jail would talk. They'd offered one convict reduced jail time on a twenty-five year sentence and the guy wouldn't budge.

I'll take the time, he'd said. *Better alive in jail than dead on the street.*

They had thrown in relocation and protection to sweeten the deal, but he'd only scoffed. *You can't take me where Delgado won't find me.*

Delgado ruled his syndicate with fear and brutal violence. Anyone even suspected of talking to the Feds was killed, their families were killed, their dogs were killed.

So far it had been a pretty effective deterrent.

"Have a seat," Walters said with a smile that was about as warm as an ice bath. She and Gordon sat in the chairs across from him and Curtis stood to the right of the phallic desk.

"What's going on?" Gordon asked, his eyes darting between Walters and Curtis.

"Delgado is on the move," Curtis replied.

He turned and hit a button on his remote and the screen on the right wall was illuminated with the face of the handsome Hispanic man who'd been all over the newspapers and television in the past few days.

"Caleb Gomez was released from the naval hospital in San Diego four days ago," Curtis said and Maggie sat back, wondering what a Pulitzer-prize winning hostage survivor had to do with one of the most brutal gang lords in Los Angeles. "According to his press release, he is planning to spend time recuperating in New York City."

Curtis clicked the remote and a bad surveillance photo of Gomez dressed out like an East L.A. native standing in front of a taco stand with Delgado filled the screen.

"What's Delgado doing with a journalist?" Gordon voiced Maggie's thoughts. "That's like suicide for Delgado."

"Or the journalist," Maggie added.

"That's what we're wondering, too," Curtis said and jerked his thumb toward the screen. "This photo was taken three and a half years ago. According to Gomez's editor at the *Los Angeles Times,* that's about when Gomez stopped taking assignments and was working on what he called his 'next Pulitzer.' The *Times* had commissioned Gomez's mystery story to run in the fall of 2003, but when Iraq really started heating up, Gomez requested to be embedded with the troops near

Baghdad. He spent the better part of two and a half years over there before the kidnapping." He shrugged, a nervous tick he had, as though he was uncomfortable in his skin and constantly wanted out. "The details of what happened to him there will be in your files."

Maggie swallowed. The whole world knew many of those details—he'd been brutalized over there. Beaten. Tortured. For three days.

But their files would hold classified—and much more grisly—information, thanks to the military and medical personnel who had assisted in Gomez's escape and recovery.

Her stomach turned.

Professional detachment could only take you so far in the face of the evil man could do.

"You think he infiltrated the Delgado gang?" she asked, shoving thoughts of torture aside. "You think that was his mystery story?"

"Three years ago, Delgado was just entering our radar. It was before he murdered Hernandez and took over his syndicate in East L.A." Curtis shrugged a massive shoulder and clicked ahead to the next photo. A closer image of Gomez and Delgado in front of the taco stand. Delgado was clearly smiling at something Gomez was saying. "Delgado was far more accessible then. He was just a soldier in the Hernandez syndicate. If a good journalist was going to get in on the ground floor, that would have been the time to do it."

"Good and crazy," Gordon muttered and Maggie had to agree, but things still didn't add up.

"That's a huge conclusion to jump to," Maggie said. "Maybe they just happened to be in line together at a taco stand."

"Well." Curtis grinned like the Cheshire Cat her colleagues claimed she was and clicked onto the next image—mug shots of two of Delgado's top men. "Hernando and Boyer were spotted in New York City yesterday outside of the apartment Gomez used to rent."

All the short hairs on Maggie's neck stood straight up.

This smelled like a break in the case.

She could see Gordon beside her, grinning in the half dark. "Delgado must think Gomez knows something or why would he send his two best thugs all the way to New York?" Gordon asked.

Curtis nodded.

"So where is Gomez?" Maggie asked. If he was in that apartment, he was as good as dead; however, a certain gleam in Curtis's eyes indicated that wasn't the case.

"Summerland, California." Curtis turned and

smiled at her while he advanced onto a photo of a stucco house behind high hedges. "He's renting a house in the foothills."

Curtis set down the remote and turned on the light behind him. Maggie could feel the electric hum of excitement radiating off him. It filled the air and she breathed it in with relish.

This was a gift. A break. A possible crack in an uncrackable case.

Now, if only it didn't require her to go under-cover again, then things would really be looking up. But she didn't get called into this kind of briefing to do surveillance or research.

She was undercover. And she was supposed to love it.

He lifted the three files from the corner of Walters's desk and handed two of them to Gordon and Maggie. The third he handed to Walters.

"What's our angle?" she asked.

"Well, Delgado is going to find out he's got his two dogs standing outside an empty apartment in New York City and start looking elsewhere." He arched an eye-brow. "And we know it won't take Delgado long to find him."

"So Gomez as bait? We just wait for Delgado to find him? Send some guys to kill him and hope we can implicate Delgado?" She hated even saying the word *bait*. Putting an innocent man in grave danger was an ugly way to break a case. And the odds of its success weren't high. Delgado's men wouldn't roll on Delgado.

"That's one option." Curtis nodded.

"What's the other?" Gordon asked.

"We find out what Delgado is clearly ready to kill Gomez to keep hidden."

"Does that mean going undercover?" Gordon grinned like a kid being taken to Walt Disney World.

Maggie felt an inevitable tide at work here and she tried not to fight it. Tried to get excited about her role, her job. She looked down at her hands.

One more time, she told herself. *For your brother. You can go undercover one more time.*

For Patrick she would do anything.

She would sell off a little bit more of her soul.

"That's the plan. Gomez has called a house-cleaning service and is interviewing candidates today. We're sending in two decoys and then we're sending in Fitzgerald." Curtis tapped her folder.

"Why two decoys?" Gordon asked.

"To make Fitzgerald irresistible."

"Thanks a lot," Maggie groused.

"In any case, you get in and during the inter-view, you plant three surveillance bugs. Hopefully you also get the job, allowing us broader access to Gomez."

She nodded and bit her lip against a satisfied smile. Finally, finally she was getting close to nailing the man responsible for her brother's death.

"Sounds good."

Walters leaned back and ran his hands over his thick brown hair and laughed, though the sound was not funny. Maggie's satisfaction dimmed and Gordon's smug smile fled.

Walters was going to give them a reality check.

"Before you kids start thinking you've cracked this case, let's look at what you are up against." He took a deep breath through his nose and it seemed to Maggie that he sucked all the air out of the room.

"Three years ago," Walters continued, "in the span of a week, Delgado takes down every drug dealer, racketeer, arms dealer and money launderer in Los Angeles who poses any kind of threat to him. He murders Hernandez and takes over his syndicate, has every Latin King from here to San Diego bowing to him."

He paused as if waiting for confirmation and Maggie, Gordon and Curtis all nodded.

"And now, thanks to this journalist, we've got two options. One, baiting a trap with Caleb Gomez in the hopes of maybe, possibly catching Delgado.

Or two, finding out what information Gomez has that Delgado is ready to kill for then somehow using it to bring him down."

"That sounds about right," Curtis said. "It's the biggest break we've had in the case in a year."

"What do we know about Gomez?" Walters asked and Maggie could have sworn Curtis got red under the collar.

"Not much," he admitted. "He was brought in for questioning regarding a burglary ring about six years ago. He'd gotten some information from one of the men for a story he was doing on the federal penitentiary system. When the Bureau tried to subpoena him, he raised such a stink he was labeled uncooperative and that the whole thing was dropped."

That's not good, Maggie thought.

"What kind of stink?" Gordon asked.

"Op-ed pieces in every major U.S. paper regarding the FBI and the swiftly diminishing civil rights of Americans." Curtis cleared his throat. "It wasn't good."

"That's our guy?" Gordon asked, almost laughing. "He's going to love us going undercover in his house."

"Well, that's why I brought in Fitzgerald." Curtis nodded, though the director seemed very unconvinced. "She's good."

"She better be or he'll be dead and we'll be no closer to catching Delgado."

"Yes, sir," Curtis said and Maggie and Gordon stood.

"You have one week," Walters said, "to turn up anything that proves this isn't a wild-goose chase and then I'm pulling the undercover operation. After that, we'll plant some protection outside his house."

"We've tried that, sir, and it doesn't work. Six months ago the female witness was killed in the safe house with two armed guards right outside her door," Curtis said. "The assailants had killed one guard and disabled the other and slit the witness's throat. The Bureau, the LAPD and ATF had huge mud on their faces for that one. We ended up with more bodies and no evidence. There's every likelihood that the Gomez case would end the same way."

"Or not. Either way you've got the Bureau out on a limb going into this guy's house. He's a public figure right now, a public figure with no respect for the necessary investigative measures the Bureau takes. This has the potential to go bad in a big way. You got me?"

"Yes, sir," they said in unison.

Before she turned toward the door, Walters's brown eyes bored into hers and she felt like a bug under glass, skewered and exposed. "Fitzgerald?"

"Yes, sir."

"Your brother was the cop—"

"Yes, sir." Maggie interrupted before he could finish. As always it was on the tip of her tongue to explain Patrick had been set up, but she'd screamed her throat raw trying to get people to believe that without proof.

Walters studied her and she did not flinch. Did not blink. He could look for any sign that she was as flawed and corrupt as everyone thought her brother was. He could look for any weakness, any soft spot that might be used against her or the Bureau.

He wouldn't find them.

Walters smiled again and a chill danced down Maggie's spine.

"What year did you graduate?"

"99-92," she said giving the year of her graduation and the class number.

"She was top of her class in investigation and fitness," Curtis said, leaping to her defense. She gave him a quick half smile of appreciation.

"You were a part of the hydroponics farm drug sting last year," Walters asked.

She nodded again.

"Well, Fitzgerald. Let's hope you can do the job."

"Yes, sir." She nodded.

There wasn't a doubt in her mind that she could do this job. Even in one week, she could do this job.

FOUR HOURS LATER Maggie, Gordon and Curtis were in place, the three of them and thousands of dollars of surveillance equipment wedged into a white utility van parked at the bottom of Gomez's street.

"You all right?" Curtis's hand on Maggie's shoulder felt like a ton of bricks, a million pounds of expectation.

"I'm good," Maggie answered. "Ready."

She had been ready for this moment for six months. Since the very moment she and her family found out Patrick had been killed—exactly two weeks before he was supposed to give testimony against Delgado.

That moment had created this moment, which she knew would create the moment Delgado either rotted away behind bars or was given the lethal injection.

These were the only possible outcomes.

She took a deep breath of the humid air in the van and held out her hand. Curtis dropped the three surveillance bugs in her palm and she slipped them into the special pocket in her khaki pants.

"How come no one asks me if I'm all right?" Gordon whined from his station in front of the monitors; his brown hair glowed red from them. "Maybe I'm a little nervous. I'm sweating my ass off and I'm starving—"

"Shut up, Gordon," Maggie said out of habit more than anything.

Curtis leaned close, his broad sweaty face illuminated by the red and green monitors. "This guy is smart, Maggie."

"I know." According to the file, Gomez had spent more time undercover than she had. His investigative journalism had taken him to some pretty scary places and the man always got out alive and with the story.

"And tough," Curtis added.

"No kidding." Gordon whistled through his teeth. "He wouldn't even tell the Iraqis his name until they broke his arm in four places."

Maggie swallowed and looked down at her clenched hands. *He wouldn't even tell the Iraqis his name.* She could hardly fathom that kind of pain. Or that kind of strength.

"Don't for a minute underestimate Caleb Gomez or let your guard down."

"I got it, Curtis." She tried to keep her frustration to a minimum. "Let me do my job."

She was good undercover. She had the ability to turn her real self off. Maggie Fitzgerald disappeared and instead she became an instrument, a camera. Something sharp and smart that collected all information and stayed solidly in character. It made her a highly sought after undercover agent.

She was good. Now it was time for her to be the best.

Caleb Gomez was not going to be a problem.

"Hey." Her boss grabbed her hand where it rested on the back door of the Municipal Utilities van she had spent way too much time in already. "I don't need to tell you what's at stake here—"

"Curtis, I was at the briefing. Benny Delgado is after Gomez—"

"No," Gordon interrupted. "He means what's at stake for us."

The two men stared at her and she tried not to roll her eyes. These two could be so damn dramatic sometimes.

"We blow this and we're back at robberies or celebrity stalkings," Curtis said.

"And I can't afford the pay cut," Gordon added. "Daddy just bought a new car."

These guys didn't know the half of it. Failing to bring Delgado down would result in things far more devastating than losing this plum assignment.

"So, go in there and—" Curtis started to say.

"Be nice?" She tried to joke around, to lighten the heavy air in the van.

"Well, that's a bit of a stretch." Curtis grinned and Maggie didn't take offense. She often wasn't nice—it wasn't part of the job.

"He was going to say shake your ass. Gomez has got to be lonely—"

"Shut *up*, Gordon." Curtis yelled over his shoulder. "I was going to say just try and get the job."

Maggie nodded, opened the door and blinked in the bright California sunshine.

She stepped down from the van and the door slammed shut behind her, somehow putting a special emphasis on how alone she was at the moment. Those guys in the van weren't going to have to look Gomez in the eye and lie to him. This case hinged on her performance.

Fine by me, she thought. She did her best work alone. Always had. Always would.

She crossed the narrow residential street to the small hatchback that was her car or rather, Margaret Warren's car.

Margaret Warren, a single mom who wanted nothing more than to raise her son away from the crime and congestion of Los Angeles.

Margaret Warren who had recently moved to

Summerland and signed up with a local house-keeping service.

Margaret Warren who knew nothing about the seedy underbelly of the largest Los Angeles crime syndicate other than what she saw on the ten o'clock news.

And she had no idea that Caleb Gomez was the key to bringing it down. That was the bait in a complicated mousetrap.

That's all. Margaret Warren, housekeeper.

Maggie checked the camera/microphone hidden in a tiny gold and rhinestone angel pin on her collar.

A housekeeper with a superstitious belief in guardian angels.

"You boys there?" she asked.

"Loud and clear." Curtis's voice was in her right ear thanks to an imperceptible receiver. The guys in the van would be able to hear everything she said and still give her instruction. She could do without the voices in her head, but Curtis was good and tweaked about this case, so she made the compromise. For today. If she got the job, there would be no camera and definitely no receiver. She couldn't work this way.

"All right, just try and keep it down," she told them.

Maggie drove up the hill toward Gomez's house. He was nestled in the foothills, away from the more popular properties closer to the beach.

I bet he's got a great view, she thought. She was able to catch glimpses of the wide blue ocean on her left between the flowering mountain laurel. On her right, wild sage and yellow wildflowers crawled up the mountain. She thought for a brief moment of her apartment and her view of Mr. Sayer's garbage can.

The views of the middle of nowhere sure beat the views of city living.

The road ended in a cul-de-sac and Maggie pulled into the only driveway, between two large jasmine bushes that provided nearly impenetrable privacy.

His house was a one-story ranch with a typical stucco exterior. She faced a garage and a nondescript back door. There were no windows on this side of the house. Just cracked white stucco and red bougainvillea growing wild.

The lawn, what there was of it, was neglected and turning brown in the heat.

Reports indicated Gomez had a dog. A big one. The last agent who supplied surveillance information said the dog was a "freaking monster."

Maggie looked around for the freaking monster but there was no sign. Hopefully, Gomez had the good sense to lock him up for their interview.

"What's the holdup, Fitzgerald?" Curtis asked.

"Looking for that dog."

"Forget the dog and let's get the show on the road. Your appointment was for one, it's now five after."

Maggie rolled her eyes and got out of the car.

She took a deep breath, adjusted the pin on her lapel and rang the doorbell. From inside the house she heard the deep bellowing of a dog.

She could also hear a distinct slide and thump sound that got louder as it got closer to the door.

She closed her eyes and sent a quick promise heavenward.

I swear, Patrick, I'll make good on everything that was done to you.

Maggie wasn't sure how to react when Gomez opened the door. Margaret Warren would have no idea that the man whose house she had been sent to by the agency had been disfigured in a fire.

Maggie Fitzgerald, of course, had seen the Army medical reports.

The door swung open before she had a chance to decide her course of action.

"Margaret Warren?" A man, a big man wearing blue jeans and boots, stood in the shadows. She couldn't even see the top half of his body thanks to the dark hallway and the very bright glare from the bay of windows twenty yards behind him.

"Oh, for crying out loud," Gordon said in her ear. "We need a better picture than that."

She blinked and shielded her eyes. "Yes, I'm—"

"Late." Gomez took an awkward step back with the help of his metal cane and waited. Perhaps it was because she couldn't see his face, but there was something about Gomez, an energy—her sister would call it an aura. Whatever it was it knocked her off her stride and she hesitated at the doorway.

"You can come in," he finally said, his deep voice laced with humor. "I only eat people who are early."

She smiled and stepped into the tiled foyer. The foyer was shadowed but the great room and the kitchen—visible from where she stood—were bathed in light from the floor-to-ceiling windows that faced the ocean.

"Mr. Estrada—" She called him by the name he'd registered with the agency. It was a fake and a bad one at that, but she could hardly tell him that.

"I'm telling you the guy is nuts. Who uses a fake name like Estrada?" Gordon said in her ear.

"Shut up, Gordon," Curtis said.

Maggie bit back a smile.

Gomez laughed, apparently very entertained with his little inside alias joke. "You can call me Caleb. Caleb Gomez."

So far so good, she thought. "It's a lovely house." She turned as if admiring the view and used the chance to case the place.

Phones. Two units. One in the kitchen beside the refrigerator. Another cordless beside the couch, facing the windows. The hallway, directly across from her and through the great room, led to three shut doors. Office, bedroom, bath was her guess.

"It's a pigsty," Gomez said and lurched away, leading her into the great room. "I wish I could claim all this mess as my own, but I rented the house unseen and the landlord didn't clean after the last tenants. I'd wondered why it was so cheap."

You're a housekeeper, she reminded herself. *Act like one.*

"I've seen worse," she said. Not really. There was some clutter—newspapers covered the sofa, a moat of coffee mugs surrounded the overstuffed chair. But dust bunnies so big her mom could use them to knit scarves floated across the filthy floor like strange tumbleweeds.

The windows were cloudy with grime and the air in the house seemed stale and musty and smelled a little like tomato sauce and dirty socks.

"You're going to have your work cut out for you cleaning that dump," Curtis said and she almost smiled. She'd done worse for her job. She didn't even want to think of those long days on that hydroponics farm.

She followed Gomez and his lurching slide-and-thump gait. From the back, his injuries didn't seem to diminish him other than the limp. He was tall and still broad, though he held his shoulder at an awkward angle. Long black hair brushed the collar of his blue T-shirt, which hugged the wide muscles of his shoulders and back.

The reports of his injuries must have been exaggerated, she realized. He didn't look like a man who had been standing at death's door a few months ago.

And he definitely didn't look like any journalist she had ever met.

He looked like a man more used to activity than sitting behind a computer. He had a magnetic force about him that she couldn't imagine allowed him to be a quiet observer.

He poked at the dust bunnies that congregated around the foot of the brown twill sofa. "I've never had a housekeeper before. I'm afraid I'm not too aware of the protocol," he said and turned to face her.

She had read the reports. She knew about the burns—the torture and the broken shoulder and arm. She had seen the grainy surveillance photos. But nothing could have prepared her for the reality.

The bright sunlight was unforgiving and the red and white scar tissue on the left side of Caleb Gomez's neck stood in violent relief. The skin was taut and shiny. His arm—the one held at an angle—was covered in similar scar tissue and his hand curled into a fist that looked unusable.

She was used to seeing injuries—had treated and caused her fair share in the field—so it was not the scars that made her feel as though she'd been punched in the stomach.

It was his eyes, as blue as the sky behind him, untouched by the fire and horrors of captivity, that made the impact. They were the most beautiful eyes she'd ever seen and they absolutely dared her to pity him.

For a moment she couldn't tolerate what she intended to do to this man. She was breathless, her stomach in knots and she knew without a doubt that he would be trouble for her.

"Holy shit," Gordon breathed in her ear.

CHAPTER TWO

FIRST TEST, Caleb thought. If she doesn't stammer or stare or run screaming, then they could commence with the interview. However, if she was going to cross herself and get all teary, the way the last woman he interviewed for the housekeeper job had, Margaret Warren could go. And quickly.

He found that his new body, as painful and ugly as it might be, was the great personality barometer. People took one look at him and their reactions told him all he needed to know about their inner workings. Their base-line take on the world.

Granted, his present appearance was more extreme than usual. Most of the time he didn't use the cane and his arm was far more mobile than people assumed. But some days his physical therapist was a sadist and Caleb felt freshly tortured all over again. Today was one of those days.

Caleb used to pride himself on his spot-on first

impressions. His editors had claimed he had the best gut in the business. But, man, this banged-up body was even better.

Survive some time in an Iraqi prison and *a helicopter crash and this is what you get.* A foolproof lie detector.

Margaret Warren took her time. She didn't look away immediately, the way a lot of women did, throwing their attention to other places and yammering on about the weather.

Her eyes widened and her lips parted, which, frankly, he liked. They were pretty amazing lips.

He read a tangle of emotions on her plain face and thus began test number two.

If she was going to pity him as the guy he first interviewed for the position had, he'd boot her out himself, bad leg or no.

He would even let his dog out of the office to chase her down the driveway.

Well, not really. But he liked to think he was that kind of badass.

She blinked and all that stunned awareness vanished and instead of pity there was…nothing. Inwardly, he had to applaud. She was good. Politicians could learn something from her rock-solid composure.

"Perhaps you should tell me what the job will

entail?" Her raspy voice went through him like good whiskey.

And that, it seemed, concluded Margaret Warren's reaction to the relative monster he had become.

Great. If she wants to pretend there's nothing strange about me, I'm all for it.

"Right." He turned and lurched farther into the living room. "As you can see I am not much for housework."

"Clearly," he thought he heard her say, but by the time he got his head turned, her face had the same slightly interested but completely removed expression.

Those lips, though. They didn't seem to belong on that plain face. The upper lip was fuller than the bottom and, while she did not appear to wear makeup, her lips were the color of the bougainvillea creeping over his window.

"I don't really like to cook, either," he said, too fast thanks to his juvenile reaction to Ms. Warren's lips.

"The agency said nothing about cooking."

"Yeah, well, I tricked you. Can you cook?"

"Sure." She continued to look around his house, no doubt cataloging the months' worth of neglect.

"Would you be interested in doing it for me?"

Good grief, the woman was worse than Colin Powell, with all the stone-facing.

"For a price."

"A girl after my own heart," he said, hoping those lips would curl into a smile, but no.

"Perhaps a tour?" she asked, all business.

Stop trying to flirt, Gomez. You're embarrassing yourself.

"Absolutely." He gestured at the cluttered room. "This is the ocean room. This is where I look at the ocean and read the paper."

He pointed over her shoulder at the kitchen. "That's where I don't cook."

She turned and walked into the kitchen and, because he was sore from the physical therapy and using a cane, it took him a moment to get all of his appendages to agree to follow her. "You'll notice the museum of pizza boxes, probably the largest in California. Again, they are not all mine, but I've added to the collection. Perhaps in—" He rounded the corner just as Margaret was hanging up his phone.

Irritation and suspicion leaped in him.

"What the hell are you doing?" he asked.

"Your phone is dirty." Margaret scraped pizza sauce off the receiver.

He told himself to calm down. He was no

longer a reporter, looking for the hidden agenda in every person he met. And, should things go well with Ms. Warren of the fantastic mouth and careful expression, he would no longer be a complete hermit.

He needed to get used to people again—or at least people who weren't inflicting pain on his person in the name of healing.

Worse, he was going to have to get used to help.

"Well, it gets worse." He smiled.

Margaret's lips twitched and he relaxed.

Score one smile for the horny hermit.

He retraced their steps through his living room, kicking aside papers and books.

"Back here is the bedroom, which is probably the cleanest room in the place." He opened the door and she ducked around him to enter the nearly empty dark room.

His clothes sat in stacks along the wall. Pulling open dresser drawers was more than he could be bothered with, thanks to his bad hand. His therapist had told him using the drawers would be good for him, but frankly being a slob made his life easier. His nicer stuff—suits and a tux he would probably never wear again—hung in the closet.

The bed, of course, was unmade. His brown comforter was tangled, the pillows were on the floor and the sheets pushed down to the bottom of the mattress. It appeared to be the site of rather athletic sex.

If only that were true.

Ah, sex. I think I heard of it once. If it weren't so damn depressing, he'd laugh.

He hobbled over to the window to drag open the drapes, illuminating the dust motes in the air.

He turned as Margaret lifted her hand from his bedside table and rubbed her fingers together.

Again he felt that spike of irritation. He wasn't good at sharing his space or having strangers touching his things. Made him antsy.

But considering it was going to be her job, he couldn't tell her not to touch his stuff. He chuckled at his own absurdity.

Clean, but please don't touch anything.

"I don't suspect the bathroom is going—" she started to say.

"It's a biohazard. You'll probably need a special suit or something."

She smiled again, a Mona Lisa curl to her lips that had devastating effects on his hermit-lifestyle suppressed libido. She really was lovely. Perhaps her features were plain, but her skin seemed to glow.

"Are you Irish?" he blurted. *Nice. Really, so suave. It's a wonder you ever got laid.*

"No," she answered and her attention drifted to the bedside table that showed that one finger swipe through the dust.

"Let's go into the other room and discuss specifics," he said and walked by her, close enough that he caught the soap-and-sunshine scent of her.

He heard her follow him into the hallway and then pause.

"What's in here?" she asked and he turned just as she pushed open the door to his office. Inside, Bear, his dog, went berserk and Caleb reached out and slammed the door shut again.

"You don't need to worry about that room," he said. "I don't want it cleaned."

"But it looks—"

"It doesn't get cleaned!" he said with more volume than was necessary with the reticent Margaret Warren. Her lips tightened and she nodded and Caleb felt like a fool.

He'd lost his touch, not just with pretty shy women who once fell to his bidding like ducks in a shooting gallery, but with other people, too. With everyone.

"Sorry," he muttered. "I just—"

"You don't have to explain," she said. "I won't clean that room."

He nodded, relieved and a little surprised by

her straightforward understanding. He could imagine that she might think he was a little nuts. Maybe he was. Most of the time, he wasn't entirely sure himself.

SHE'D PLACED two of the three surveillance bugs. There was no way she was going to get into his office considering the way he'd flipped when she opened the door.

Obviously there was something in there he didn't want people to see.

I need to get in that office.

"I think he likes you, Mags," Gordon said in her ear. "Dude can't stop looking at you…ouch… Man, stop throwing stuff at me."

Gordon was right, Gomez was lonely. Really lonely if his awkward sideways glances were any gauge. She was not a woman men stared at. She was a woman men glanced at and forgot.

Apparently, not Gomez.

The back of her neck burned and her fingers tingled and she told herself it was the job. It certainly had nothing to do with that dynamic energy that surrounded him, that seemed to reach out to her with every glance.

That's good, I can use that.

Things were going well. She seemed to have

passed some sort of test when she didn't react to Gomez's injuries. She had handled the situation when he caught her bugging the kitchen phone. It had been close, but luckily there really had been pizza sauce on the receiver.

They seemed to get along, if his corny jokes were an indication. Except for his privacy issues about the office, which she planned on stepping all over, she guessed she had this job in the bag.

She followed him from the dark hallway back into the bright room with the view of the ocean. She didn't pay much attention to what lay outside the window, instead planning to get her third and final bug planted under the table beside the over-stuffed sofa.

"Your ad said mornings two days a week," she said, breaking the silence in the room.

"Right. Eight to noon." He limped over to the large armchair hidden underneath newspapers. He brushed them all to the floor then collapsed into the dark blue cushions with a groan. "I'll be home most of that time, but I'm usually working in my office."

"We need more time, Maggie," Curtis said. "We'll be here weeks if you keep to that schedule."

"I'm afraid that's not going to work, Mr.—"

"Gomez," Gomez said, "but please call me Caleb."

"Okay, Caleb." She swallowed, his first name felt thick and awkward in her mouth. "It's going to take me about a week of four-hour days just to get this place cleaned to a livable standard. And that doesn't include the cooking."

"Good point." Caleb looked around and grimaced. "What do you propose?"

"Two weeks of eight-to-one and then we'll see."

Caleb smiled and Maggie glanced away from the twist of that wounded mouth and the humor that poured out of those eyes. "*We'll see.* I like that. It's been my motto for two and a half years."

Maggie was startled by her desire to ask what he meant by that comment, but she quickly focused back on business. "Did you want to call my references?"

"Already have, they couldn't say enough good things about you."

Considering Curtis and his secretary had been her two references, she wasn't surprised. Still, she smiled as though she was pleased.

One step closer, she thought. *I am one step closer, Patrick.*

"Great. So, is there some paperwork you want me to fill out?"

"Not so fast." Gomez grinned again, the wry tightening of his face looked more like a grimace than an expression of pleasure. "Why don't you clear a seat and tell me why you are so eager to work for slave wages for a disfigured cripple?"

Maggie inwardly winced. Though his tone was casual, joking even, it was very clear what this man thought of himself.

"I need the job," she answered. *More than you'll ever know.* "I have a son."

"You're married?"

"No."

"Divorced?"

Maggie narrowed her eyes. "Is it important?"

"No." Gomez wearily rubbed the scars on his neck.

Does it hurt? she wondered.

"Sorry. Old habits die hard, I guess." He looked out at the ocean, his face touched by the sunlight and Maggie had the strangest feeling that he was searching for composure.

"So, Margaret with one son," he finally said, turning back to her. "What brings you to Summerland?"

"Will is getting older and his influences were getting worse at school and in the neighborhood."

"Where were you from?"

"Los Angeles." The lies came fast, natural. "Long Beach."

Gomez nodded. "Spent a little time there myself. Some neighborhoods there can eat a kid alive."

She knew all of this, of course. Long Beach and Will, her fictitious son, were all part of her cover designed to elicit reactions from Gomez, to create a sense of common ground. She needed him to want to talk to her.

It was what being undercover was all about. Building trust and then destroying it.

"How old is your son?" he asked.

"Ten."

"What—"

"You mentioned a pay increase if I agreed to cook," she asked, interrupting his twenty questions. Best to keep some mystery about herself, keep the journalist engaged in her story. Spilling all of her made-up beans wouldn't do that.

Gomez did not miss a beat at her change of subject.

"An extra $150 a week. If it's edible."

Maggie nodded, clueless as to whether that was fair or not. "Sounds fair."

Gomez watched her, unabashed, and the air slowly filled with tension like a gas leak. She could feel his regard, like fingers reaching out to stroke her hair, her face. His eyes probed hers and for a moment, because she knew, at least in words, all of the things that had happened to him, those beautiful eyes shook her.

She knew people torn apart, absolutely devastated by things not half as bad as what this man had suffered and survived. Her mother for one. Destroyed by what had happened to her golden son.

"So, do I have the job?" she finally asked, acting as the composed Margaret Warren once more.

"Yes, Ms. Warren, I do believe you do."

She, Curtis and Gordon all sighed in relief. "That's good news," she told Gomez.

"Well," he said with a wry chuckle, "you haven't seen the bathroom."

IN THE END Margaret wanted to write down a list of cleaning supplies but didn't have a pen so he had to go into the kitchen to grab one.

Giant suitcase of a purse and she doesn't have a pen? What do they carry in those things?

When she drove away Caleb stood at his back door and watched her crummy little hatchback until it vanished down the hill.

There was going to be a woman in his house. A woman with a gorgeous mouth and unreadable eyes, touching his things. Making him dinner.

Caleb didn't know how to feel.

Bear, still locked up in the office, bellowed to

be let out. Caleb propped the cane on the wall and limped as fast as he could and flung open the door.

"Oh, Bear," he groaned when he saw the mess his big dumb dog had made. "I'm gonna take you back to the pound."

Bear sat in a nest of shredded paper, fragments of newspapers and magazine pages dotted his fur. One triangular strip hung from his lolling tongue.

Even after more than a week of seeing the beast every day, Caleb wasn't used to his looks. Half of the dog's right ear was missing from a fight that also took out his right eye. Because of a skin condition, he was hairless except for a couple of clumps of fur along his sides. Those clumps were coarse and wiry, the fur constantly falling out. He had a bad temper toward strangers, which was the main reason Caleb had bought the damn dog, but that didn't make him any more endearing. Bear adored chewing paper, but left shoes alone, which was nice except Caleb often liked what was on the chewed-up paper more than his shoes.

Caleb reached out and peeled the piece of paper off the dog's tongue.

Bear licked his hand and Caleb stepped over him to the sliding glass door that led from the office to the patio and Bear trotted out the door, knocking over the books and magazines Caleb kept piled on his office bookshelves.

Dumb dog. Caleb followed and pushed open the screen door so Bear could flop down on the deck in the sunshine. Caleb flopped down as well in the padded lounge that faced the water.

Bear sighed and scooted around so he sat within petting distance and Caleb flexed and stretched out his bad hand to stroke Bear's single hairless ear.

"A woman's coming, Bear." He long ago stopped feeling stupid for talking to his dog. "You've got to behave yourself."

Bear barked, once, a succinct reminder. "Me, too," Caleb agreed, thinking of Margaret Warren's pink mouth and those other soft womanish things that he longed to sample but were no longer within his limited reach. "I have to behave myself, too."

"WHERE THE HELL DID HE GO?" Benny asked. He watched Hernando squirm and gasp. It made Benny feel better to know that the pain in his belly was also in the bellies of his men. Benny looked down to the floor, where Boyer lay in a slick of his own blood.

Well, he did not feel much of anything anymore.

Benny had to come all the way to New York from L.A. to deal with this Caleb Gomez problem when it should have been dealt with three days ago.

He wanted Hernando to feel the pain.

"*Jefe,* I don't know." Hernando shrugged and licked his upper lip, beaded with sweat despite the frigid temperature in the warehouse.

Good. Good. Be nervous.

Benny nodded at Ramon who held Hernando's arms behind him, twisted high behind his back. Ramon lifted Hernando higher off his toes and Hernando screamed in pain.

"He left New York, *jefe.* That's all I know. Nobody knows where he went. All those reporters that were hanging around his house don't know either. Trust me." Hernando was crying, snot trickling down over his lip and into his mouth like a river.

Disgusting. It was so damn hard to find men who would behave like men rather than scared little schoolgirls.

"Did you talk to the reporters? Did you ask them where they think Gomez went?"

"Of course…I…"

"Did you ask them like I am asking you right now?" Benny cocked his gun and Ramon lifted him again and the screams echoed through the empty warehouse.

"No," he finally gasped. "No, I didn't, *jefe.* Give me a chance and I will. I will find out. I swear."

The little bitch was crying in earnest and Benny thought about shooting him just on principle. Instead he uncocked the gun and put it back in the waistband of his pants.

He could be benevolent.

"Do it," he said. "You have ten hours."

Ramon dropped him and Hernando landed in a heap on the cold cement, sobbing.

Five hours later the sound of Benny's cell phone cut through the canned music being piped through the speakers behind his head.

"He's on the West Coast," Hernando said. "North of Los Angeles, no one is sure where. That's the truth, *jefe*. I swear to God."

Benny flipped his cell phone shut and put the biography of Mussolini on the floor for some minimum-wage bookstore employee to pick up. He kicked Ramon's foot to wake him up. He'd been dozing in the chair in the empty non-fiction section of the bookstore since they'd arrived after dinner.

"Wha—?" Ramon sat up, blinking and huffing like a man coming up from under water. "What's going on?"

"He's on the West Coast." Benny stood and picked up his leather jacket from the back of his chair. "North of L.A."

"You want me to go find him?" Ramon stood,

too, his giant six-foot, three-hundred-pound frame uncurling like black smoke against the book-shelves behind him.

"No," Benny said. "You take care of Hernando. I know who to call to take care of Gomez."

CHAPTER THREE

MAGGIE MANAGED to slide open the lock and get through the front door of her new temporary apartment without dropping her overnight bag, her dinner bag, her laptop bag, her purse or, most importantly, her jumbo root beer.

Once inside she put as much of her load as she could onto the floor and surveyed her new home.

Just once she wished for an assignment that required fancy digs. Some place furnished with real furniture that didn't smell like cat pee. Some place that might actually have a view of something other than a Dumpster.

"Used to wish," she muttered. She hoped this was her last job. It had to be. She had to get out of the Bureau while she still had something left of herself to get out with. And if Gomez had the stuff to bring down Delgado, she could solve her brother's murder, clear his name and move on.

It was time—probably past time if her mindset

today had been any indication. She wasn't as focused as she usually was. Something about Gomez kept her off balance, a little too aware of the fact that she played a part.

She'd regroup tomorrow. Stay on task.

Tonight, however, I can enjoy my luxurious surroundings, she thought.

Her apartment, located in an old building off what appeared to be the only nonresidential street in Summerland, was small. Very, very small. She turned right and saw the blue tiled bathroom with the naked lightbulb hanging from the middle of ceiling. She turned left and saw the kitchen-dining room-living room area, complete with Formica kitchen table and chair. She hoped it wasn't her bedroom, too.

She could have stayed in her own apartment, but she and Curtis had hopes that with proximity she might be able to run into Gomez around town—should he actually leave his house.

She needed to increase her possible points of contact in whatever way she could considering the time frame. One week. It was practically a joke.

She held on to her drink and the brown bag that contained her dinner in one hand and dug from her overnight bag one of the few things—besides her clothing, computer and gun—that came with her from the outside world.

The cruise brochure.

She took the single step required to move her from the hallway to the center of her kitchen. Her heart sank to see the mattress in the middle of the main room. The tiny space was indeed her bedroom, too.

She tried to look on the bright side but couldn't find one.

Maggie hiked herself up onto the counter, dug out her burrito, and spread the cruise brochure with its gorgeous, shirtless, brown-skinned man out on the counter faceup.

"Hola, señor," she cooed to the man who could be considered her dinner date most evenings.

At some point Maggie had stopped fighting the sad state of her life and embraced it. She was a workaholic who dreamed of taking a cruise but probably never would because she was too busy working. She also dreamed of having a sex life with a real man, instead of fantasies originating from a New Holiday Cruise brochure. But that was about as likely as Margaret Warren sprouting wings and flying around to dust Gomez's house.

After Patrick's murder was solved. Then. Then Maggie would actually take a vacation. Maybe she'd take a vacation and not come back. She'd settle down on some Mexican beach with a beautiful, shirtless man and a lifetime of umbrella drinks. She'd throw out her clothes and wear only bikinis. All day. Regardless of who she blinded with her Irish white skin.

Maggie bit into her bean and cheese burrito with gusto. It'd been ages since her last meal. That coffee at the briefing had been about it all day.

Man, the morning seems like years ago, she thought and took a slurp of her root beer. Odd how meeting Gomez today had messed up her perception of time. Anything before looking into those startling blue eyes set in that even more startling face seemed like a long time ago. She'd gathered from reading his file that he was a pretty dynamic guy, but meeting him was a whole different story.

Caleb Gomez was one of a kind.

Now, he was bait.

She cringed just thinking about it. Gomez didn't deserve this treatment from the Bureau and she hated being the person to set him up. Not after what he'd already been through for his country. But she and her family were carrying the emotional scars as proof that sometimes life was not fair.

"Patrick." She said his name out loud and listened to it echo around this empty place that his death had led her to.

Her voice bounced back from the window with its view of the Dumpster to the tiles in the bathroom, reaffirming all her reasons for being in this shabby apartment in this shabby town, ready to betray a good guy who clearly only wanted to be left alone.

Saying her brother's name kept the driving edge of her pain and commitment sharp. She would not be swayed by Gomez, by fear, by anything.

Delgado would pay for killing her brother.

She only had to prove that Delgado had been behind it.

She took another bite of her burrito, licked the salsa off the corner of her mouth and forced herself to consider brighter subjects for a while.

"*¿Cómo está usted?*" she asked the guy on the brochure. "*Usted es muy hermoso. Puede usted traerme una bebida con sabor a...*" She couldn't remember the words for a fruity umbrella drink. Her poor Spanish echoed around the empty apartment and she cringed.

"I am crazy," she told the brochure and jumped off the counter to grab her laptop. A little conversation with the outside world was what she needed, even if it was in cyberspace.

She unzipped the case and opened the thin computer, locating the available phone jacks and outlets. She ate a little more while listening to the soft hum and whir of the booting computer.

She opened her e-mail program, thinking she could get a little work done but was immediately sidetracked by an e-mail from Liz Meisner with the word *Emergency* in the subject.

Maggie rolled her eyes. Of course. Her sister could be counted on for at least two emergencies during every case.

Luckily, Maggie had never been in such deep cover that some family contact wasn't allowed. The provision was that her real life never threaten the integrity of the case.

This could be another one of Liz's not-so-urgent emergencies or it could be real. Dad's health was bad, Dan, Liz's husband, was working overtime, Mom was exhibiting manic behavior in her effort to counterbalance her husband. The truth was they were a family living in a state of semi-emergency.

Maggie grabbed her cell phone and dialed her sister.

"Liz, here," her bright perky sister answered.

"Emergency?"

"Oh, my God! Mags! I'm so glad—"

"The Starbucks north of Zuma Beach on Highway 1 in exactly a half hour."

"Uh…okay."

Maggie hung up and picked up the remains of her burrito. The cheese was cold and her hunger had turned to a dull ache in her stomach.

"You don't have any sisters, do you?" she asked shirtless man, and tossed the burrito in the garbage.

LIZ WAS TEN MINUTES LATE. Which, in Liz time, was practically early. She entered and scanned the palatial coffeehouse located just off the beach like a starlet looking for her public. Most of the men in the place looked back.

Liz attracted attention to the same extent that Maggie didn't. Tall, with long legs, and brown hair cascading down her back. Big brown eyes that screamed "Help me" and suckered even her smarter-than-that older sister into offering assistance. Not even the giant rock on her left hand deterred the interested male glances in the coffee shop.

Maggie put up her hand and waved Liz over.

"Mags!" she cried, throwing her purse onto the chair. "Thank God—"

"Where's the blood?" Maggie asked.

Liz blinked.

"This is an emergency and emergencies while I'm working require blood."

Liz winced but then smiled—sorry, her smile

said, but aren't I charming and I am your younger sister and who else could help me out but you?

Maggie looked up at the painted ceiling and blew out a big breath. She hadn't really expected anything different. "Go get me a latte. A big one," she said and shrugged out of her coat to settle in for whatever tale of woe Liz had for her this time.

If she ever went in deep cover Liz would be beside herself.

"Dan's cheating," Liz said a few minutes later, setting down the large lattes and sliding into her seat.

"On you?" Maggie asked, jaw on the floor. Men didn't cheat on women like Liz—they cheated on other women with women like Liz.

Liz nodded and Maggie suddenly saw the tension and strain on her sister's face and felt the age-old big sister desire to make whatever was wrong better.

"Are you sure?" she asked, leaning forward and brushing Liz's hand with her own.

Liz nodded. "He's gone all the time. He's getting these phone calls late at night and then he leaves. Just gets out of bed and goes."

"He's a cop, Liz—"

Liz shot her an acrid look under her eyelashes. "I've been married to him for six years, Mags. I know what the life is like and I'm telling you this is…different."

Maggie sighed. "Maybe it's got something to do with Patrick."

Again, his name aloud straightened her spine and she saw the small muscles in Liz's jaw flex. The whole family suffered from the same helpless rage that had settled in their muscles and stomachs. Their father already had atrophied so much that no one could even say Patrick's name in front of him. It was as if their dad was trying to erase her older brother from the family.

Liz shook her head. "He was warned away from the case."

"When did a warning ever stop Dan Meisner from doing something?" Maggie asked with a smile, trying to tease one from her sister. "If I remember correctly, Patrick tried to warn Dan away from you. That didn't do much good."

Finally, Liz smiled and took a sip of her latte. Her brown eyes no longer dull. "True." Her smile was coy and Maggie sighed. Liz and Dan were a solid couple. Any woman would chafe at being married to a cop—the hours and the job stress weren't easy. But Dan and Liz made it look easy. The Meisners were a dream couple.

"So." Maggie finally took a sip of her own latte, the ulcers groaning in wretched protest. "Dan's just doing what Dan does best, stirring stuff up and trying to solve his best friend's murder."

Liz didn't look convinced, but at least the fine lines of tension were gone from her face and her hands weren't white-knuckled around her cup. "Is that what you're doing?" Liz asked, looking at Maggie sideways. "Trying to solve Patrick's murder?"

"You know I can't tell you anything."

Liz shrugged, looking somehow smaller. "I wish I could do something, too. I feel helpless."

"We all do."

Liz sighed and then pasted on a counterfeit smile. "I guess I should leave things to the professionals."

Maggie nodded. "Please do."

They sipped their coffees in quiet for a moment. Each of them staring out different windows. This was a good Starbucks. Lots of view to be had. Lots of staring out windows to be done.

"I was surprised when you said you were going back undercover," Liz finally said and Maggie braced herself for the inevitable question. "We all were."

"It's my job," Maggie said.

"Yeah, the job you were going to quit."

"Liz—"

"What about law school?"

Maggie swallowed the bitter coffee and stood to find a sugar packet and to avoid the remainder of this conversation. "What about it?" she asked over her shoulder, casually, as if they were talking about nothing important.

Liz shook her head when Maggie got back to the table, stack of sugar packets in hand. Maybe the ulcers would like the gut-rotting caffeine sweetened.

"Don't pretend like this isn't a big deal."

"It isn't." Maggie lied.

"Pepperdine Law is a big deal. You've wanted to be a lawyer since you were a kid—"

"Yeah, and I think Patrick wanted to have children and watch them grow up," Maggie snapped. Then she felt as though she'd just kicked a poodle. "I just deferred. I can go later."

"Later when?" Liz asked.

"Later, later. This is hardly worth discussing right now."

"Patrick would want you to be happy," Liz said.

Maggie felt the hot lump of emotion assemble in her throat. She coughed and took a sip of her now-way-too-sweet coffee.

"Mags—"

Maggie pushed the cup away. "I can't talk about this now."

"You are just like Dad," Liz said.

Maggie nodded. So she'd been told most of her life. Recently she'd stopped pretending it was a compliment.

"Just because he wanted a kid in the Bureau didn't mean it had to be you."

"Were you going to sign up?" Maggie asked, laughing at her sister. Liz was a gifted magazine stylist—about as far away from special agent as one could get.

"None of us had to sign up. That was Dad's deal. You didn't have to take on the job. And moreover you should be able to leave it when you want to."

"I don't want to just yet." Maggie shrugged as if it were that simple. And it was, mostly.

"That wasn't your story seven months ago."

"Things changed, Liz. I can't talk about this now. Let it go."

"Fine."

"Fine."

They both stared out the windows again.

"Are you okay? Emergency over?" Maggie asked, her temper slightly cooler thanks to the rolling waves on the other side of the highway.

Liz nodded, pulling her gaze back to Maggie.

"Something is wrong with Dan, but you're right, I don't think it's another woman." The shadows that lingered under her sister's bright eyes indicated something serious was amiss in her sister's stylized life. Some detail was not going as planned and Maggie did feel bad about that, but she had her own amiss details to sort out.

"It's only been six months, Liz. Dan lost his best friend."

Liz nodded, her brown hair gleaming in the low light. Maggie wondered if it was genetics or expensive hair products that created such a shine. Maggie's hair usually looked like a springer spaniel's coat—after he'd chased some animal into a hole.

"Okay, I gotta go." Maggie stood. "No emergencies unless there's blood next time."

Liz smiled. "Okay."

Maggie leaned down and kissed her sister's head and grabbed her coat.

"Oh, hey, can I borrow some movies? Dan's been working late and there's nothing but reality TV on in the summer." Liz assembled herself to go, too. Flipping her hair and slinging her bag over her shoulder. She looked like a perfume commercial.

Maggie nodded; her sister had her own key to Maggie's apartment. "Just put them back when you're done." It was a useless request. Chances were Maggie would never see whatever movies Liz borrowed again.

"Do you have something with Hugh Grant? I feel like something Hugh Grant-y."

"Third row down on the bookcase. I've got them all." Truth be told Maggie was often in the mood for something *Hugh Grant-y.*

"Thanks, Mags," Liz said. Maggie heard a lot of gratitude in those two words.

"No problem."

Someone had to handle the emergencies, keep the family together, bring murderers to justice and lend the Hugh Grant movies when they were desired.

Once again, Maggie was the woman for the job.

CHAPTER FOUR

ON HER FIRST DAY as GOMEZ's housekeeper, Maggie stood outside his open door and tore the sticky note off the glass.

Come in. Supplies in kitchen. I am in office. Please do not disturb.

"Right," she muttered with a grim smile. "Like that's going to happen."

She kicked the door open the rest of the way. It was actually good news that the guy planned on staying locked in his office. It gave her ample opportunity to search and to learn a little more about Caleb Gomez.

She was looking forward to the opportunity.

Gomez had made a token effort at straightening the place up. Magazines, papers and shoes were stacked in piles rather than left scattered about. But still, there were a lot of piles. And underneath the piles was the filth.

Uncle Sam owes me for this. He owes me a lot of umbrella drinks.

She dropped her purse on the couch and spared a glance for the stunning view of morning sunlight over the choppy waters of the Pacific Ocean visible beyond the ravine and the houses on the next street west before starting her rounds.

A quick check of the phone and the table next to the couch confirmed the surveillance bugs were intact.

She grabbed the mail from the stack sitting on the table by the couch. "Pizza, pizza, home renovations," she muttered, setting down each flyer as she read it. "Phone sex, YMC— Hello." There were five envelopes from the University of California, Santa Barbara. Security envelopes with plastic windows, the sort that paychecks come in. The dates on the envelopes spanned from two months ago to yesterday. She held the latest one up to the bright sunlight but the security pattern did its job and she couldn't see the amount written on the check.

Nothing to do but Nancy Drew it.

She put a pot of water on the stove to boil and while she waited, she ducked into his bedroom. The hushed dark room breathed with a musky intimacy. A sleepy scent that was spicy and warm filled the room as if Caleb were still in it.

She ignored the rumpled bed, the stacks of clothes and checked the bug under the lip of the bedside table. Still good.

She pulled open the drawer, looking for anything. Any clue. Never on one of her cases had she simply opened a drawer and found what she needed to solve a crime, but legends abounded in the Bureau about murder weapons being stashed in kitchen drawers and stolen, marked money found under beds.

The drawer was empty but for the smell of wood. *That's my kind of luck,* she thought.

She walked around the bed to the other table, checking over her shoulder, listening intently for sounds from the office.

Nothing but silence.

She slid open the drawer to find an iPod as well as an old *Playboy* magazine.

She quickly grabbed the iPod and shut the drawer, a painful heat flooding her face. That magazine was too much information about Gomez's personal life. Unless he was the only man on the planet who actually read the magazine for the articles.

Considering the warmth of his regard for her own very average self yesterday, she doubted he read many of those pages.

She returned to the kitchen, grabbed her cell phone and text messaged Gordon that she would put an iPod in the mailbox and she needed it back pronto after he duplicated the contents.

The water was boiling so she held the oldest envelope over the steam until the adhesive became damp enough and the envelope popped open for her. She smiled and slid out the pay stub. It was too bad that credit card trick with locked doors wasn't as effective.

The pay stub—a thousand dollars a week directly deposited into his account at the Bank of America in Santa Barbara—was for an online class. Journalism and Ethics. She nearly laughed. Caleb Gomez, the man sitting on information needed to bring down the biggest crime leader on the West Coast was teaching a class on ethics. Ludicrous.

But good for her. And good for Gordon. If Gomez was teaching an online class, Gordon could hack into the course instructional area and monitor Gomez that way. Pose as a new student perhaps, ask some sly questions. And, Gordon could access Gomez's bank records for the past few years to see if there had been any interesting activity while he'd been undercover with Delgado.

Again checking over her shoulder, the iPod and

check stub tucked in her fist, she ran out the door to the mailbox and slid everything inside.

Maggie returned to the house and made a point of closing the door hard enough to rattle a few windows.

Perhaps that would draw the guy out of his cave.

But the door remained shut. The hallway empty. The house silent.

She opened the door and slammed it again, her eyes on the hallway.

Nothing.

Is he even in the office?

That idea perked her up. Maybe he'd lied and said he was in the office so she wouldn't make off with his... She glanced around the room. He didn't even have a TV to make off with.

In any case, it was a little too silent in the house for there to be human and a dog inside.

She stepped lightly across the room to the corner of the hallway, where the light turned to shadows.

A narrow beam of sunlight seeped out from beneath the closed office door.

She shut her eyes so she wouldn't be distracted and listened for a sound—the groan of a floorboard or a chair, the clatter of keyboard keys, a sneeze—anything that would indicate that she wasn't alone. That the room she needed to get into was occupied.

She breathed deeply, held it.

Silence.

Nothing but silence.

She opened her eyes, controlled the sudden heavy pound of her excited heart and stepped closer. She watched the strip of sunlight from beneath the door and reached out a hand to touch the knob. A smooth twist and she'd know if it was locked.

The muscles of her shoulder, her arm twitched with the adrenaline rush. She released the air in her lungs to ease the tension.

The brass ball was cool in her hand. She took another breath and started a slow rotation.

A shadow passed through the light under the door. *Could be the dog,* she told herself, but she paused anyway. The floor creaked. *Could still be the dog.*

She heard a muffled cough. A very human muffled cough and the floor creaked again, this time closer to the door.

He was in there. And he was on the move.

She stepped into the bathroom and prepared a slightly expectant look on her face, but the office door remained shut.

She shook her head at her aggressive eagerness. It was one of her better qualities as an agent, but she knew she was walking a fine line between being aggressive and being stupid in this case.

Don't be stupid, she told herself and turned to case the bathroom.

The medicine cabinet door squawked when she opened it to reveal toothpaste, a red toothbrush, a razor and shaving foam.

The bottom shelf was filled with prescription pill bottles.

Pulling her phone from her pocket she text messaged Gordon the name of the prescribing doctor—Herrara—and the address of the dispensing pharmacy in Goleta, California.

He had a bottle of liquid morphine with a syringe still wrapped in plastic, unused. No prescription. She swallowed a hard lump in her throat and wondered if he was afraid of addiction, or if he had it around because he was so afraid of pain.

A bottle of Vicodin, with the prescription fill date nearly a week ago and the bottle was full. He was either no longer taking his medication or he had another bottle somewhere. She glanced toward the office. The guy could have untold drugs in there—a meth lab, though the air did not smell of cat urine so probably not. But still, morphine, Vicodin…Gomez wasn't fooling around with his pain.

The pharmaceutical inventory also contained a potent anti-inflammatory and a high-dosage antibiotic, probably to fight infection in the burn wounds.

When she shut the cabinet door, her face was reflected in the water spotted mirror. Plain. Hair scrapped back, no makeup, her thin lips nearly disappearing into her pale face. Not a face worth looking at twice or remembering.

She wondered for a moment what Gomez would do if Liz were here cleaning his house. The man wouldn't hide, that's for sure. He'd probably camp out in the kitchen.

Maggie switched her phone to vibrate, closed it and tucked it back in her pocket. About twenty rolls of toilet paper were stacked up against the wall. He clearly did not intend to visit the grocery store any time soon.

Two towels, both brown, hung over a plastic rod

A stool sat in the bath-shower and a generic bottle of shampoo-conditioner rested on its side on the floor of the tub.

A bar of white soap rested in a small purple dish.

Nothing good here, she surmised looking around. After the initial casing she realized that the bathroom was very dirty. Scary black stuff stained the tile grout and gray soap scum coated the tub. She didn't even want to look at the toilet.

Maggie checked her watch. Gordon should be done by now. She pulled out the front door, saw the red flag up on the mailbox and smiled.

Good old Gordon. This was why she put up with his inappropriate comments and tendency to whine—the man was an efficiency genius.

After grabbing the iPod and check stub, she replaced the electronics in his drawer—trying not to notice the worn magazine with the beautiful brunette on the cover. Then she put the pay stub back in its envelope and licked the corners of the flap—spots that most postal machines missed sealing the adhesive—closed it then stacked it among the rest of his ignored mail.

She paused, listening for him, but the house was still silent.

Excellent, she mentally cooed and as quietly as possible she slid open the patio door and stepped out onto the wooden deck. The ravine butted up against the patio, giving the house an extraordinary level of seclusion, which wasn't so good considering someone wanted to kill him.

She noted a sliding glass door that led from his office to the deck. A giant hunk of dog pressed tight against the glass and Gomez sat at a desk beyond the slumbering animal, Gomez's back to the door and view.

She turned the other way to be out of sight should he suddenly decide to look out his window and saw the garage nestled among the trees of the ravine.

She checked her watch then jogged across the burned grass toward the building. The door creaked hideously as she opened it, revealing the musky near-emptiness of the shabby garage.

Empty but for a motorcycle, parked in the center.

She whistled between her teeth and approached the Ducati Multistrada 1100 S. It was like finding the Mona Lisa in someone's basement.

That is a hell of a bike, she thought circling it, admiring its lines, its lovely power and feline grace. The 1100 S was a very expensive, elite racing bike. She shook her head sadly. Gomez probably couldn't even drive it anymore. And that was a shame because, of any bike, this one deserved to be ridden well and often.

Oh, man...I could, she thought with near hunger for the chance. Her fingers practically twitched with the sudden urge to straddle it just once.

She and Patrick used to race Nighthawks. The year of her high school graduation they drove up the coast on their bikes, camping and drinking too much beer along the way.

Thinking of Patrick, his smile beneath his beat-up helmet, was enough to kill her distraction.

She turned, noted the brand-new washer and dryer in the corner and left the garage.

Halfway across the lawn her pocket began to vibrate and she pulled out her phone.

Sooner or later you're going to have to clean, the text message read. I'll be thinking of you. Gordon.

Her partner thought he was hilarious.

But he was right. She was hired to do a job and she'd never get a chance to finish her real job if she didn't get her hands dirty.

Maggie smiled, thinking of his note, his wish not to be disturbed and she walked to his office door and knocked. Loud.

There was a scuffle. A dog's bark. Something hit a wall or the patio window. And finally, a few moments later the door eased open.

A dog's snout pushed out into the crack and Gomez's hand cupped it and jerked it out of the way. "Get lost," he muttered. Maggie's eyebrows climbed.

"Are you talking to me?" she asked.

"No." Gomez laughed and then pulled the door open wide enough for her to see him. He faced her and, in some deep place, she braced for her first glimpse of the man, wondering if her memory had somehow made him worse or better than reality. But the sunlight hit the scar tissue and the deep blue of his eyes and Maggie realized he looked the same as she'd remembered.

Startling. In several different ways. His eyes met hers and a tingling rush of blood whooshed up her spine. Her neck went hot. Just the kind of reaction she was trying to control.

"What do you need?" he asked. Not rude, but not polite, either.

"Nothing." She shrugged. "I just wanted to let you know I was here, in case you heard me banging around or something."

"Great."

He smiled.

She smiled.

"Okay," he said, stepping away from the door as if he'd like to shut it.

She waved and stepped back into the darker shadows of the hall. He closed the door, cutting off the light.

What a weird guy, she thought.

JESUS, CALEB. Do you have to be so weird?

Caleb pressed his forehead to the door. *You're like the Phantom of the Opera or something.*

He nearly laughed. At least that guy got the girl

for a little while. Caleb was the Phantom of the Opera without the *cojones*.

He'd heard her come in. She practically slammed the roof down tromping in and out of his house. And from the moment he'd known she was here, in his house, touching his things, he'd been battling his urge to go out there.

And do what? he asked himself, pushing away from the door and limping toward the chair.

Stare at her?

As nice as that might be for him, it would be creepy for her. Weird. She'd probably leave. Report him to some house-cleaning union. Best to just stay in the office and work.

It was safer that way. And that was the way he liked things.

Safe.

He clicked open the FreeCell icon on his desktop and got to work.

MAGGIE TOOK DEEP BREATHS watching the sunlight break into diamonds over the crests of the waves and turned very slowly from special agent Fitzgerald to Margaret Warren, housekeeper.

It was time to clean.

Her mother, Bridget, in her efforts to make her two daughters care as passionately about a clean home as Bridget herself did, always said that the easiest thing to do was to start at the worst spot and move outward.

Gazing at the mess and clutter surrounding her, Maggie wondered where ground zero might be. She peeked into the kitchen and the pizza-box museum.

Boxes stacked on every flat surface, a sink filled with dirty coffee cups, some terrifying smell wafting from the garbage.

This, she thought, pulling a big black garbage bag from the stack of supplies in the middle of the room, *has got to be it.*

By lunchtime she'd finished cleaning the kitchen. It gleamed and smelled like a chemical pine forest. There were no traces of the pizza-box collection and the mugs had been scoured and put back in the cupboard. She'd wiped out the cupboards, amazed that someone actually had a worse-stocked kitchen than she did. He had two plates, four forks, five one-pound bags of coffee, some cans of chicken noodle soup and a big restaurant-sized shaker of red pepper flakes. For the pizza, Maggie surmised.

At one o'clock, her work done for the day, she considered faking a fall in an attempt to startle him out of his cave, but she dismissed the idea. He might tell her to take tomorrow off, insist she go to a hospital or something.

That was a delay she couldn't really afford. Now that she'd figured out the lay of the land—not to mention had done some damn fine cleaning—tomorrow she could push things, manipulate events to work in her favor to dig for the information they needed, although they had a respectable start. She had the contents of the iPod, after all, and the check stub. Gordon was probably already in Gomez's class, asking important questions about keeping information away from authorities.

While the hounds in her howled for more, she had to admit, for a first day it wasn't bad.

She stored her cleaning supplies then pried the frozen lasagna from the freezer-to-oven container and put it into a glass cooking dish with the hope that it would pass as homemade. She hadn't had time to put together a meal last night, although perhaps if the offerings were bad enough, he'd actually come out of his cave tomorrow and complain about the quality of the food versus the amount of money he was shelling out for it.

Low blow, but time was of the essence.

Swinging her purse over her shoulder, she headed for the office, intending to let him know she was leaving. Just then Gomez emerged from the shadowed hallway.

She paused, knocked off her stride for a millisecond by his sudden appearance. She hadn't heard the door open. Had he been there for a while?

"You're off?" he asked. He tucked his hands in his pockets and looked, despite the injuries, like a little kid.

She nodded. "Dinner's in the fridge and cooking instructions are on the counter."

"Excellent." He looked over her shoulder at her handiwork, eyeing the kitchen that was no longer a potential biohazard.

"Nice work. Wow, the place looks livable. More than livable."

"Well." She practically laughed. The guy was easy to please. "I wouldn't eat anything off the floor, but it's better than it was."

Oh, the umbrella drinks I will be owed.

"Thank you, Margaret." Caleb's voice was so sincere, his gratitude so real and palpable that guilt welled up in her belly.

Don't thank me, she suddenly wanted to say. *Don't be kind.*

"See you tomorrow," he said and ducked back into the hallway.

"Tomorrow," she murmured, watching him go and ruthlessly suppressing all the insane urges for honesty that were clamoring in her brain. She was here to do a job. A job that could save Gomez's life, even if he didn't like the means. It was the result that counted, she reminded herself as she climbed into Margaret Warren's beater of a car. Results for Gomez, for her.

For Patrick.

"Nothing?" Maggie asked Gordon over her cell phone at midnight that night. She'd been trying to reach him for hours, but he hadn't been answering his phone, usually an indication he was hard at work. She'd hoped that meant he'd been hard at work cracking the case. "Nothing was on the iPod?"

"The guy loves Bruce Springsteen and NPR."

"That's it?"

"Oh, right 'Born to Run' and all his secret Delgado files. Didn't I say that?"

"You're hilarious. What about the pay stub?"

"It was easy enough to get the bank records. Dude is pretty rich. But I had some trouble on the university end."

"Trouble? You?" She mocked him.

"Yes, trouble, *moi*. Hours of it. I've got the chat room and I can open every other chat the university uses except his. He must have changed the code. And I think his new code is Arabic or something. I'm running a languages program right now."

"How about his Internet connection. Can we track what sites he's going to?"

"I'm on it," Gordon confirmed. "I should know more tomorrow morning when he gets back online. How about you? Anything?" Gordon asked. She heard the pop and fizz of a can opening and she imagined him consuming his eighty-ninth Mountain Dew of the day.

Maggie sat, leaning against the wall of her shabby digs, her tired and sore legs stretched out and her notes on Gomez spread out in puddles of paper around her. Earlier she'd gone for a run trying to hammer out that aggressive eagerness that made her feel reckless. She'd tired her body but sleep, she knew, was a long way off.

"The guy's got a serious coffee habit but never pees. And given the stash of meds, is either a drug addict or has a pain tolerance I've never seen before. What about the doctor? Dr. Herrera."

"Now that's interesting. Herrera's been retired for several years. But apparently he's a friend of Caleb's father."

"That's interesting?"

"Well…relatively. I'm thinking if he's using a retired friend of the family as his physician, he's got limited contact with strangers. Add that to the teaching online and the food delivery services and you got a guy who's keeping a serious low profile." He paused and Maggie could almost see him shrug. "Could help with the security part of the case. Low profile, minimal external contact might make it harder for Delgado to find him. I stress the *might*."

"Did he make any calls? Talk to himself? Did you get anything from the bugs?"

"I tapped into his phone line at the box, but he's not using it. Not a single call in or out," Gordon said. "I almost called the guy just to make sure the lines were working. It's weird but does keep him off the radar."

Maggie rolled her head against the wall.

"We knew he was going to be tough," she said. She'd been foolish to hope that the info would fall in their laps. Gomez was too good to be careless.

"Yeah," Gordon said. "There's tough and then there's…" He trailed off. "Britney Spears stalkers."

She sighed, nudging the desk lamp she'd put on the floor with her bare foot. She tucked the ball chain between her toes and pulled until the circuit broke and the room went dark. She pulled again and the light turned on.

If only that was all I had riding on this.

"What did you make him for dinner?" Gordon asked, his tone mocking.

"Nothing good."

"Good. Maybe he will come out tomorrow to complain."

"That was the idea," she said.

"I'll talk to you tomorrow night," Gordon said and hung up.

Maggie continued to play with the lamp to distract herself.

Why am I doing this? The small voices, the ones she usually ignored or could shout out were whispering in her head again. In moments such as these, when her job seemed far too daunting, the small voices were the loudest, the most compelling.

She opened the lockbox she kept in her closet and took out the pictures. Her answers. Her reasons for everything. She carefully placed tape at the corners and then hung them on the white wall.

Every night she performed this ritual, and every morning she carefully took them down, tucked them in the box and hid them. Should her cover be blown, her real life might stay hidden.

Patrick's graduation picture from the academy was the first photo. The twinkle in his eye barely subdued and just the hint of his copper-red hair showing underneath his service cap.

He'd been a good cop. The kind of cop who lived for his job. Landing a spot on the Delgado task force had been, for him, a dream come true. A sign he was among the elite of his profession.

The photo next to Patrick's was a surveillance shot of Delgado from six months ago—the day after her brother was killed. Delgado had been photographed coming out of a Denny's restaurant with his arm slung around his sister.

They were both smiling.

The drumbeat of frustrated rage pounded in her head. That that scum lived while her brother and his pregnant wife were dead made Maggie breathless with anger. She wanted to punch down walls and drive up to Gomez's house and demand he let her search his office. Force him to tell her everything he knew.

That he had the information and either didn't know it or, worse, knew it and willfully withheld it made her burn.

She needed solid proof that Gomez actually possessed substantial evidence—it was all supposition, but Maggie's gut instincts said he did— before the Bureau would be able to seize his property. Which—she nearly smiled thinking about it—he would not like.

Serves him right, she thought, perhaps unfairly.

She looked down at a photograph of Gomez and the doubts resurfaced.

What if he didn't know anything? What if he didn't have any information?

What if she couldn't put Delgado away?

Her brother's solemn face and dancing eyes gave her the answer—she'd work this case until Delgado went down.

She thought about calling her family, finding out if things were better with her sister. She wanted to call her dad and tell him that she was going after the bad guy, that she was going to make things right.

She stared at her phone and imagined his face. Imagined the pride shining in his eyes. A smile on his lips. She imagined a hug. Basking in the warmth of fatherly love and acceptance.

But that's all it was—imagination.

She shook her head.

Being undercover always messed with her head. Too much time to think about the problems in her life, the distance between her and her father and the fact that she wasn't the child for whom he'd dreamed of the Bureau career. She was the replacement, the second best. Sadly, being the second choice didn't reduce the pressure for her to get to the top, to be the first female agent in charge.

She frowned at the tension that coiled in her gut at this train of thought. This was why she wanted out, why the straightforward, uncomplicated rules of law beckoned.

But not yet.

She dropped her phone and picked up the Gomez file, flipping through the pages until she got to the two photos. One before Iraq. One after Iraq.

There was tough and then there was Caleb Gomez.

In the before shot his eyes were just shy of cocky. He had a sort of I-know-my-place-in-the-world look about him in the slight curl of his defined lips.

Post-Iraq, the cocky look was still there in those blue eyes. But the rest of it was gone.

It seemed the only place in this world for Gomez these days was a locked office on a mountain in California.

She grabbed some tape and tacked the post-Iraq photo on the wall next to her brother.

The three men, a dead cop, a gangster and a journalist, were connected. She knew it. She just had to prove it.

THE NEXT MORNING she arrived at Gomez's armed with frozen enchiladas. Vegetarian enchiladas.

A duplicate sticky note was stuck on the door and she pulled it off with a growl.

Not an auspicious beginning.

She dropped her purse on the couch and headed into the kitchen to disguise her frozen enchiladas as homemade. She was brought up short by what appeared to be a lasagna massacre.

The glass dish was upside down on the floor, surrounded by what appeared to be smears of blood, but what Maggie guessed was actually tomato sauce. In the middle of the sauce, like a fingerprint, was the clear imprint of a giant paw.

Maggie, who had never thought herself particularly attached to a clean house felt her blood boil.

"I spent hours on that floor!" she muttered. She yanked the bucket out from under the sink, making as much noise as possible as if to telegraph to the silent ghost and his dog that she was very, very unhappy.

The sauce clung to the linoleum like glue and it took close to a half hour to eliminate all traces of it, even with anger lending a certain strength to her scrubbing.

She wondered, pressing on the lever to squeeze the water from the mop, if this was Gomez's way of complaining about the food. As soon as she finished this she was going to knock on his door and let him know—

Snick.

The office door opened. The center floorboard in the hallway squeaked.

Of course, she pretended not to hear it and continued to mop. She could feel Gomez in the other room watching her as she backed out of the kitchen. His gaze, intense as it was had a palpable weight. She could feel his eyes on her back, her legs, her hips and, despite her best efforts, she was discomfited. He wasn't simply watching her, she knew that. The guy, alone and damaged beyond repair, was practically salivating.

Suddenly she was all too aware that she was acting. That she was playing a role designed to trick him into doing what the Bureau wanted. And with that acute contemplation of his, he might see through her guise as Margaret Warren to the truth of her.

She wiped her forehead with the back of her hand, overdramatic and awkward but she had to do something to break the silence and his intense study.

It worked. Gomez cleared his throat.

She jumped, the picture of a woman startled out of a hardworking focus.

"Oh, my God," she breathed. "You scared me."

"Sorry." One half of Gomez's face lifted in a smile, the rest remained twisted. Frozen. "I didn't mean to startle you." He wore jeans and a ragged Chicago Blackhawks T-shirt. His feet were bare and somehow that was more startling—more intimate—than the scars and the eyes.

He had big feet. Long toes.

Maggie dragged her eyes away from them and smiled, getting herself back on track.

You are hired to clean his house, not analyze his feet.

"No problem." She pulled the bucket of dirty water out of the kitchen and plunked the mop into it, leaning the handle against the wall.

"I was just going to get a cup of coffee," he muttered, gesturing toward the kitchen with his empty mug. He took a step in that direction, and while Maggie Fitzgerald didn't really care what the guy did with his floors and coffee, she figured Margaret Warren would. So she channeled a bit of her mother on cleaning days.

"If you try walking across my clean floors, it won't go well for you," she told him, setting her hands on her hips.

Nice, she thought. *Mom would be proud. Wouldn't believe it for a second, but she'd be proud of the effort.*

Gomez lifted one eyebrow and he smiled again, that ruined smile.

"All right. No coffee." He turned to retreat to his office and Maggie thought fast.

"Fine. I'll get it for you." She held out her hand for the cup. She couldn't gather intelligence with her subject locked up in the room she needed to get into.

He handed her the mug and she tiptoed carefully along the edge of the clean floor to the state-of-the-art coffee machine in the corner.

"Feel free to help yourself," he said. "You deserve a medal for cleaning that kitchen."

Twice.

"Thanks," she said and reached into the cupboard with the mugs.

She tiptoed back into the main room and handed him a steaming mug.

"The only addiction I've got left," he said.

They stood there awkwardly, smiling politely, she in no position to make time-consuming small talk since she was supposed to be cleaning and he clearly unsure of what to do with someone in his house.

Crap, she thought. *This is going to take forever.*

"Was that your review of dinner?" she asked, pointing toward the kitchen.

"I meant to clean that up." He winced. "Bear very much enjoyed your lasagna."

"It's okay," she said and waited for him to say

something else about the frozen dinner, but he remained silent.

"Bear?"

"The dog."

"Oh?" She raised her eyebrows, an invitation to further conversation.

"Well," he said and lifted his cup in a half-hearted toast, ignoring her invitation. "Back to work for me."

"Okay." She took a sip of the coffee and wondered how hard or fast she could push things. "What are you working on?" she asked, eager to see what answers the question would yield.

"I teach some online classes."

"On what?"

His brow furrowed as though he couldn't quite understand why she suddenly had so many questions.

"Sorry," she said, interpreting his look. "It's pretty quiet here. I guess I'm a little starved for conversation."

"Understandable. Bear and I aren't great company." He managed to look sheepish. "I teach writing courses."

"Are you a writer?"

"Are you a cop?" he asked.

"What?" She laughed incredulously. Not an

unheard of question in her line of work. She wouldn't be investigating him if he didn't have something to hide and people with things to hide tended to be paranoid about questions.

Caleb Gomez had more reason than most to be paranoid.

"A cop?" she said. "Hardly."

"Sorry." He appeared sheepish. "It was a joke. A bad one."

"So, are you? A writer? I mean do you get paid?"

"Ah. Not a cop," he said, lifting a finger. "A woman worried about her paycheck."

"Something like that."

"You know—" he looked at her, then at the wall and then back at her as if she'd stumped him "—not right now. I keep surfing the Net and playing FreeCell."

She laughed in total understanding. She'd had to have FreeCell taken off her laptop, because for about a week, her high score had become paramount in her life.

"It's hard to stay focused when it's so nice out," she said, nodding her head toward the sunlight and fresh air on the other side of the window. *Go.* She silently urged. *Walk. Smell some plants. Get out of that damn office.*

"We're in Southern California," he said,

looking out the window. "It's always sickeningly nice outside."

"Spoken like a guy from New York."

As soon as the words left her mouth, she froze. Prickly heat exploded in her body as the conversational air disappeared.

She moved a quarter turn away from him so he wouldn't see the crimson heat of her disgust on her face.

"Did I say I was from New York?" he asked.

She swallowed, her throat in knots. "No," she managed to say. She even flashed him a weak smile. "Your accent. It's East Coast. And don't most East Coast writers live in New York? I just presumed." Awkwardness filled the space between them. She shrugged. "I've always been good with accents."

Rookie mistake. Goddamn rookie mistake. She took a sip of coffee to hide her grimace. She'd been flustered by his intense scrutiny, the way he watched her with those eyes.

I'm sorry, Patrick. I'm sorry.

Her brother deserved better than this. Her mouth, as her father had always said, was nothing but trouble.

"That obvious, huh? I spent years trying to get rid of my accent and now I think it's coming back."

Gomez clearly didn't notice her blunder and her gut, clenched in horror, eased a bit. *Get your shit together, Fitzgerald.*

"Why'd you try to get rid of it?" she asked, her voice stammering slightly as she scrambled to get her feet back under her. "The accent, I mean."

"Hard to blend into a crowd when you sound like a guy from Queens."

She furrowed her brow as if not understanding, even though she had gone through similar voice training to remove any trace of regional accent. "Why'd you need to blend into a crowd?"

"A good question," he said, not answering it. He turned away, wincing as he pivoted on his damaged leg and walked toward the office, clearly trying to control his limp.

Maggie sighed in defeat, staring at her reflection in the dark surface of her coffee. Here she was flailing about like a bull in a china shop. Bad enough on its own, but made worse by the fact that she knew Gordon was listening.

"I, ah…" He paused between the shaft of light from the windows and the darkness of the hallway beyond. "I was a journalist," he said. His shoulders stiff under the soft gray of the T-shirt.

"Was?" She held her breath. The tension in Gomez snaked toward her, coiling around her stomach and lungs. She could sense his discomfort, knew without being told that what he was saying cost him something.

She inhaled, a quick breath of exaltation. For a man of so few words—and even fewer around her—she was relieved and surprised to feel so attuned to him. There were times in her past when subjects hadn't been so available to her, times when there had been no connection at all.

With Gomez she could read in the stiff line of his shoulder that this admission was not an easy one.

He nodded.

"Not anymore?" she asked.

"Not right now," he said, then shuffled into the shadows.

Maggie watched him go. Low in her belly, where she carried those emotions her father and the Bureau insisted she get rid of, something trembled in sudden sympathy.

I will not like him, she told herself, worried it was too late. *I will not.*

CHAPTER FIVE

CALEB EASED OPEN THE DOOR to his office, hoping not to startle the beast snoring on an old sleeping bag.

Bear snorted and huffed, his giant rib cage undulating like a wave.

Soon Caleb was going to have to take Bear out for a walk and he wondered how Margaret Warren would react to the monster.

He wondered how Margaret would react if he stripped naked and did the hula in front of her. If he pulled out a gun and shot up the ceiling, she'd probably still stare at him with that unruffled, slightly expectant look on her face, as if to say, "Is there anything else, you giant idiot?"

He felt a little bad that he wasn't better company for her. But then he hadn't hired her to make small talk and, frankly, she was lousy at small talk. He, on the other hand, had been a master at chatter. A bit of flirtation, a few coy questions, the subtle harvesting of information without the other person ever knowing. Margaret made conversation as if she were interrogating a witness.

He smiled grimly and sat in the old desk chair behind his computer, his back to the view of the sunny day outside.

I was a journalist.

He sighed and leaned back in the chair, ancient springs and hinges silent due to frequent oiling. Journalists write. That would be a requirement of the job.

When he'd first been released from the hospital, he'd been on fire, burning from the inside—that familiar storm of ego and desire to tell a story, to reveal a certain truth in a way that he felt only he was able to.

And he'd written a three-part feature about his time in Iraq, his rescue and his rescuer, Jesse Filmore.

The series was received with great fanfare, huge buzz, discussion of a Pulitzer.

Then he had sat down to work again, his dog and the view at his back, his first Pulitzer on the shelf beside him. And…nothing.

His head was a vast desert. Empty.

No ideas. No storm. No ego.

Which made him a writer with nothing to write.

He had an editor dying for something to publish.

He had readers dying for something to read.

But unless there was a sudden interest in his FreeCell score, he had nothing to give them.

He clicked through the screens on his computer to the chat room his class on ethics used for class discussion.

This morning his question to the class had been "If you were the editor of a newspaper, to what degree would you show the victims of violent crime on your front page."

Amanda Groser, his young Geraldo Rivera—pre-Al Capone's vault—had already chimed in with her emphatic, All the way. For too long gang violence, domestic abuse and the casualties in Iraq have been underreported. Show the public some body bags, some blood on the streets of their cities, and let's get some outcry for change.

Gomez smiled reading her post.

He could have written that ten, hell, even five years ago.

That had been his motto at one time—create change.

He wondered what his motto was now? Turn in your papers on time? I'd like a large extra-cheese pizza?

Not quite change inspiring.

Thanks, Amanda, he posted back. Murrow would be proud. Anyone else? These are just opinions, no right or wrong answers.

It was silent on the boards, so he'd check back later. The discussions usually lasted all day and he generally did a quick summary and round-up around midnight.

He enjoyed the teaching, really enjoyed it. Surprising, considering how much he'd hated school. And conducting the course online was a tremendous benefit. He imagined that if he were actually in a classroom, students would be so horrified by his face they wouldn't pay attention to his words.

This way he could hand out assignments on Monday, discuss related topics throughout the week and the students e-mailed their work to him on Friday. There were many hours in there where he had nothing but FreeCell to fill his time.

He couldn't go undercover anymore, which robbed him of what he'd loved most about being a journalist. The immersion in a story, the experience of living events firsthand, revealing that truth, that honesty to everyone. After that exhilarating life, how could he be a beat reporter, attending press conferences and relying on other people to distill the facts for him? That wasn't journalism to him, that was being a simple scribe. And he wanted no part of it. If he couldn't be in the field undercover, he couldn't be a journalist.

His father, the esteemed psychologist Dr. Gomez, had had a field day with Caleb's preference for the life of an undercover investigative journalist—psycho-babble about masks and fluid identity and self-deception. But Caleb didn't listen. He just missed his old career. The way he missed his old face. The way he missed his old ability to move without pain.

"Caleb Gomez," he sighed, tired of this familiar trip down self-pity lane. "Sad sack."

There was a war on. Men were being killed. Innocent—and not so innocent—people were being beaten and tortured. On both sides of the conflict.

But he'd written that story. He'd told Jesse Filmore that his demons were exorcized, and they were, for the most part. Caleb had the odd nightmare, the occasional heart-dropping startle when he caught sight of himself in a mirror. But for the most part he was okay in a soulless bored kind of way.

Sadly, the sight of Margaret Warren backing out of his kitchen had been one of the few inspiring moments in his life of late.

The woman had a world-class ass.

An awful cook, but not too hard on the eyes.

Bear put his wet nose against Caleb's bare foot—a strange camaraderie, but the best he would get these days.

Margaret Warren stuck in his mind like a splinter. *Good with accents? What kind of house-keeper is good with accents?* She was a mystery, that was certain.

And nothing got his juices flowing like a good mystery.

He should go back out there and investigate his cleaning woman. Find out her secrets. But he could imagine her nonplussed disinterest. Her placid face and raised eyebrows expressing only polite concern. Her probable reaction dammed the flowing juices.

He minimized his class chat. Behind that screen the Internet was open on the black, white and green backdrop of the POW/MIA page.

He clicked on Forums. And as he had done too frequently of late—even though he knew that this fascination with the chat rooms and forums focusing on captured or missing civilians and soldiers bordered on an unhealthy obsession—he immersed himself in the only world he could understand right now.

He grabbed the amber plastic bottle from his desk and shook out a Vicodin, which he swallowed dry.

Tomorrow, he told himself, *tomorrow I'll work on mysteries.*

ONCE AGAIN Maggie sat on the floor of her apartment, perfecting her skill of turning off the lamp with her toes. Any moment now her cell phone was going to ring and Gordon was going to ask some very tough questions that she didn't have answers for.

She tugged the lamp's small chain and plunged the room into darkness. Another tug and a pool of light filtered through the lamp shade to light up her corner of the room. From the wall Patrick watched her.

She plunged the room into darkness again, unable to tolerate his gaze.

I'm blowing it. I know. I'm sorry.

Her cell phone rang. Gordon.

She let it ring until the last possible moment.

"Hello?"

"Maggie? What the hell?"

"Sorry, Gord—"

"What happened with you today?"

"Nothing. I just—"

"You all but told him you know who he is. The

guy hasn't lived in New York in years. *I'm good with accents,* my ass. Are you losing it? You're an FBI agent. Not a kid playing detective."

Oh, man, she thought. *That's totally how I felt talking to him.*

"And those questions—"

"I know Gordon. I know. I blew it today."

"What am I supposed to do if Curtis asks for those tapes?"

She swallowed. She wanted to tell him to erase them so that they'd both be complicit in the possible downturn of the investigation. So that he'd have as much at stake as she did and would fight to keep their boss from discovering what had happened. She wanted to, but couldn't. She'd learned to take responsibility for her actions, regardless of the outcome. "Give them to him."

"And we'll both get pulled out of there."

Maggie sighed and rested her head against the wall. "I know. Look, tomorrow will go better."

"Tomorrow he probably won't even come out because he's scared you're gonna tie him up and interrogate him."

In the dark, her eyes sought out the picture of the tortured Gomez that she'd tacked on the wall when she came home. She couldn't see it, but she could feel his gaze in such a tangible way that the short hairs on the back of her neck stood up, and low in her belly anxiety coiled.

"That's not funny, Gordon."

"I know, Fitzgerald."

She took a deep breath, found room on her shoulders for the blame. This is what good agents did—learned from their mistakes and moved on. "I screwed up today. I get it. We still have three days."

"You better make them count."

"You know I will."

Maggie hung up and bounced her head against the wall once as if driving home Gordon's words.

She stood and faced her wall of motivation where she'd taped everything she had on Gomez beneath the photos. These three men who seemed to control her fate as much as she tried to control theirs.

The surveillance photos of Gomez with Delgado three years ago. The surveillance photos taken the same day she took the job as housekeeper. The photos of him in the hospital and the ones of him wearing a tux at a Washington, D.C., fund-raiser seven years ago.

The many faces of Caleb Gomez.

She'd written out the time line and that was affixed to the wall above the photos. She studied it all again. The problem was she had all of that information memorized.

And it didn't help.

Staring at it didn't help.

How am I going to get to you? she wondered, knocking her knuckles lightly against one of the photos of Gomez and Delgado.

She knew Gomez was hiding from something. The world? Himself? Probably both and that was a conundrum she didn't have time to probe.

But she wanted to know. She cleaned his house, sorted through his sparse existence and the experience only left her wanting to know more about him. She wanted to know if he hurt. If he had nightmares. If he missed his old life. She wanted to know things about him that made her uncomfortable.

Not the point, Fitzgerald. Concentrate on what you know and what you need to know to get Delgado.

She opened the file to the blue transcript pages of his military debriefing. Even with her security clearance there were confidential parts of the interview removed, which left some basic location questions. Oddly enough, he'd been able to answer these with clarity.

Q: Are you sure about the time frame.

A: Absolutely. From the time I was taken to the time we arrived at prison it was six hours.

Q: You'll have to forgive me for doubting you, but you were blindfolded. Time has a way of—
A: The sun is hot in the desert and they had me in the back of a transport truck. Lots of sun. So, I sweat during the day and at night I got cold because the sweat dried. I was kidnapped at two in the afternoon. The sun had been setting around seven these nights and I didn't get real cold until about an hour after that. Time slips away only if you let it. I stayed pretty focused, Sergeant Drury.

She smiled, able to hear him saying that.

The influence of the heavy-duty painkillers they had him on as well as his general smart-aleck sense of humor was in full evidence throughout the interview.

Q: At what point did you know you were being taken hostage?
A: I imagine some people might figure it out when the black hood appeared, but I was never the sharpest knife in the drawer. Perhaps the solid kicks to my groin and chest should have clued me in, but I didn't fully get the fact that I was a hostage until I saw the

menu at my hotel. Gruel and rat are a dead giveaway every time.

Q: We can stop the proceedings if you are in pain.

A: Well, then, I'll see you sometime after I die. Because, according to my doctors, the pain should ease by then.

But at the end Gomez's true patriotism won out over sarcasm and irony.

Q: It is truly an honor to have spent this time with you, Mr. Gomez.

A: Thank you Sergeant and thank you for all the work you guys are doing over there. I am forever in debt to the United States Army.

Maggie spread her hands out at her sides and studied the ceiling, thinking of all the questions she wanted to ask him—about Delgado, about his work…about his life.

She was getting ahead of herself. Plotting conversation strategies did very little good when the man didn't come out of his office.

Tomorrow, if he didn't come out on his own, she'd smoke him out. It had worked like a charm in the

Hollenbeck case, which had been part of what earned her the promotion to Curtis's task force.

She turned off her light, patted her brother's picture and headed for bed, her heart cheered by her plan.

IT WAS COLD. Freezing. She tucked her hands in her armpits and put her chin to her chest to try to keep warm. The shadows in the alley were long and deep. The buildings obscured all but traces of sunshine.

"Patrick!" she screamed.

Her voice echoing back to her was her only answer. She thought she detected movement behind a Dumpster and her heart leaped. But it was only a rat.

Suddenly the sound of someone running after her cracked the silence of the alley and she knew without having to look that it was Delgado. If he caught her, he'd kill her.

She started to run. Legs pumping, breath bellowing out of her chest, she ran as hard and as fast as she could.

"Patrick!" she screamed. "Patrick this isn't funny!"

Delgado gained on her. She could feel him behind her, his malice physical and terrifying. She forced her legs to move faster, as fast as she could.

She screamed her brother's name, even though she knew he wasn't going to answer.

MAGGIE HAD HER GUN in her hand before she fully woke up.

"Who's there?" she asked, her voice a croak as though she'd been screaming. Even as she asked the question she knew her apartment was empty—it was her head that was filled with ghosts and phantoms.

She uncocked her gun and set it down beside her mattress, pushed her sweaty hair off her face, then cradled her pounding head in her hands. The muscles in her arms protested, cramped from her day of labor. Her jaw hurt and her ulcers were churning acid and bile.

One week left. Three days left to find whatever scrap of information Gomez had that would bring down Delgado. Or she'd have to set up Gomez as bait to bring Delgado to her. Time was something she couldn't change, like the past, like her brother's fate and, she feared, like Caleb Gomez's tortured silence.

The question of *what then* that she hated to think about and the *plan B* she hadn't yet formulated taunted her, whispering insidiously *You're never going to avenge your brother this way.*

She had to focus. She had to lure Gomez out of his office long enough to search it. No more rookie slip-ups. No more indulging in regrets and thoughts of what might have been. If she had to use Gomez's attraction to her as a way to get past his guard, she would. She'd been ruthless before and she would be now.

She got up to get a glass of water and to look at her time line again. Sleep, like her brother in her dreams, eluded her.

DAY THREE as Margaret Warren and Maggie again had to clean up a mess in the kitchen from the dog. This time green chili salsa was splattered across the lower cupboards, as if the dog had put his snout in last night's meal then sneezed.

Something, she thought, eyeing the carnage, *has got to give.*

And hopefully it would give before she had to clean that bathroom.

The phone in her pocket vibrated and she grabbed it, scrolling through her in-box for Gordon's text message.

Problem with bedroom feed, it read. I think the stupid dog might have knocked loose the bug. Fix.

She took a look in the oven, which appeared to

have never been cleaned, and cranked the temperature as high as it would go before heading to the bedroom. The gross black bits layered on the bottom of the oven would incinerate, creating a nice thick smoke. But it would take awhile.

She headed down the hallway toward the bedroom, slowing in front of the office to press her ear against the door.

No sounds but the muffled snoring of the dog.

She wondered what would happen if she kicked the door in. Announced that she was FBI and that his old buddy Benny Delgado was hunting him down.

Well, she knew what he'd do. He'd press charges, the way he had in the past. The Bureau would freak and she'd be assigned to desk duty fielding calls about alien sightings.

That meant she had to play Gomez according to plan. *So do your job.*

With her foot she pushed open the bedroom door. It slid soundlessly over the beige carpeting.

She took in the image of him in a split second. The woman in her responded to catching him unaware, embarrassed yet intrigued. Then the swift analytical cataloging of particulars she'd been taught at Quantico took over.

Gomez stood, his back to her, in a shaft of

sunlight from a gap where the thick curtains didn't quite meet.

The T-shirt he struggled to put on was caught around his injured shoulder blade. The bottom hem evaded his damaged hand, his arm not able to reach far enough to grasp the fabric.

The brands the Iraqis had laid against the skin of his back had healed into shiny red divots, perfect circles all along his spine, a trail of torture.

His shoulder had been smashed, the bones set incorrectly, requiring the medical teams to break them again, then reset them properly. The result was a mass of scar tissue and bumpy cartilage.

"Aha!' he muttered and shimmied slightly. The blue shirt unfurled, obscuring his back. He ran his good hand through his dark hair and limped, sideways, rotating slightly to grab the jeans laid out across the bed.

One leg was thinner than the other, bent inward at the knee at an awkward angle.

He didn't wear underwear.

She ducked back into the hallway, pressed herself flat against the wall. Slowly, she let out the breath she didn't realize she'd been holding.

He was scarred, damaged and yet, somehow… beautiful. Bathed in shadow and light, he was beautiful. To her. Dark and dangerous and…appealing.

She forced herself into action, shaking off her reaction and reached across the hall into the closet and grabbed the vacuum so it appeared she had a reason to be wandering into his bedroom.

She took a deep breath, waited until she thought she'd given him enough time to get his pants on—and herself enough time to act like a professional—then turned into the doorway, making sure to bang the vacuum against the wall.

"Oh!" Gomez said, pulling up the zipper on his jeans. "Hi, Margaret."

"Caleb!" she cried and looked away as if she hadn't been ogling him moments earlier. "I'm so sorry!"

"Don't worry about it," he said. "I'm just getting a late start."

He grabbed his cane from where it was propped against the bed and, leaning heavily on it, he crossed the room past her.

Say something. Say something. Say something.

But he was gone, only the smell of soap lingering.

It was the wrong time, she told herself, yanking on the vacuum with too much force. *It would have been forced.*

But the truth was a little too obvious.

Caleb Gomez was under her skin.

Shaken by her failure to manage her feelings for him, she braced herself against the bedside table and checked under the lip for the bug.

It was gone.

She went down on her knees, searching the beige carpet for the device. Ran her hands under the bed and table, but coming up empty. They could replace it—surveillance bugs got lost or damaged all the time. Once in the Ciglioni case in New York, the flowers in which the bug was delivered were thrown against a wall. It stuck there—inoperable—literally a dead fly on the wall for two months before anyone noticed it.

But if Caleb found this bug... Well, that would jeopardize everything.

She stood: checked the bed, ran her hands over the sheets, shook out the pillows. Nothing. Absolutely nothing.

She whirled, searching for his shoes. He could have stepped on the bug and tracked it...the dog could have eaten it.

Christ, it could be anywhere.

Gordon was going to lose his mind.

She put her hands to her head. *Think, Maggie.*

Think! But before she could search further, she smelled the smoke from the oven.

One disaster at a time, she thought and took off for the kitchen.

*When, her fingertips tight, . . . in a flutter, the . . . slid in an array from her own. . . .

. . . one above . . . for now, she . . . moved . . . into the future.*

CHAPTER SIX

MAGGIE PULLED OPEN the oven door and smoke poured out in choking thick curls. She tucked her face into the neck of her shirt and waved the smoke out of the kitchen into the hallway and in mere minutes the house was filled with drifts of the blue-gray stuff.

She coughed. Loud. Theatrically. And kept her eye on the hallway while the smoke detector wailed.

Jeez, she thought as the minutes passed. *The guy is either asleep or doesn't care that he's about to go up in flames.*

Bear howled, adding to the cacophony.

She leaned out of the kitchen and waited to see the patio door from the office open. Instead, his office door opened. She quickly turned to wave the smoke out into the yard through the door she jerked open.

Maggie wondered how to best play this situation with the dog. Before she could formulate an answer a monster—no lie, a monster—barreled out of the dark hallway straight for her like some demented hound of hell.

As she'd only seen his snout and his back as he slumbered, she was in no way prepared for the ugly beast and before she could stop herself, she kicked the garbage can to act as a barrier between them, then grabbed the vacuum as an improvised weapon.

"Whoa! Whoa! Bear. Chill out." Gomez hurried after the dog—hard to do with his injuries no doubt—and managed to grab Bear by the collar before he lunged over the garbage and got beaned by Maggie's vacuum.

"Just relax, dog." Gomez raised his voice to be heard over the still-screeching smoke detector and kept a firm grip on Bear's thick red-canvas collar. "He won't hurt you," he said to Maggie.

Maggie turned incredulous eyes on him. "Does the dog know that?"

Gomez chuckled. "I think so."

"That's not very reassuring," she said, letting a slight tremble of apprehension fill her voice as she dropped the vacuum. It would seem a bit suspicious if Margaret Warren, mild-mannered housekeeper, snapped the dog's neck. Caleb yanked on the collar until Bear sat back on his haunches and Maggie got a good look at the animal.

"That's some dog. It is a dog, right?"

"That's what they told me at the pound. His looks are the most effective thing about him as a guard dog."

"He's pretty scary," she agreed. Bear appeared to have some terrible fur-eating virus.

"What happened?" he asked, waving smoke from his eyes.

"I thought your oven was self-cleaning."

He limped toward the patio and slid open the glass doors, one hand clutching the dog's collar.

"We're going to have the fire department here," he said as the curls of smoke reached across the ceiling toward the open doors.

"I hope not," she said and ducked back into the kitchen to turn the oven off.

Caleb coughed and his grip on Bear's collar loosened. The animal made his break for freedom, racing onto the patio and attempting to wiggle beneath the bottom slat of the railing.

"Oh, crap," Caleb muttered and lurched after the dog, who heard him coming and veered away.

Caleb shot her a beseeching look and she knew there was no way she could let him hobble after his mutant dog while she ransacked his office or searched for the missing bug as she'd hoped.

"Let me help," she said and they both stepped

out of the smoky house into the bright sunlight of the California morning.

"Bear, you stupid mutt! Get over here!" he shouted as she shot him a dubious look.

"Does insulting him usually work?" she asked, trotting out into the barren yard where the dog had industriously set to digging a hole.

"I don't think he knows the difference," Caleb said with a sheepish grin.

"I've got a ham sandwich in the fridge," she said, ready to sacrifice her meal in order to bring this episode of *Animal Kingdom* to an end so she could start plotting another way into the office.

"Excellent idea," he said. "I'll grab it, you make sure he doesn't eat any children wandering by."

Caleb limped away and she slowly closed in on the dog. She crouched, held out her hands.

"Hey, you big sweet dog," she said in those low tones she'd learned at Quantico for use when dealing with a skittish armed man. "Come on over here."

Bear growled at her. His fangs looked lethal.

She circled him the other way. Skirting the edge of the ravine, she noticed a thin, worn footpath winding through the ferns and pines. She jerked upright, peering through the woods to see where the trail went.

The house wasn't as secure as they'd thought.

Someone could get here without driving, which eliminated using Gordon's van sitting at the bottom of this street as an early warning of trespassers.

"Hey, dog," Caleb cried from the porch. He held half the sandwich in the air while the other half—*the jerk*—was in his mouth. "Come and get it!"

Bear abandoned his hole as though it meant nothing to him and charged Caleb, knocking the man onto the wooden Nantucket chair nearby.

Maggie eyed the trail one last time before joining man and beast on the deck. She couldn't tell where it went—perhaps the view from the elevated deck would be better.

"You just let him run wild?" she asked.

"Good God, no," Gomez said. "Usually he's chained up." He leaned off the seat and grabbed the heavy chain bolted to the side of the house and clipped it to Bear's collar.

She sat on the step next to his chair and watched the dog eat her lunch. Caleb tore off part of the sandwich he'd been eating and handed her the rest with a sheepish grin.

"I'm starving," he said, his mouth full. "I'm sorry."

All three of them munched the ham sandwich intended to feed only one.

"Well," he said, swiping at a patch of smoke that hung in the air. "Nothing like a little excitement in the middle of the day." He looked at her, his eyes penetrating, piercing as though she was smoke he was trying to see through.

"So, tell me, Marg—"

She put her fist to her mouth and coughed in a desperate and hackneyed effort to stop him from trying to focus the conversation on her.

"Are you okay?" His concern was real and she felt the usual bite of guilt when a subject expressed concern over fake moments of weakness.

In fact, seeing the worry in his blue eyes was worse.

I gotta get out of this job, she thought. *Caleb Gomez is going to be the last person I trick. The last person I lie to and hurt.*

"I'm okay." She waved him off, but coughed to negate her own words. "I must have swallowed a little too much smoke."

She bent double and put all her effort into hacking.

"Let me get you something to drink," he said and stood, shuffling into the now quiet house since the smoke detector had stopped screeching.

Maggie stood and rushed to the edge of the porch to peer into the woods. She could see the trail cross the stream and then climb the opposite bank to the hilltop and another residential street. She'd have to get Curtis to put some men on that street.

She heard Caleb returning and resumed her seat. Bear watched her out of his sad, red eyes.

"Shut up," she muttered to the dog, projecting her guilt. "I'm doing my job."

"Here you go," Caleb said. He handed her a glass of water and sat back in his chair.

"I hope the whole house doesn't smell like smoke," she said, watching him from the corner of her eye.

"It's not too bad. I think if we leave the doors open, it will be okay."

Gomez scratched his dog's ear and Maggie opened her mouth to ask him about stories he'd worked on without publishing but he spoke up first.

"Where's your son?" Gomez asked, turning slightly to watch her. "Will, you said?"

Coughing up a lung doesn't seem to distract the man. She decided to create some connections between them to draw him out.

"He's with his father until I get settled." The prepared lie fell from her lips. As well as training to remove any accent from her voice, she also trained to control all of her "tells," the small unconscious ticks and gestures people had that gave away lies.

"Long Beach?"

She nodded. "You lived there, right?"

He nodded, but she couldn't be sure he was answering her question. The guy was so evasive he could give agents lessons. "I hope you get settled soon," he said, kicking at a dried leaf. His scarred, red face was turned toward her. "For your son's sake."

"He's there for the summer." Will was a necessary part of Margaret Warren's character, but not having him around was equally necessary.

"What's he like?" Caleb asked.

"Good kid, bad student."

He laughed. "I can relate."

I know you can.

"How is the—" she started to ask but he interrupted.

"So, what do you do for fun? I mean, with your son gone."

Ah, Jesus. What does Margaret Warren do for fun? Does she have any? "I knit. I read."

"Oh?" Caleb asked. "What are you reading now?"

"Well, I read your articles," she said trying to get things back on track. She even smiled in an effort to disarm him. "I looked you up online after you told me your real name, Mr. Estrada."

She joked, proving Margaret Warren had some life in her.

"Boring stuff." He dismissed his work with a wave of his hand. "What else?"

"Biographies." That was the truth; it tasted weird coming out of her mouth. "When I have the time."

"Did you read the new one on Elizabeth I?"

"I did," she said with perhaps a bit too much enthusiasm for Mild Margaret. But she'd loved the book. Gobbled it up in one weekend a few months ago.

She jumped in with her own questions before he could chip away at her cover to the woman underneath.

"How is the work going today?" she asked.

His shoulders rose in a small shrug. "Same as yesterday and the day before and the day before."

"Not so good?"

"You could say that."

She idly ran her thumb nail along the grain of the wooden step. "You're a serious journalist. I mean, that's what it looked like on the Internet."

"I was." He nodded.

"You should write about Long Beach," she said, plunging into the common ground she'd established between them. "About the crime there."

He turned to face her, his face so still it

seemed to be made of wax. His eyes focused and penetrating.

"You did live there?" she asked, feigning confusion at this blank expression of his. "Right?"

"Sort of." He was clearly distracted, his eyebrows knit together as he thought about something.

"So you must have been exposed to it, or at least seen how bad it was."

He nodded again.

"Well, you should think about it now. It'd be a good story. People should know how bad it is. And you can make the politicians fix it."

But Gomez wasn't listening to her. His eyes had a far-off, yet totally focused look in them.

And she wondered if she'd managed to pull him out of his mental cave. She ducked her head and reached across the step to scratch Bear behind the ear. Was it her imagination or did he seem to like her a bit more having eaten her sandwich? While she bonded with Bear she watched Caleb from the corner of her eye. She could practically see the mental wheels turning, the slow forward roll out of inertia.

"That's a good idea, Margaret Warren." He smiled at her, this time his whole mouth lifted and changed his face. The scars seemed insignificant in the light of such a smile.

He wasn't handsome, would never be considered handsome with the damage done to his face. But he was captivating. The space between them shrank and the air suddenly became humid, hard to breathe.

Before she could stop herself, in the soft silence of the backyard, she smiled back at him. Not one of Margaret Warren's thin-lipped grimaces. But one of her own—Maggie's—full, heartfelt smiles. He appealed to her. As a man.

I wish I'd met you a different way.

The thought, like something washed up on the tide, was a surprise. She never saw it coming.

She coughed and he looked away, breaking the intimate bubble they'd created.

"Well, if we leave him, he'll go back to work on that hole," he finally said, referring to Bear. He was obviously as discomfited as she was. "That should keep him busy for a while."

They both stood. Maggie busied herself by brushing off her pants, flustered and embarrassed by her attraction to him.

He limped past her carrying with him the slight scent of soap and, oddly, black licorice.

"Oh." He turned around. "What did you bring for dinner tonight?"

"Baked macaroni and cheese," she said, forcing

herself to look at him with the same distance she'd managed to perfect before.

"Is it still frozen?" he asked, with a sly look indicating he'd known all along that she was feeding him crap and he'd let her get away with it.

She nodded. "I'm sorry," she said. "I just haven't—"

"Keep it frozen," he said. "I'll go get something tonight."

She blinked at him, stunned.

"It's true," he said, reading her expression. "The hermit does actually leave his house."

"That's great," she said and then inwardly winced at the awkward amount of good cheer she'd forced into her voice. *That's great,* the cheer seemed to imply, *the cripple gets out.*

Gomez's smile fled his face and his eyes shuttered. He shuffled off into the house.

Maggie watched the ocean and cursed her inability to keep herself in line. She'd made some headway and then ruined it with a strained pity she didn't even feel. She wanted to apologize to him, assure him she didn't see him that way. As a cripple. As someone to pity.

He…amazed her.

But she couldn't say that, either.

Maggie sat down on the step and Bear put his

giant head in her lap. She patted him awkwardly, all too aware of his skin condition. But there, sitting in a glob of dog saliva stuck to his fur, was the missing surveillance bug.

"I don't believe it," she whispered and pulled the device from the dog's face. He whimpered and licked her hand and Maggie started to laugh.

She put her head in her hands and let the relief pour through her, obliterating the confusion of her feelings for Gomez. "This whole thing is a circus."

GOOD FOR YOU. Her tone rang in his ears. *Good for you, you poor man. You poor, pitiful man.*

You have no idea what I am, he wanted to yell at her. He wanted to yell that to everyone he caught looking at him with pity in their eyes. He couldn't believe she'd done that to him. Especially after that…moment out there. That man-woman thing that sparked between them.

He collapsed into his chair and hung his head over the back. *What's happened to me?* he asked himself. A few months ago he had been so happy to be alive that every breath was something to celebrate. But now…? Now there was nothing to celebrate.

There was just…nothing.

He eyed the pain meds on his desk. They were

probably a reason why he felt nothing. They made his sleep dreamless, his days painless and his brain fuzzy.

The drugs kept him comfortable in this highly uncomfortable life of his.

Maybe a little discomfort wouldn't be amiss. His hip hurt, his skin felt tight and the itch along his neck was nearly unbearable.

And his pride. His pride stung and burned in his chest. Of course he went out. What he didn't share with her was that he only went out on his motorcycle, alone with his face covered by his helmet. He would never sit in a restaurant again, letting everyone get a good look at him. He didn't even pick up his own pizzas.

Ah…what the hell.

Caleb shook out a Vicodin and ignored those voices in his head that told him he was hiding.

Bored and soon to be numb. He'd grown partial to this state of being.

But something Margaret had said stuck in the back of his head.

Crime in Long Beach.

It seemed like a million years ago, but he'd once been obsessed with gangland violence. Back in the days before heading to war. And… He turned looking for his boxes of tapes and notes.

He usually kept his research around after a story ran in case there was a follow-up or a criminal investigation.

He eyed his shelf, considered the amount of work, of heavy lifting and possibly squatting required to locate the right box.

*Ah...*he thought, the painkiller entering his bloodstream and twisting with his consciousness. Care drifted from him, the reality of his life, of his injuries seemed very far away.

The story could wait. He'd sit here and think about Margaret and let life keep going on without him for a little while.

FOR SOME REASON, his mother, who sat at the Palm Restaurant in Los Angeles and cut his steak for him, kept knocking on the wooden table.

"Mom," he said trying to catch her hand in his, "stop doing that."

"Well, you can't," she said, pointing the steak knife at his ruined hand.

"No, not that. Stop knocking."

"Sweetheart," she said, cupping his hand with hers, "I'm not."

Caleb woke up with a snort and nearly propelled himself out of his swivel chair.

The pounding in his dream was at his door.

He shook his head, trying to clear the sticky cobwebs of narcotics.

"Hel—" His voice came out a croak. "Hello?" he tried again and sounded more human.

"Caleb?" Margaret's voice came through the wood door, muffled.

He wiped his face for drool and pushed himself upright. The loose disconnected feeling from the painkiller was gone and now he was simply pain free. He stood and opened the door with barely a limp.

"Hi." He made sure to smile, hoping he seemed to be a man who had been hard at work rather than asleep and dreaming of his mother and steak.

"I was wondering." She licked her pretty pink lips and seemed less straightforward and more demure. Caleb blinked hard, thinking this was just a new chapter in his dream. "Did you expect laundry service?"

Not quite the kind of dream he had in mind.

"Uh…" He leaned against the door frame. "Sure? I mean, are you offering?"

She heaved a sigh and her breasts pushed against her worn T-shirt. Caleb forced himself not to stare. "I can do it, it's not a problem. I just need you to show me where everything is."

"Well, the washer and dryer are in the garage and the soap is on the shelf next to it."

She nodded. Licked her lips again and Caleb swallowed hard. Uncomfortable as all hell.

"Thanks!" he said and leaned away from the door, giving her the cue to take her breasts and lips and leave his vulnerable person alone.

"Okay." She stepped back. Smiled. He nearly groaned at the prettiness of her and shut the door before his drug-addled and dream-drunk self did something stupid.

He bounced his head off the door's surface a few times to knock some sense in.

Once upon a time when he was interested in a woman he would spend time with her. Talk to her, flirt with her. Ask her to dinner. Find out what made her tick.

Now he stayed locked his office.

Good idea. That's sure to work.

He turned and came face-to-face with his bookshelf of boxes.

What was I going to do with these? He remembered an interest in those boxes before the nap.

Right. Delgado.

The bite of an untold story clamped down hard on his gut and he nearly rubbed his hands together.

Caleb checked out his intricate box-filing

system—which consisted of setting big, unlabeled boxes on top of small, unlabeled boxes. He pulled the lids off a few crates and read the names in the notebooks, hoping Benny Delgado would pop out of nowhere. On the bottom shelf beneath stacks of phone books and take-out menus he found a green box and yanked it onto the floor.

He flipped off the lid and found four miniature tapes and seven pocket notebooks.

The Delgado story.

A little more than three years ago it had been his plan to shadow a soldier in the Latin King gang. He'd done as much research as possible through arrest records and targeted Benny Delgado, an up-and-comer in the Hernandez syndicate. He had been arrested twice for carrying a gun and once for conspiracy to commit a felony. The charges weren't interesting, but the fact that he managed to beat all three and never do jail time was pretty out of the ordinary.

Caleb had followed Benny's sister, Lita, for two months and finally made contact at her church in East L.A.

Two dates later he was introduced to Benny in their backyard in Long Beach.

The notebooks and tapes had six months' worth

of investigation that he'd dropped suddenly when the chance to go to Iraq had come up.

He'd forgotten about it. He wondered what happened to Delgado. Was he running the organization as he'd so intricately planned years ago? Or had he been shot down as was more likely.

A quick check of the *Los Angeles Times* online archives told him that Benny had been busy and gruesomely successful.

This, his gut told him, *could be a story.*

And it was a story he could write, even without his old face and body.

Margaret Warren seemed to think he could.

For some reason her belief lit a fire under his confidence. The regard of a pretty woman was a powerful thing.

He opened the first notebook filled with impressions he'd had of Benny.

The guy sure does love his mother, he read. And he does not trust his brother. Drug Addict. Lita gets overlooked and she likes it that way.

He flipped to another page with a reasonable transcription of a conversation he'd had on July 2, 2004.

Delgado: Gangs need to be run like businesses. That's the problem right now. Too many thugs thinking it's all about street cred and respect, when it's really all about money and keeping shit in line.

Me: What would you do different?

Delgado: You got to get the politicians in your pocket. This dude in Mexico, Reyes, the ambassador? That guy controls drug and gun trade. Hernandez (Gang Leader—Eduardo Hernandez, Benny reports directly to him since the death of Alvarez) he doesn't get that shit. He needs to have meetings, set up some pressure so that we control Reyes and we control the guns and drugs out of Mexico.

Me: Sounds like you've thought about this a lot.

Delgado: It's all I think about, dude. I gotta take care of my family, man. For generations. I don't want my nieces and nephews dying like my momma because no one can afford medicine and doctors. I want someone with my blood to go to college. To become a doctor or a lawyer. That shit takes money.

Caleb closed the notebook and pulled the box up onto his desk.

An hour later, a storm of ego and the desire to tell the story brewing in his belly, he called Robert Louis at the *Los Angeles Times*.

"Robert," he said when his old friend answered. "I've got a story."

"Finally!" Robert cried. "Front page above the fold. No matter what."

"That's why I call you, Robert." Caleb laughed.

"What's the story?"

"Remember my mystery story from three years ago?"

"I remember you had one. But I also remember you not telling me what it was."

"I got close to Benny Delgado."

There was a long gratifying pause on the other end of the line and Caleb sat back, a smile on his face.

"How close?" Robert asked, like a dog latching on to the scent of something good.

"Very. I need some holes filled in from your crime guys. They'll get bylines."

He heard Robert's feet hit the ground and the clatter of keys. "I just e-mailed them," Robert said. "They'll send you all their recent stuff. Delgado has been busy since you were gone. He's tied to some nasty work that happened six months ago."

"Give me everything you've got. And the name of your source at the police station. I think once I start piecing this together, we might have enough to do some damage to the guy. Get him off the streets."

"'Atta boy. So, what do you say you come down to the city and we can get lunch and—"

The pride fizzled and went dead in his stomach. Leave?

Walk out the door among people?

Among his old colleagues? The men and women who had revered him and hated him and respected him and wanted to be with him? Let them see what had become of him? The limp and the face and the FreeCell games and the online classes?

Not a chance.

"Sorry, Robert."

"Everyone here would love to see you, Caleb."

I'm sure they would, he thought, unkindly.

"Soon." He was lying and Robert knew it.

"I'll order every photographer to take the day off. No pictures. No story. Just a colleague coming back to see some friends. My secretary misses you."

Caleb swallowed and grabbed one of the stress balls from his desk that was supposed to help him gain strength and mobility in his hand. So far they'd been good chew toys for the dog.

"I…ah…maybe it's too soon," he said. "I'm in therapy and driving is—"

"You don't have to lie to me," Robert said, his voice low.

I'm not lying to you, he wanted to laugh. *I'm lying to myself.*

"When I get the first draft done," he said forcing the old cheer back into his voice. "I'll come down and make you take me to the Palm for lunch."

"Done."

Caleb hung up and watched his hand shake. A strange mix of emotions coursed through him. A recklessness, a heady sense of who he was and what he was capable of, filled him like a drug.

He buzzed with deadlines and the realities of the job he more than loved. The job was as much a part of him as his bone and blood.

An idea, dangerous and stupid, took root in the soft tissue of his soft head.

Lita.

As helpful as the stories from the crime reporters would be, Caleb knew that there would be one person even more helpful. One person who could fill in the three-year gap in his Delgado story.

Lita Delgado.

He eyed his phone and tapped his fingers against his suddenly smiling lips.

A risky move for sure. Possibly a suicidal one. His photo had been plastered all over the news the past few months and if Delgado was still a news junkie, he'd seen it.

Granted, Caleb looked different than he had then. But a photo of him before the fire and kidnapping had made the media rounds, too. Making the connection between Ruben Villalobos, a regular nobody, and Caleb Gomez, journalist, was huge and he couldn't know if Delgado had made it.

A thin river of fear cut through his adrenaline and made the hair on his arms stand on end. He nearly closed his eyes to embrace the feeling. This feeling, this tense measure of anxiety against excitement, was what made him drop everything to follow the war. It was what made him love motorcycles and going undercover. This feeling made him remember what it was like to be alive. Really alive.

The dangerous unknown lured him from the other side of this decision.

He could not pick up the phone, go about his life—

That thought stopped him. What life? Ordering pizza and ogling his housekeeper? It was hardly a life.

Or, he nodded, *I could pick up the phone and stir up a little trouble.*

The surge of excitement in his bloodstream, the part of him that longed to have some measure of himself back with powerful intensity, made the decision.

He called Benny Delgado's sister.

LITA'S BLACK EYE had faded to purple. Just looking at it made Benny feel like smashing things. Smashing her. Again.

She made me do it. Bringing that man into our lives. She brought that beating on herself.

You take care of your brother and sister, his mother had told him when she was dying, hacking blood into handkerchiefs so he couldn't see it.

If Momma knew he'd hit Lita, she'd kill him.

Guilt, anger, rage—it all ate at him like the cancer that killed his mother.

The stupid bitch brought a reporter into my home! The devil in him howled, defending the beating he'd given his baby sister. The devil in him had been howling a lot. He couldn't keep himself calm these days. He felt juiced, electric.

Ruben, Gomez, whatever the hell he'd been calling himself, was nowhere to be found and Benny buzzed and shook with rage. He couldn't sleep. Food tasted like acid. He could smell himself because he hadn't showered in two days. His beard was so itchy he scratched incessantly.

He'd beat his little sister like a dog.

"What do you want?" he asked Lita. Too harsh. She flinched and he wanted to hug her, pull her ponytail the way he used to. He wanted to be the brother she'd loved before he hit her a week ago.

She looked at her hands, timid, afraid. His beautiful sister who used to fight with him, tell him he should comb his hair, try to be nicer to her friends because they all thought he was good-looking. Her knuckles were white. Her lips shaking.

"What the hell do you want!" he yelled, angry at her for making him angry.

"He called me," she stammered.

"Who?" Benny barked.

"Ruben...I mean...Gomez or—"

"He called you?" Benny stood. "When?"

"On my cell phone...just now." She held up the small phone and he charged around the desk to grab it from her. She cowered against the wall. The bruises on her arms, revealed by her sleeveless shirt, matched his shaking fingers.

He paged through screens to the recently received calls screen.

Stupid ass, he thought, victory slipping like

tequila into his bloodstream. *I've got you. I've got you. I've got you.*

Blocked number.

He tried to call the number but it didn't register. The line rang once then went dead.

"What did he say?"

"Nothing…I mean…I didn't answer. He left a message."

"What did he say on the message?" He spoke to her as though she were stupid. Talked to her as though she was nothing. He hated himself for it, but he couldn't stop himself. The devil in him was in control.

"Here." She took the phone from him. Pressed a few buttons then handed it back. "You can hear for yourself."

"Hey, Lita. It's Ruben Villalobos. I don't know if you remember me from a few years ago. We met at church and had some fun? Ring any bells? Anyway, I'll try you again later."

He played the message again, hoping for some clue. But it was the same heavily accented voice he remembered.

The bastard was probably faking that, too.

"Damn it!" he growled, throwing the phone into the corner that held his sister. The phone exploded over her head and she shrieked in fright. "I'm sorry," he said. He reached out a hand, brushed a broken piece of plastic off her shoulder. "I'm sorry Lita—"

She jerked away from him.

"Why'd you do this to me?" he asked, managing to refrain from yelling. He'd asked her before, screamed it in her face and hadn't been satisfied by her answer. "Why'd you do this to us? To the family?"

"I told you, Benny," she whispered. "I met him at church. I didn't know. I didn't. I swear."

That was the knife twisting in his gut. He believed she didn't know. He believed Ruben-Gomez was that good.

And that's why he had to die.

"Get out of here," he told his sister, who was running before he even finished saying the words.

He fisted his outstretched hand and hammered it through the cheap paneling.

I'm falling apart. He could recognize it. The temper he'd spent years harnessing so he could be a strong leader was unleashed and eroding away at his control.

He had to find this guy. And he had to find him fast. It wasn't just about Reyes anymore.

If he didn't find this guy, he'd turn into one of those butchers, those thugs he hated.

He grabbed his own cell phone to call the guy who was supposed to be figuring this out.

Dirty cops, Benny thought, *can't trust 'em to do anything.*

MAGGIE WAS JUST OUT OF SIGHT of Caleb's house when she called Gordon.

"Nice work, Fitzgerald!" Gordon said upon answering.

Maggie pounded the steering wheel of her crappy hatchback with her fist. Fierce pleasure—pride and a relief that bordered on pain, like swallowing back tears—overwhelmed her. "I could hear him in his office talking most of the afternoon, but I couldn't hear anything through the door."

"He made two calls. One to the editor of the *Los Angeles Times.* He told the guy that he got close to Delgado. Very close. He's doing the story."

Maggie tipped her head back and laughed. It worked. The nudge worked.

"Yeah, but get this," Gordon said. "The second call was to Lita Delgado."

The laughter died in her throat. "Benny's sister?"

"The one and only."

Maggie swallowed. "Wow." That was all she could say. The relief and pride vanished.

"*Wow* is right. This thing may be over faster than we thought if Gomez waves red flags around like that."

Stupid man, what is he trying to do? she wondered. *Does he have a death wish? Does he think he's invincible up on that mountain?*

"Hey, Fitzgerald, this is good news." Gordon's tone snapped her back to the present. Gomez was bait and he'd set the trap better than the Bureau ever could.

"Curtis wants a meeting with us today at five."

"Because of the calls?"

"The calls and the missing bug—"

"I replaced it."

"Yeah, and the feed is good, but—" he paused "—Curtis asked for the tapes." Maggie grimaced.

"The tapes?" she asked dreading the worst.

"The New York mistake, Fitzgerald." Gordon's tone said it all. "You're not on top of your game."

Maggie cursed silently. "He said he was going to go out tonight to get some food. I thought I'd circle the eating—"

"Gomez just ordered a pizza."

She sighed, there was no avoiding the ass-chewing she rightfully deserved.

"Okay. Five?" She glanced at her watch.

"You want me to tell him it's gotta be later?"

She had just enough time to change and get down to 11000 Wilshire Boulevard. "No, I'll be there."

She hung up the phone and cut across the small town to her apartment. Caleb had given them a major break in the case, but the bitter taste in her mouth was not victory or satisfaction.

It was fear. For both of them.

CHAPTER SEVEN

THE LAWN in front of the Los Angeles field office was the greenest, lushest grass Maggie had ever seen. Every time she pulled into the sea of free parking surrounding the white building she wondered if whatever the agency did to make the lawn so ultraviolet green was legal.

She parked and hustled into the side entrance to the office, her files, all the pictures and time lines pulled from her lockbox tucked under her arm. She wasn't late, but she definitely wasn't early.

The meeting with Curtis was being held in the main conference room in the center of the building and when she arrived, Gordon wasn't outside. The door to the boardroom was cracked open, so, courage in hand, she peeked in.

Gordon sat facing the door, Curtis stood facing the windows that looked out at the labs.

They were listening to the surveillance tapes, she recognized her voice saying "Spoken like a guy from New York."

She watched Gordon cringe and suddenly she wanted to walk away. Just leave her badge with the receptionist and go to law school, or maybe go with the cruise idea.

Curtis's old lineman shoulders seemed particularly big at this moment. Particularly able to crush her career in the Bureau along with any chance she'd have at clearing Patrick's name and putting his killer behind bars.

For a split second, faced with the huge tongue-lashing she was about to get, she didn't care. Dan Meisner could avenge Patrick. The other agents doing hundreds of things to bring about the downfall of Delgado could avenge her brother better than she could right now.

She was tired of it. Tired of lying and sneaking around and pretending to be someone she wasn't. She was tired of manipulating a good man. A man she liked. A man, who once this was over, would loathe her.

But Gomez had put himself in the line of fire and someone had to protect Gomez.

"Fitzgerald," Curtis said, having turned from the windows and seen her. "Come on in."

She stepped into the impressive boardroom. It was equipped with giant plasma screens and the very latest in conferencing technology.

She slid into a seat opposite Gordon who gave her a little wince of a smile.

"We've just been listening to some of the Gomez tapes." Curtis said. "Interesting stuff."

"We had a major break in the case today," she said, quickly jumping on her successes.

Curtis nodded. "The phone calls. Good work."

"Regarding the call to Lita Delgado, I recommend we put Gomez under twenty-four-hour watch. There's a trail through his ravine, we need some men on the next street west."

Curtis hummed and pulled out the chair at the head of the table. That hum made her wildly uncomfortable.

"A car perhaps, at the entrance of the cul de sac," she said.

"Do you want to do it?" Curtis asked. And Maggie's eyebrows hit her hairline.

"I can," she said, unsure of where Curtis was going.

Curtis nodded, steepled his big hands together in front of his lips. "Let's get down to why I called you here, Fitzgerald."

Maggie braced herself for Curtis's comments.

"I put you on this task force because you are good. I ignored the fact that you believe your brother was killed by Delgado, and that the allegations that he worked for Delgado were falsified."

"He was, sir," she said quickly. "I can prove it. With time—"

"The LAPD already determined that your brother and his wife were victims of random violent crime. No gang involvement."

"Curtis, you know that's not true." She protested. Again. The way she had for months. "They dropped the investigation because of the rumors that he was dirty. They didn't want to find any more connections between him and Delgado."

"Your brother—"

"Patrick is—" She talked over him and Gordon signaled her to shut up with a finger across his throat. She couldn't.

"Fitzgerald, let me talk." Curtis's soft tone belied the tension that radiated out from him in choking waves. "Your brother was a valued member of the gang violence task force. His death affected every single person who knew him and every single person he worked with including the police, the Bureau and the ATF." Curtis stood and prowled the area in front of the windows. "I believe you, Maggie."

The use of her first name made something inside of her melt.

Maggie swallowed her emotions and stared at her hands.

"So, when this Gomez opportunity came up, I put you here because I thought that your involvement, your personal stake, would make you diligent. Would make you tenacious and careful and exacting." He turned to her, his dark eyes splitting her open and laying her bare.

"But it seems the opposite is true."

He pressed a key on the laptop that operated the audio equipment and her voice filled the air.

"Are you a writer?"

"Are you a cop?"

Curtis fast forwarded.

"Did I tell you I was from New York?"

Curtis stopped the recording and the silence threatened to squash her under its massive weight.

"He's astute," Maggie finally said in her defense. Her knuckles were white and her fingers ached with the force she was using to clench them. "We knew that going in."

"And you're acting like a novice agent in Hogan's Alley," Curtis said, naming the training facility for all FBI agents. "Now, Walters hasn't heard these tapes and won't. But I can pull you off the case without his authority."

He watched her in silence until, finally, her

throat dry and rough, she asked, "Is that what you're doing?" *Perhaps this is for the best,* she thought. *I'm not doing a good enough job. My head is screwed up, my heart is—*

"No." Curtis shook his head. "I'm as worried as you are about what Gomez is doing up there. Calling Lita was dangerous and even with all available agents watching his house, I'm still worried. You were right in the briefing—Delgado doesn't leave clues, just bodies, and I'm tired of chasing this maniac."

"What do you need me to do?"

"Find a way to be in the house longer. I need someone there, in the house next to Gomez. Otherwise the guy will be dead before we get our act together."

Relief buzzed through her body chased by adrenaline. A second chance.

"No problem," she said. "I've got a plan."

"Really?" Gordon mouthed to her, looking worried.

"Good." Curtis nodded and waved his hands, as though he was scattering birds. "Go. Stop screwing around and let's put this guy away."

"About the car in the cul de sac, sir. Delgado could already—"

"It's done, you don't need to worry. And we'll put people on the next street west and in the ravine."

"Thank you."

Curtis nodded at Maggie's words.

She and Gordon stood and nearly ran from the room. She felt like a convict given clemency and was doubly determined to put Delgado away. For her brother's sake. For Curtis's and now for Gomez's.

THE SMELL OF FOOD COOKING—real food, meat and the tangy bite of vinegar and cabbage—slid under Caleb's door in intoxicating waves. He felt as though he was in a cartoon and the scents had formed a finger beckoning him and Bear—who was actually licking the floor in front of the door—to a feast.

His stomach growled so loudly Bear turned a cocked ear toward him and whined deep in his throat.

"Okay, okay," he said to his dog, pushing away from the desk and computer screen filled with articles from the *Times* crime staff. Benny had been busy while Caleb was following the war. He'd been very busy and now, according to what Caleb had read, Benny was untouchable.

Knee-deep in research for a story and he felt good. It was better than food or sleep or even sex. It felt as though he had a small sliver of himself back.

"Bear," he said, moving toward the door. "I'm serious this time, no screwing around. She's a friend. She's cooking us real food." He nudged Bear with his cane.

"Got it?"

Bear barked once and Caleb doubted they'd shared any sort of understanding but he nodded anyway. "Good boy," he muttered, and opened the door slightly only to have the massive mutt nose it open the rest of the way and barrel into the hallway.

Caleb didn't even bother going after him. He could barely move.

Last night he'd sat at his computer too long and his leg was killing him, cramping and sending sparks and radiating fingers of shocks down to his foot and across his pelvis.

There was a way out of this agony. He could pop a pill or two and drift. And thanks to his doctor and some friends with loose standards regarding prescription medicine, he had enough to keep him pleasantly pain free for a long while.

But eliminating the aches came at a price. He'd be numb. His drive, his ego storm would be gone. The story would slip into the abyss…and he wouldn't even care.

I can live with the pain, he decided. *It's not that bad.*

He limped into the hallway to find the highly unlikely sight of Bear sitting like some sort of prize poodle at the feet of Margaret Warren as she scratched his head.

"Wow," he said, emerging from the shadowed hall into the bright mid-afternoon sunlight. "Beast-master."

"Hardly," she said, looking up at him with a smile. She was flushed from whatever slaving she was doing over the stove and her hair, blond and curly—a breathtaking surprise those curls—had come free from the tight band at her neck and made a soft halo around her thin face.

The smile, the curls, the bright flags of color on her previously colorless and stern face combined to blow a hole through his chest.

"I gave him a piece of meat," she said patting Bear one last time. "I hope that's okay."

"Fine by me." He took a great sniff of the air. "I do believe you are cooking something."

"Well, you did hire me to do that," she said and the roses on her cheeks turned crimson.

He waved off her embarrassment. "I would have been happy with those frozen dinners, as long as it was something I didn't have to think about."

"All you have to think about tonight is whether

or not you'd like a beer with your corned beef and cabbage."

"Beer? Corned beef and cabbage? Good God, I'm in heaven." He lurched farther into the room, the swish and thump of his foot and the cane a strange staccato rhythm he'd grown used to. "I knew you were Irish."

"My dad's from Dublin—" She stopped, her smile fading into something tighter, more restrained.

Well, well she does not like to talk about her father from Dublin. He added that to the very little he knew about Margaret.

"So, when will this magical meal be ready?"

She winced. "Well, about a half hour actually. I am sorry, I got a later start than I had hoped. I can leave you with instructions and get out of your hair."

"Cook?" he asked, pretending to be horrified before easing himself into his overstuffed chair. He set his bad leg on the ottoman with a grimace. "Me? Sorry. You're going to have to finish the job. Unless—" he looked up at her "—you have to go…."

"No." She waved him off. "Will's with his father. I'd only go home and be lonely."

"Can't have that," he said, a swell of bonhomie filling his chest. That hole she'd blown through him grew larger at the thought of her being lonely.

I'm lonely, you're lonely... It was a bad line he might have used a million years ago on a woman like Margaret. Actually, he watched her from the corner of his eye, a woman like who he used to think Margaret was. He didn't really know who she was right now.

"You have beer?" he asked. A heady thrill eased soft and slow into his bloodstream. It was time to resume his investigation into this woman who distracted him and made him foolish.

"I do." She grinned and headed into the kitchen. *Jesus, the woman looks good in Levi's.*

"Get one, too," he said. "For yourself. We can have a beer and discuss things."

"What things?" she called back.

He looked out over the waves and smiled. "We'll think of something."

The smell of food filled the air. His homely dog chewed on a piece of rope from the garage. The buzz of a good story churned in the back of his head. And a pretty woman was bringing him a beer.... Suddenly things felt right. In a way they hadn't in a long, long time.

"How did the work go today?" she asked, returning with two cold bottles of Harp.

Oh, he thought with a grin, *that cinches it, she's Irish.*

She looked like a working man's beer commercial—worn jeans, faded purple T-shirt that clung just enough to the right places, clear pale skin, freckles not covered by makeup, hair a little messy as though she'd been making out with—

Caleb sighed.

Hair a little messy as though she'd been cleaning a bathroom.

Let's not go overboard here, Gomez. Maybe you should just get a hooker and leave poor Margaret alone.

"Work went better." He took one of the bottles from her and lifted it in a toast. "Thanks to you."

"Me?" She sat on the edge of the sofa.

"Gang crime in Long Beach has organized and a story I was working on years ago is almost more relevant now than it was then."

"Well." She smiled and sat back, looking pleased with herself. "I'm glad I said something."

"How about you?" he asked, taking a sip of the cold, crisp beer and nearly sighing in pleasure. Beer was something he couldn't get delivered and he'd forgotten how good a cold one tasted at the end of the day.

She shrugged. "I worked. Your bathroom is clean."

He grimaced, theatrically, then worried how

macabre he must look and stopped. But she smiled in response.

"Not as bad as expected," she told him and took a sip of her own beer.

They watched the waves for a moment and he felt as if he'd taken that Vicodin. He practically melted into the chair. He rolled his head and saw her staring at the waves, the most relaxed he'd ever seen her.

"Do you have a lot of clients in the area?" he asked.

She shook her head. "You are my one and only."

"I should pay you more."

She pulled at the label on her bottle. "I'm planning on going to the community college in the fall. I didn't want to start a bunch of jobs and then have to quit them."

"What are you going to study?"

"Criminal justice. A friend told me the state is always looking for female parole officers or prison guards."

He recoiled before he could help it. He'd done a story on women in prison, from the guards to the inmates—it wasn't an easy life for anyone. "That's tough work."

"So is cleaning your bathroom."

He should let it go. He barely knew her, maybe criminal justice was right up her alley.

But of course, he couldn't.

"Sorry, you just don't seem the type for prison work."

She cocked her head. "What do I seem the type for?"

The air got so heavy so fast it felt as if a thunderstorm brewed in the hallway. What she asked opened up a level of intimacy between them that seemed dangerous considering his fascination with the fit of her Levi's.

But he was never known to be cautious.

He watched her. Drank some beer. Kept watching her. She didn't blink or demure, she looked him head-on.

"An eagle-eyed, no-nonsense prosecutor," he finally said with a definitive nod.

Her face washed white and her mouth fell open for a moment before she lifted her beer and took a drink.

"I considered that." Her voice sounded husky, as if the beer had gone down like a ton of bricks.

"So? Why not?"

"Family issues," she said.

"Hard to go to law school being a single mom?"

She nodded and then stood to go to the kitchen.

I'm gonna ask her to stay, he thought, watching

her go—his new favorite thing. *Share some food with me and the dog.*

"How's the class going?" she asked from the kitchen. "That online thing you do."

"It's good. I like it."

"How many kids do you have?"

"Ten, though it looks like I might have gotten a new one yesterday. I forgot to e-mail the school to find out who joined."

"Do the kids know who you are?" She came back to the room with another beer in her hand, which she passed to him. His first was nearly empty and he hadn't realized.

"Nah," he said. "I thought if word got out that the journalist tortured in Iraq was teaching a class I'd get a lot of people registered who only wanted to find out more about what happened to me."

He took a swig of his beer, to wash down the distaste those words had spawned. Part of the reason he hated leaving the house was those unasked questions that dogged him. From grocery store to gas station people watched him, unspoken whats and whys threatening to spill from behind closed mouths.

What happened to you?

The question was in the room right now, a pink elephant doing backflips on his coffee table. For the first time, Margaret seemed on the verge of articulating that familiar query.

"Did you want to ask me something?" he finally said, the elephant and her Levi's making him crazy.

She pursed her lips, tilted her head. Opened her mouth then finally shut it.

"No," she said, finishing her beer.

"You can ask me anything," he said, wondering what in the hell had gotten into him. He ignored his family, his friends. He made sure his phone number was unlisted and untraceable. But he was opening himself up like a suitcase for this woman.

"I'm really okay talking about it," he said. A bigger lie had never been spoken. "I mean, you must be curious."

"I read about you on the Internet when I looked you up," she said. "I know about the kidnapping. And the helicopter crash."

"Well, as long as you've seen my highlight reel, I guess—"

"What are you hiding from?" she blurted out.

"Hiding?" As if he hadn't been asking himself that very question.

She smiled at him, no trace of pity, just a slight give-me-a-break curl of the lips. "You don't think you're hiding?"

"It's not that easy for me to get around," he hedged.

"And you really love pizza?"

"I do love a good pizza," he said, hoping to joke away the tightness in his throat.

"Then why not go out—"

"Do you have a vision problem you should have told me about?" he interrupted, tired of talking about the sad state of his life in terms of take-out or eat-in pizza.

"No, of course not—"

"Then it should be pretty obvious why I'm not too eager to head out into the public eye." He lifted his ruined hand to his equally ruined face as if presenting evidence to the jury.

Margaret looked down at the bottle cradled in her hands. "I'm sorry," she finally said. "It's none of my business."

She stood, again heading for the kitchen, and Caleb felt as though the elephant in the room now sat on his chest.

He wrapped his good hand around his throat and pretended to choke. What an idiot. She was being nice, had been nothing but honest and...cool.

Here he was drinking beer with a pretty lady who didn't seem to see his scars and he had to go and ruin it.

"Everything's ready to go." She came back in the room, her car keys in her hand and her purse over her shoulder. He wanted to kick himself for making her leave. "It's in a pot on the stove."

"Great," he said, mustering far too much cheer for corned beef and cabbage. He stood, too fast, too much weight on a bad leg, too much beer on an empty stomach, and nearly stumbled forward. His own embarrassment, like steel rods up his legs, kept him upright. "Thanks, Margaret."

He waved at her, a jaunty sort of salute that seemed stupid, then turned toward the safety and sanctity of his office. He couldn't remember feeling like such a giant boob.

He had a hand on the doorknob when the floor squeaked behind him and he felt the cool press of Margaret's palm against the crook of his right elbow.

Touch.

That was all his body could register for a moment. Every nerve ending and neuron and blood vessel expanded with a sudden physical joy.

Another person…a woman…touched his flesh.

He pulled away before he made a further ass of himself. "Did you forget something?" he asked.

"You're amazing," she said or he thought she said because she was practically whispering.

"I'm sorry. What?" He leaned in and she stepped

closer, her breath, warm and beer-scented brushed his face. He was seconds away from blacking out thanks to the rush of blood heading south.

"You're amazing," she said, no louder. "I'm inspired by you…."

He put up a hand to stop her. He was on fire with lust for her and she was thanking him as though he were a member of the VFW and she was student body president. He couldn't stand to be so naked and needy for her while she *admired* him. It was humiliating.

She grabbed his hand and her eyes, pale blue, nearly gray, lifted to his. Again the rush of blood and sensation through his body rubbed like salt in a wound. And he knew how that felt.

"Nothing about you is diminished by what's happened," she said.

He squeezed her hand involuntarily. A spasm of incredulous desire clenched him, rocked him. He wanted to grab her, pull her warm, whole body to his.

"I wish I'd met you a different way," she whispered and before he even knew she was doing it, she pressed those lovely rose lips to the wreckage of his.

Sweet.

Soft.

And then gone.

She ran down the hallway and out the door of his house before he even managed to breathe.

He didn't know how long he stood there, his lips tingling and burning, his erection subsiding. After a while Bear came and sat on his feet.

"That was my first kiss," he murmured. While patently untrue, it seemed no less real. Like champagne across the bow of a new boat, that kiss was a sweet call to action. A soft welcome to the new world he never thought he'd get.

He was happy to be alive, even with the pain. The teaching filled him with a sense of purpose and the story he worked on led him to believe that one day he would be useful in the way he wanted to be.

But he'd given up on things like kisses, the brush and press of skin against his. He'd given up not just on sex, but on himself, on his manhood. Suddenly here it was, given back to him by his straightforward cleaning woman.

The gods had been kind when they led Margaret Warren to his dirty door.

"I still got it, Bear. I still got it."

MAGGIE GOT INTO HER CAR and drove out of the foothills with hands that shook. She watched her cell phone where it sat on the passenger seat like a snake coiled and ready to bite, waiting for it to ring. Waiting for Gordon to tell her he'd heard every word of what she'd said in that hallway, even though she knew it was doubtful the surveillance bugs would pick up sound at that distance.

At the stop sign before where she turned left toward her apartment, the adrenaline finally seeped out of her and she rested her head against the steering wheel.

What have I done?

She lifted her forehead and pressed her lips hard against the knuckles that gripped the wheel. She could still feel his mouth. The lush bottom lip that bloomed away from the scar tissue at the corner. The deep dent in the upper lip, the narrow scar that ran through it.

Utterly ruined and totally beautiful.

A car behind her honked and jerked her out of her reverie.

Good God, Fitzgerald. Get your shit together.

It was too late for that, however. The kiss had happened. The words she never should have said were out there, spoken and she'd seen what they meant to him. She'd seen the hope and life, the incredulous delight and wary gratitude they'd sparked in his eyes.

Worse somehow were the sharp fragments of her own feelings.

Maggie Fitzgerald was too present, too much a part of Margaret Warren. She couldn't look at him, talk to him without her own feelings getting involved. And it wasn't only the job she no longer wanted to do. It was the injury she would cause Caleb that she didn't want.

Why didn't I meet you another way? she wondered. *Why did you come into my life like this?*

She shook her head and felt the bite of tears. She would have to fix this somehow, get things back on track for Margaret Warren and this investigation.

She'd worry about Maggie Fitzgerald later.

CHAPTER EIGHT

CALEB BURNED the candle at both ends and by dawn he felt the way Bear looked. But still he couldn't stop. Between the story and the kiss from a pretty woman, he was far too worked-up to sleep. He'd transcribed his notes from years ago and read all the current articles about Delgado's rise to power.

He realized that not only did he have the makings for a great story, but that he also had the makings of a case against Delgado. Granted the evidence was years old, but from what he'd read the Delgado task force—consisting of the FBI, ATF and LAPD—had come up empty-handed.

Except for more bodies: the female witness who had been killed in the safe house, the cop and his pregnant wife.

While the articles claimed Patrick Fitzgerald was a victim of random violence, there were just a few too many connections to Delgado to make it totally random. The guy intends to testify against Delgado but suddenly turns up dead?

The stories ended there. As soon as the words *dirty cop* hit the headlines, the police department shut its collective mouth.

Caleb would bet ten to one the guy had been framed. It was all a little too pat. The stories went from fallen hero to dirty cop a little too fast. He'd looked at Patrick Fitzgerald's photo and there was no way that guy was dirty.

His legendary gut said so.

He leaned back in his chair and rubbed his gritty eyes.

"Oh, man, Bear." He turned to look at the trusty slumbering lump behind him, but the sleeping bag was empty.

He heard the sound of a heavy pot being slid across the linoleum in the kitchen. Bear, it seemed, was having breakfast.

He smiled, checked his watch and grimaced.

He'd been letting the online class slide the past few hours. He didn't do his nightly round-up yesterday and hadn't checked the chat room in about ten hours.

He clicked through his screens and refreshed his chat room screen and pages of conversation appeared. He scrolled through, his mind already on coffee when the last line, typed in neon green text, jumped out at him.

Who are you?

A cold chill skittered around Caleb's head and down his neck to sit in the small of his back.

Who are you?

Something about it seemed strange. Almost menacing.

He checked the screen name of the person who wrote it and didn't recognize it from his class list. The phantom addition he'd never checked up on.

"Great," he muttered. Some intrepid journalist or scandalmonger had found him.

He opened an e-mail message and sent a note to everyone in the class, except his neon-green friend, that the pass code to the chat room was changing.

He smiled.

The new pass code was: Irish.

BENNY LOVED MORNINGS. He sat in the plastic lawn chair in his backyard, smoked a joint and drank his orange Gatorade. Every day. And while he sat, he counted the many ways in which he'd made his life better.

Normally he thought about his mom—if the weed was particularly good, he might have a conversation with her. But since smacking Lita, he didn't think about his mom. Much.

He drank at night so he wouldn't see her face. He'd made Miguel take all the pictures off the wall so he wouldn't feel her eyes watching him.

When things were made right, he'd put the pictures up again. He'd go to church and pray for forgiveness. He'd light candles in her memory and scour his soul in penance for his crimes. But not until this Gomez thing was behind him could he seek forgiveness. Until then there would only be more blood on his hands.

Something in him was chewing him up, eating away the parts of himself that he'd worked so hard on for three years. He could feel himself becoming what he'd been before.

The two months when he'd killed everyone above him in the Hernandez syndicate in order to take control—it was as if he'd been in a trance. He barely remembered it now. In dreams sometimes, or when he smelled blood or heard a woman scream on TV, then bits of it came back to him.

He was like Dr. Jekyll and Mr. Hyde. Monster and man.

And the monster was coming back.

He checked the time on his cell phone and decided that if he was awake, the scumbag dirty cop who was supposed to be solving all his problems should be up, too.

He hit ten on his speed dial. Chief of police was number three.

He got such a kick out of that.

"Watcha' got for me?" he asked as soon as the phone picked up.

"I'm close," his rat said. Dude sounded tired, but Benny didn't care. He needed this done. Yesterday.

"How close?"

"In an interview he said he was going to teach some classes and the man who used to be his writing partner—"

"I don't care about this shit. Did you find him?"

"He's teaching an online class for the University of California in Santa Barbara. I managed to hack into the class but he changed the password on me."

"So? Go up there and get rid of him."

"I plan to check out the faculty at the university, but it's not that easy. He can teach the class from anywhere. He could be—"

"But we know he's on the coast north of L.A." Benny hated having to do the work for the retards he employed. You'd think a guy who went to college, got a degree and passed the police academy exams would be able to see the writing on the wall. But Benny had long since stopped being amazed at how stupid people could be.

"There's a lot of land between here and there," the cop said, subdued like a good little dog.

"I don't care if you have to knock on every door from here to Alaska. Find that journalist."

He flipped the phone shut and threw it onto the grass next to his chair.

Benny took another drag of his joint hoping to keep the peace in his morning, but he could feel the pit in his belly start burning and his hands made fists.

Kill him. Kill him. Kill him, the devil whispered in his ear

When this was done, he was going to have an exclusive agreement with Reyes regarding the guns and drugs that came out of Mexico, one dead journalist and, it couldn't be helped, another dead cop.

MAGGIE TOOK A DEEP BREATH, focused her attention on the center of her body. She felt her strength radiate from her abdomen, through her arms and legs. Into her hands. She curled her fingers into her palm.

I can do this. I can do this.

It had been a long time since she'd had to resort to the feel-good, self-actualization hooey she'd learned in a class on relaxation at the academy. But she felt loose and unfocused, caught in a current she couldn't control and she didn't like it at all.

She was torn right down the middle by a mistake. One that, in the cold dark center of the night when she could be honest with herself, didn't seem like a mistake at all.

Stop it. She tried to conjure that river of strength the teacher had insisted lived in all of them.

Finally, she quit when the attempt to relax only spiked her tension. Margaret Warren would deal with whatever came her way today as it happened. Maggie Fitzgerald was going to keep her mouth shut and her hands to herself.

When she arrived, the house was silent, as it had been for the past few days. She allowed herself to hope that they could continue as if nothing had happened between them, no emotional confessions had been shared.

She checked the kitchen. The pot with the corned beef sat on its side in the middle of the room, uneaten cabbage scattered around the floor.

The dog didn't like vegetables.

She walked to the hallway, listening for Bear or Caleb—

She closed her eyes. Gomez. *Gomez.* Not Caleb.

Silence stretched out from the back rooms. She eased past the closed door of the office, to the bedroom. She carefully tucked her head into the crack left in the door, bracing herself for some intimate scene she shouldn't see—Caleb dressing or sleeping perhaps, mouth open, slightly snoring.

But the room was empty.

She turned and realized the bathroom door was shut. She stepped to it and, as she pressed her ear to it, she heard the sudden rush of water from the shower.

The shower curtain snapped back and then, muffled but still audible, she heard Caleb humming and then singing.

He was loud and cheerful. He sang the drumbeat, adopted a thin falsetto that was awful and messed up some words of the oldie.

Maggie pressed her head to the door, shaken by affection for him, by her desire to take care of him.

She turned, forcing herself to bury those feelings. The best way to protect him was to get into the office, figure out what he had then leave the man alone.

At the office door she wiped her damp palms on her pants and reached out to open the door.

Sure it was locked she nearly stumbled when the door opened under the weight of her hand.

She checked behind her, listening for water turning off, but Caleb had progressed to "Blueberry Hill" and didn't appear to be in a hurry. Controlling her heart rate and the sudden guilt that nearly immobilized her, she slid through the half-opened office door, not trusting the hinges to stay silent.

The office was a disaster. Papers and books stacked everywhere, some, having clearly fallen off shelves, were lying in heaps on the floor.

Dog hair an inch thick swirled across the hardwood. She stepped over a nest of it and sat in front of his computer, which was nearly obstructed by a box filled with tapes and notebooks.

She touched the computer mouse, hoping the computer was just sleeping, and the screen sprang to life.

Relief surged through her.

Four windows were opened. Three for the Internet and one word processing.

The first window was his online class. Her guilt had prevented her from calling Gordon to see what he'd learned joining the class. That student Caleb…*Gomez* had mentioned had to be Gordon.

She clicked on the next window which was the POW/MIA Web site.

Her heart clenched at the distinctive black and white symbol of a man, head bowed behind the barbed wire.

Caleb Gomez had been a prisoner of war. It only made sense that he would search out other people in the world who knew what it had been like. People who would understand the horrors he lived with.

Suddenly, the part of herself that was so taken by Gomez, felt chagrined. A fool. Who was she to offer up her admiration and respect? What would it mean to a man such as him? A man who had done his part to change the world, who had suffered for his efforts.

She was doing a job she was growing to hate because she'd once longed for her father's approval so much that she made his wants her wants. She snuck into people's lives, befriended them then betrayed them. Maggie doubted that if they'd met a different way—ran into each other on the street or were introduced at a party—he'd care much for her.

He hated the FBI. And she, despite wanting to leave, despite her law school aspirations, was very much the FBI.

She minimized the screen and tried to do the same with her feelings. The third screen was a front-page article from the *Los Angeles Times* five months ago about the death of her brother.

Her heart stopped.

Detective and Wife Killed screamed the headline. Investigators reveal tie between Detective

Patrick Fitzgerald and gang lord Benjamin "Benny" Delgado.

It was as if she'd run into a brick wall. To be confronted by this slice of her real life made her nauseous. Worse even that it seemed Gomez was investigating her.

She swallowed nausea and bile, tried to shake off the vulnerability, and, finally, clicked to the last screen.

Notes June 12, 2004 Delgado backyard, family barbecue

Benny: What the hell is wrong with you, man?

Me: I told you Benny, I'm not selling drugs.

Benny: It's not drugs. I need you to carry some packages for me.

Me: What's in the packages?

Benny: If I told you, you wouldn't be able to tell the cops you had no idea what was in the packages.

Laughing.

Me: Dude, you're not selling the job to me.

Benny: Come on, Ruben. Why don't you want to work for me? I'm going to run this city one day. I might run the whole state. Don't you want in on that action?

Me: No, man. That action is dangerous. I just

want to find a nice girl, keep my job and get myself some babies. I'll leave the drugs and guns to you.

Benny: No one said anything about guns and drugs, man.

Maggie's breath stalled in her dry throat. This was it. The evidence. She looked in the box at the tapes and notebooks. She scrolled through the document on the screen. Thirty-five pages. Single spaced. Dates. Times. Gomez had it all.

She skimmed the notes, but most of it was written in a shorthand that she could not decipher.

If this was what she thought it was, he had enough evidence here to fill the major gaps in their Delgado case.

Patrick's name could be cleared. He'd be vindicated.

She nearly laughed. With a little time, maybe she could figure out—

The shower stopped and the pipes over her head thunked once.

She weighed her options in a nanosecond. She could grab the boxes and confront Caleb as he came out of the shower, gambling that she could persuade him not to go after the Bureau, to give up his notebooks and tapes.

It could be over. The D.A. could finish the case, issue a warrant for Delgado's arrest. Patrick's death would be avenged and she could move on with her life.

But that was a gamble without being sure of what she had.

And if she came forward now, revealed herself, Gomez would start hating her.

She clicked on all the screens, putting them back up on the monitor and ducked out of the room, before her head fully realized what she was doing.

It's not like I really know what I've got, she rationalized. *He could be working on a novel, or filling in blanks in his own story. It's unreliable. I need more time.*

But she knew that wasn't the truth. Something dark and personal and wrong was behind this behavior, this stalling. Maggie Fitzgerald was behind this.

She wasn't ready for him to hate her. Not yet.

Not without all the information, she told herself, embarrassed and angry with herself.

Patrick would have done the same thing. He had been even more cautious than she was. He'd have made sure there were no what-ifs.

She stepped into the hallway and pulled the door shut with a quiet snick just as the bathroom door flew open. Steam and the smell of Irish Spring soap flooded the hallway.

Caleb…*Gomez,* she corrected herself for the hundredth time since kissing him last night, stood in the doorway, a brown towel wrapped around his waist and another around his neck.

"Oh, hey," he said, for the moment taken aback by her sudden appearance. He pulled on the brown towel around his neck, using it to cover up the worst of the scars that licked across his chest and up his neck in a fiery caress. "I didn't hear you come in."

He crossed his arms over his chest, his fingers fidgeting with the end of towel like a nervous teenager at a school dance.

It was endearing. Sweet.

And she shouldn't care.

"You were too busy singing." She smiled at him, a quick moment of eye contact that, despite his seeming discomfort and embarrassment, threw kerosene on all the awkward emotions between them.

She wanted to pull the towel from his neck and kiss his wounds, telling him in a way he had to believe that he was beautiful.

The hallway, with his naked chest, all of her lies and his tortured past, was crowded.

She took a step back, leaving the hushed space for the safer ground of the kitchen. "I'll let you get dressed."

THE SITUATION WASN'T QUITE what Caleb had hoped for. He had wanted to be a bit more in control the next time he saw her after their brief kiss.

Singing and nudity had not been part of his plan.

He shimmied into his clothes. His skin, all that had been naked and imperfect and exposed in the hallway, was hot to the touch. Hot where she'd glanced over him, touching him with her gaze.

Get. A. Grip. He lectured himself as he eased his right leg into his jeans.

The truth was, he used to be a pro at these conversations. The loaded and dangerous words between two people who had shared some intimacy, who wanted to share more intimacy. He used to navigate these troubled waters with ease when he'd had half-decent looks and a whole body to back up the talk.

Now, to beat the nautical analogy to death, he couldn't even get his boat started.

Dressed, hair combed, deodorant on, he stood at the doorway to his bedroom shaking with nerves.

What should he say?

Should he pretend nothing had happened?

Would she pretend nothing had happened?

Jesus Christ. Maybe I should attach a note to Bear and send him out there.

He looked around for his dog, who never strayed too far from his feet, but the beast and his drool were nowhere to be found.

With nothing to do but face this himself, he headed to the main room.

I am an adult, he chanted. *I am an adult.*

Margaret stood facing the windows, a lithe silhouette against the shimmering backdrop of morning sun across the Pacific.

He couldn't make out her features and that only added to the mystery of her. The dangerous allure of Margaret Warren.

"Good morning," he said and she turned to smile at him. Reserved but friendly and that's all it took to send his blood chugging harder.

"Morning. Sorry—" she gestured to the hallway "—about earlier."

He waved her off. "Don't worry about it. I should have known you'd be coming, I just didn't check the time."

She smiled.

He smiled.

Silence drifted between them like heaps of snow.

"Look, Margaret about last night—" He stopped. The look on her face was not horrified, but it wasn't happy. She sprinted to the dust cloth and can of polish that sat on the side table.

She covered the surface with spray, filling the air with lemon-scented fumes.

"Margaret?"

"Don't worry about it," she said, practically scrubbing at the underside of the table, which—due to the law of gravity—he doubted collected much dust. But now didn't seem the time to question her cleaning methods.

"But I wanted to tell you how—" He stepped closer to her, nearly brushing the table with his leg, but the movement only sent her into greater, Herculean efforts on the bottom of the table. She went down on her knees, even.

"Please." She looked up at him. Those blue-gray eyes, normally so straightforward and unflinching all but begging him to say no more. "It's all right."

He retreated. Juvenile feelings of inadequacy and nerves coalesced into something bitter and hard in the back of this throat.

Something like shame. And regret.

Apparently, Margaret Warren's feelings were unsettled. Perhaps a night of sleep and the sight of his disgusting body on an empty stomach were enough to change her mind about his undiminished status.

He held up his hands, letting her know he'd say no more.

"My physical therapist is coming today," he told her. "I don't need you here."

She blinked at him.

"Too many people," he said by way of explanation. He didn't want her to leave, particularly not without cooking. He'd had this nice fantasy of having the two women in the house, one cooking something delicious, the other torturing him but he would take it in a manly way. Margaret would see, perhaps, how manly he was, grinning and bearing it while Nicole manipulated his knee and forced him to do leg lifts that ignited infernos in his hip joint.

But he couldn't stomach Margaret being here right now, with his fantasies leaking air, even if he stayed locked in his office. Tomorrow, they could go back to whatever they'd been before. Today he needed his home back. His house free of her scent and touch and presence.

"Okay," she said, her mouth a tense white line that barely moved.

He turned, mindful of his leg, and headed to his office. His story. His class. His solitary life.

CHAPTER NINE

MAGGIE SLAMMED shut her car door and started the engine before she called Gordon. She was halfway down the hill when he picked up.

"Hey," he said, not sounding the least bit happy. "What the hell is going on? I've lost the feed in the living room."

She looked down at the disabled bug in her cupped hand. She couldn't tell if she'd just saved herself or ruined everything.

"I know, I'll replace the device later." She turned right at the bottom of the hill where she normally turned left. The winding road led back up the mountain.

"Replace it? What happened to it?"

"I had to remove it."

"Uh…why?"

"Look." She pretended to be harried as she eased the car onto a gravel fire road that branched off the main one. "I'll replace the bug later, but he's asked me to leave for a few hours while his therapist comes in." It was a lie. A small white one that hurt no one, but managed to save her a lot of time answering questions. She braked beside the utility van that came into view and climbed out. "I need you to set up a conference call with Curtis."

"Okay? When?"

Maggie yanked open the back of the van, catching Gordon picking his fingernails.

"Now," she said.

THE CONFERENCE CALL WAS BRIEF. She told Curtis about the transcripts, the notes and the tapes and accepted the congratulations all around.

"Why didn't you just call him out then?" Gordon asked.

She'd prepared herself for that question.

"I want to be absolutely sure of what he's got before I blow my cover. He won't let us back in if we screw up now."

"If he's got what you say, we could get a court order," Gordon insisted.

"And a heap of bad press," she snapped, frustrated with him for being right.

"Where is Delgado?" she asked Curtis, throwing the attention away from her decision. "He sent any men out?"

"Not since the failed New York trip," Curtis answered. "I don't know if he's lost interest or if he's got people we don't know on the job."

Maggie nodded. The pressure was off. Slightly. It gave her and Gordon enough time to get into that box again.

But it also meant those FBI agents staking out the neighborhood could be less vigilant due to boredom. And that's when mistakes happened. As she well knew.

And she was too close to the end for there to be any more mistakes.

"Tell the men to stay sharp," she told Curtis. "We know Delgado's going to do something—it's just a matter of when."

"Good work, Fitzgerald," Curtis said, his tone about a thousand degrees warmer than the last time she'd talked to him at the office. "What's next?"

"I'm going to head back with dinner. He's been with his therapist and I think he might load up on the meds when she's gone. I'll see if I can get back into that office."

"Sounds good. Call me if you find anything. Anything at all."

Maggie nodded and disconnected the satellite phone that connected the van to the Los Angeles field office.

Gordon rubbed his hands together and looked like a weasel in the artificial glow of the monitors.

"We're getting close," he said. "I can feel it. Dude is going to go down."

Maggie nodded and stood to leave.

"Hey." Gordon stopped her. "Considering what you're seeing you should go back to this."

He held out the guardian angel pin with the camera that she'd worn to interview with Caleb.

Maggie eyed it like a worm.

"I don't think so, Gordon. Curtis authorized cameras for the first day only. I can't work with you looking over my shoulder."

His mouth fell open. "If I had been able to see what you saw this morning—"

"What?" she asked, determined not to wear the pin. "Nothing would have changed."

"But we could break down the images and it would be another set of eyes."

"Are my eyes not good enough?"

Gordon swallowed, his gaze darted to the ground and never came back up to meet hers. Gordon had a million tells and this was one of them—he was uncomfortable, but he was sure he was right. "What happened last night, Maggie? Gomez said something about last night before I lost the feed. Something is going on."

Maggie called upon all of her acting skills to appear frustrated and put out, rather than guilty.

"Gordon. I got the go-ahead from Curtis to have no camera and no two-way mics. I can't work with you in my ear or with you second-guessing everything I do."

"I know, but you've got my ass on the line here, too."

"Trust me, your skinny butt is the least of my worries if this thing goes sour." She tried to make it a joke, even reached out to punch him lightly in the arm. "You've got to trust me." She nearly choked on the words. "You have to trust me like I trust you."

Finally, he looked at her, sheepishly. "I do trust you. You've just got me sweating bullets here."

"You need to get out of this van a little more often. Breathe some fresh air."

He recoiled in horror at the suggestion and they both laughed, the tension and doubt and confusion gone. They were partners again.

"I'm gonna run back to his house and make some dinner."

"Replace that bug!" He pretended to be stern, but his goofy appearance ruined that.

She slammed the van door shut behind her and climbed into the hatchback. Now that business was done, there seemed to be a surplus of empty space in her mind and thoughts of how Caleb's face looked this morning bore down on her like a train.

She'd pushed away his wounded expression, forced herself to forget the way he'd jumped to the only conclusion he'd think of: that having seen him more clearly—scars and burns and broken bones—she'd rejected him this morning.

It's the way it's got to be, she told herself. *It's better. Easier. For us to continue on as employee and boss.* This was the opportunity she needed to remove Maggie Fitzgerald from that house and to keep her out.

THE DOOR WAS LOCKED and Maggie could see him on the couch, or rather, his handsome naked feet hanging over the arm.

She knocked but the feet didn't even flinch.

She rang the doorbell and Gomez jerked upright. She could hear his muffled cursing and winced, hating to disturb him when he must be sore. But there was far too much work to do. Bridges to repair and trust to rebuild.

All so she could burn it down when her work here was over.

She watched through the small window as he shuffled to the door, using his cane, which he hadn't been using as much. He looked haggard, pale, his injured hand curled into his chest and held there, a bird protecting a bad wing.

He threw open the door and stared at her. "What are you doing here?"

She ignored his inhospitable welcome and hoisted the bag of groceries. "I figured you'd be hungry."

He looked at the bag, at her, then finally turned away, leaving the door open.

I guess that's a "Come on in."

Maggie stepped into the foyer and shut the door behind her. The surveillance bug in her pocket weighed a thousand pounds.

"Are you okay?" she asked. He eased onto the couch, grimacing and breathing carefully through his mouth.

"I will be in about ten minutes." He laid back and put one of the throw pillows over his face to block out the late afternoon sunlight coming in through the windows.

"What—?"

"I'm glad you're here," he said, though it was muffled through the pillow. "But can we hold off any conversation until the drugs kick in?"

She nodded, suffering again that stab of tenderness, that whispery longing to care for him.

But she snuffed it. As if to prove how unaffected by him she was, how single-mindedly focused on her job she was, she put the bag of groceries on the counter then stood in the kitchen doorway to watch him.

She forced herself to count the seconds between his breaths without noticing anything else about him. And when he appeared to be sound asleep she eased out of the kitchen, past the couch to the hallway and finally stopped in front of the closed office door.

Holding her breath and listening for the sound of him stirring she turned the knob.

Open. Again.

She exhaled, jittery and victorious, and slid inside.

Bear leaped up from his sleeping bag and charged her, teeth bared, a growl rumbling out of his chest.

She had no bribe on her, no meat or crunchy dog treat and so she tried to grab his collar, but he twisted and nearly clamped onto her wrist with his powerful jaws.

She lifted her foot and planted it in his chest, pushing him backward. He slid across the hardwood floor, nails scrambling for purchase. He righted himself and charged her again, but this time she shut the door in his face.

He barked once then was silent.

A guard dog with a short attention span; she nearly laughed through her heart attack.

She rested her head against the door and gave her pulse a second to return to normal. There was no sound from the living room and when she peeked at Caleb, he hadn't even moved. The pillow had slid to the floor, his face, relaxed in slumber, was turned to the window, where the last of the dying day gilded his dark complexion and red scars.

He was knocked out cold if he could sleep through *Animal Kingdom,* she thought wryly.

She went back to the kitchen and grabbed a slice of the roast beef she'd bought so Caleb could make sandwiches instead of living on coffee all day and returned to the office.

Maggie took a deep breath, cracked open the door, chucked in the meat and waited until she heard Bear scarfing it down before entering the office.

"Good dog," she said, patting his head.

At the desk, she pushed the chair out of her way and jiggled the mouse to get the computer screen to come to life.

A genie appeared on screen, wafting up from a magic lantern, bubble letters erupted from its mouth, "What's the password?"

Maggie blinked, stunned by this strange locking mechanism on his computer.

She thought for a second of what she knew about Caleb and then typed Vicodin.

The Genie tipped back his head and laughed. "Try again," he said.

A sudden bolt of inspiration hit her and she quickly typed Ducati.

"Welcome," the genie said and vanished in a poof of computer-generated smoke. Caleb's desktop appeared but she couldn't find any icons on the green screen except for a small wineglass in the corner with the words *drink me* next to it.

"Holy crap," she muttered. The guy lived alone in a house on top of a mountain. His phone was untraceable, he never left, rarely let anyone in... who was he trying to keep out?

Well, her, for one.

After double-clicking on the icon another password screen came up. She rolled her eyes and reached behind her for the chair, but Bear's meat distraction was over and he growled at her.

Hoping a trip outside might get him out of her way she slid open the patio door. "Go," she muttered. "Outside."

But his growling increased. He barked once low and deep from the back of his throat. Okay. She could lure Bear outside with more meat and continue her efforts to crack another password to get to his files. But hacking systems wasn't her strong suit—Gordon's expertise, not hers—and chances were that a guy who put two locking devices on his computer would also have software that shut down the entire system with too many incorrect password attempts. Plus, she'd have to worry about the racket Bear would raise after he'd consumed the beef and she remained at Caleb's desk. No, better she abandon this particular mission to plot a more effective plan with the knowledge she now had. Never turning her back on Bear, she left the office.

If Maggie Fitzgerald couldn't do her job, it was time for Margaret Warren to take over.

Back in the kitchen she started dinner—fish tacos.

She'd had a craving for the Southern California delicacy and in no time, the pieces of red snapper had been dredged in cornmeal and were frying on the stove.

She chopped cabbage and peppers and carrots for the slaw that topped the fish and heated a pan in order to warm up the corn tortillas.

She had stopped cooking for herself years ago yet here she was preparing food for a man who needed it. And part of her enjoyed it.

Not the work so much. Her back hurt and the

frying fish spat at her, leaving small burn drops on her hands. But the idea of doing something for him.

She realized the danger of this catch-22. She needed to spend time with him to protect him, to gain access to the office and the information he had. But the more time she spent with him, the more she liked him.

She'd studied the psychology of going undercover while in training at Quantico. It was hard to compartmentalize one's life to the degree demanded by undercover FBI work. But frankly, she'd never had a problem before. It's why she was so good at her job—she could gain trust and empathy without ever getting involved or jeopardizing her cover.

Until now.

Further proof, she told herself, *that it's time to get out.*

The phone rang behind her and shattered the silence of the little house.

"Caleb?" she said, ducking into the main room to see if he wanted her to answer the call. But he didn't move. The phone rang again, an electronic jangle that seemed too loud. Still, he didn't stir.

Maggie answered it by the third ring.

"Hello?"

"Hel—Caleb?"

"No, this is Margaret."

"Margaret?" The man's voice nearly squeaked with what was clearly surprise. "Is this 805-555-4833?"

"It is. Are you looking for Caleb Gomez?"

"Yes, but—"

"I'm the housecleaner." She smiled at the man's embarrassed chuckle.

"You'll have to excuse me. The last thing I expected was to hear a woman's voice at my son's house."

All the short hairs on her neck stood at attention.

"You're Caleb's father?" Her memory pulled up details from the file. Dr. Eduardo Gomez, clinical psychologist. Board member at Mount Sinai. Married for thirty years to Marguerite, kindergarten teacher.

"I am. Is he around?"

She looked over to where Caleb snored, unmoving on the couch. "He is but I think he's passed out in a drug stupor."

The silence on the other end echoed with reproach.

"I'm sorry. That was sort of a joke."

"You've been spending too much time in my son's company," Dr. Gomez said.

"I guess so. Mr. Gomez—" She made sure not to call him doctor.

"How often are you there?" Dr. Gomez interrupted, his deep voice touched slightly with a Spanish accent.

"Every day."

"Is he usually passed out from the medication?"

"No. Honestly, that was just a joke."

Finally Dr. Gomez sighed. "Perhaps years ago I might have laughed."

"Your son had physical therapy today, which is why he took the drugs."

"So, he's doing the therapy."

"He is. Do you want me to try to wake him?"

Dr. Gomez paused and Maggie read a million moments of disappointment in that pause. "He wouldn't speak to me if you did."

"I'm sure—"

"Trust me…I'm sorry. What's your name again?"

"Margaret."

"Trust me, Margaret. His entire family has spoken to him, to persuade him to come home so we can care for him. But he won't do it."

"He's pretty stubborn."

They broke his arm in three places before he'd tell them his name. It seemed as if they were both thinking it in the silence of the phone line.

"How does he seem?" Dr. Gomez finally asked, his voice low.

"Good." She scraped at a bit of green salsa that had somehow landed on the wall near the phone. "He's teaching and working."

"Working?"

"On a story."

Dr. Gomez broke into an incredibly long and imaginative string of Spanish cursing. Seriously, the man pulled out all the stops. Dogs. Mothers. Forked tongues. He hit them all.

"I take it you don't like that?"

"Would you?"

She nearly laughed. *Hell yes! Go Caleb Gomez!* "Perhaps as his father I would be wary of seeing my son chase after more trouble."

"Exactly."

Margaret didn't agree with Dr. Gomez, however. She'd seen the intensity working on the story had given Caleb and wouldn't want him robbed of that again. Suddenly she became aware of the position she was in—standing between father and son—and the confidences she'd revealed. "I could wake him up and you could swear at him."

"I'm sorry," he said and blew out a long breath. "I am. Margaret, I've been calling him every week and this is the most I've found out about him."

"Doesn't he answer the phone?"

"No, he answers the phone. But he only talks about college football the whole time."

Maggie could picture Caleb countering all inquiries about his well-being with stats and scores. "That would be frustrating."

"I'm a clinical psychologist, Margaret." For some reason she'd never considered how frustrating it must be for a father, a psychologist father, to have to deal with Caleb who wore armor so thick he could barely move. And how frustrating it must be for Caleb to have to fend off the well-meaning questions and intrusions because he had no desire to get any better.

Caleb was alive and that seemed to be enough for him.

No wonder he didn't stay in New York with his family.

They wouldn't have let him be a recluse. They'd have forced him into the land of the living. And he would have hated it.

Maybe after she'd betrayed him he'd seek out the shelter of his family. She could only hope that heaping more pain on his already painful existence would break him enough to seek out help and love and…

Who am I kidding? she thought bitterly. *He'll*

take all that hurt and sharpen it into knives to use on me and the FBI. She knew him enough to know that.

"Margaret," Dr. Gomez said. "Perhaps you and I could make a deal. I will call back at this time every week and hopefully talk to you for a few moments. Find out something about my son other than his college football picks."

Betray him twice over? Spy on him for the government, whom he hated, and for his family, whom he clearly was avoiding.

Maggie chafed at the thought. Giving Caleb more reason to hate her seemed like overkill. Plus, this nice man, this father worried about his son would be another victim of her lies. She wouldn't be here next week. His trust and hope would be ill-placed in her.

Good God, I haven't even met the guy and I'm failing him, too.

However, there could be an upshot to this. An angle she could use, a way into the very private mind of Caleb Gomez.

"I'll try," she said and Dr. Gomez heaved a sigh of relief.

"Wonderful. Now, his mother wants to know— is he eating?"

Reminded, she whirled to see her fish smoking

in the pan, dangerously close to burning. She yanked the pan off the stove-top and then waved her singed hand to ease the sting.

"He is." She swore silently and sucked on the sore flesh at the base of her thumb.

"Is he going out?"

"Outside. Sure. Once in a while."

"No. I mean, is he leaving his house?"

She shook her head. "No. He says he does, but I don't think that's true."

"Well, Margaret, see what you can do about that, would you?"

She chuckled. "Right. Because that will be easy."

She heard a heavy sigh from the great room and peeked in. Caleb stirred, tossed his head on the cushion. His feet seemed restless against the arm of the couch. It was either a nightmare or the meds were wearing off. She checked her watch. It had only been thirty minutes. The drugs would just be really kicking in.

Caleb had nightmares. Something low in her belly flipped over and squeezed in pained sympathy.

"He's waking up. I've got to go."

"It was a delight talking to you," Dr. Gomez said.

"You, too," she said, hung up then headed into the living room.

There were important things in play here.

Things bigger than Caleb Gomez and much bigger than her ulcers and guilt.

Justice.

Vengeance.

She reached over and touched his shoulder, shaking him a bit.

He woke with a start, his hand grabbed her wrist with surprising force.

"Don't touch me!" He growled the words. His eyes were cloudy, unfocused and she knew he was caught between dream and reality.

"Caleb," she said, her voice sharp. He gripped her wrist tighter, yanking her slightly off balance. She caught herself against the couch, so she wouldn't tumble onto his prone body.

"I'm an American citizen," he yelled, his breath hot against her face, his eyes wild and hurt. "Don't touch me!"

CHAPTER TEN

"CALEB." Maggie wanted to brush his cheek, feel the life and strength and heat of him until reality burned through the clouds of his nightmare and he released her.

Dangerous ground, Maggie. Don't be an idiot.

"Wake up, Caleb," she said brusquely. "You're dreaming."

"What the—" He jerked and dropped her wrist. He struggled to sit upright, while she fought the urge to help him.

"Dinner," she said, her voice loud in the hushed room. "I thought you might be hungry so I made dinner."

He blinked at her a few times as if wondering how she'd gotten there. Or perhaps who she was? He sighed and scrubbed at his face, groaning. "Yeah, I am. That's great." He finally shook his head then turned to look at her, his eyes crystal clear and chagrined. "Thank you," he said.

"For what?"

"For coming back. I would have just slept all evening and woken up at two in the morning starving with nothing to eat."

"Well, not tonight."

She went into the kitchen to make up a plate of tacos. Her absence would give him time to orient himself. Grabbing a plate and a drink, she headed to the living room.

His eyes went wide and he rubbed his hands together. "Fish tacos? Guacamole? Again, I've died and gone to heaven."

"Well, hardly. I'll let you eat—" She stepped away, pausing long enough to see if he would offer—

"Sit," he said, confirming her instincts and not letting her down. "I mean stay. If you want. You could eat. With me."

She checked her watch and pretended to think about it before nodding.

"That would be great," she said. She made up a plate for herself, before sitting in one of the overstuffed chairs. She had to dig out a coffee cup that had been wedged between the cushion and the frame.

"Sorry," he said, his mouth full. "My cleaning woman just took off today."

"Just out of the blue?" she asked, grinning at him.

"I know, I know. I should fire her. But she's an awesome cook." He winked at her and she practically blushed.

He was good at this, good at making the awkward moments easier. She could tell he didn't think so, especially after he'd kicked her out of his house today. One more way she felt attuned to him.

He took another bite of taco and rolled his eyes dramatically. "This is a good taco."

"Thank you." She took a bite herself and had to agree. "So how was the physical therapy?" she asked.

"The woman is medieval."

"Does it help?" she asked. "I mean in the long run?"

"They say it will. In another year maybe I won't walk with a limp and I'll have almost full use of my hand."

Her eyes went wide. "That's amazing."

He nodded and dunked a chip in the guacamole. "We'll see."

"You don't sound very excited. Or hopeful."

He shoved the chip in his mouth and chewed. "I'm not."

"Caleb—"

"Mobility would be nice. Typing with both hands would be great. But even if I could do the hundred-yard dash or make origami, it really wouldn't change much about my life."

"Well, not with that attitude."

He rolled his eyes and took another chip. "Please, let's not talk about my attitude. Nicole's favorite topic is my attitude."

"Nicole?" A strange ping shot through her. Not quite jealousy, but close.

You thought you were the only woman in his life? She mocked herself ruthlessly, trying to burn out these soft emotions that threatened everything. *I doubt Nicole is setting him up, she probably really is his friend. Whoever she is.*

"My therapist. She's like a demented kindergarten teacher. All good cheer and inside voices. She makes me crazy." He drained his glass of watermelon water. "You got anymore of this?" he asked and she stood to get the container.

"Why wouldn't better mobility change anything?" she asked from the kitchen.

"Well." The sarcasm was rich in his voice and she almost cringed listening to him. "It doesn't change my face. Or the fact that I can't do the job I love—"

"I thought you were working on that story

about crime in Long Beach," she asked, perhaps a shade too fast.

"I am, but I can't go out and do any legwork. I can't go undercover."

She replenished his glass then sat.

"What's so great about going undercover?" She was relieved to be the one directing this conversation before he had the chance to start asking her more of his own questions. She hadn't given any thought to Margaret Warren's childhood and he would no doubt head in that direction eventually.

Caleb took the last bite of taco then leaned against the cushions. He stretched his arm across the top of the sofa and considered her question. She liked that about him—he was deliberate with his words. He rarely talked before he thought.

"I love the moment when people let their guard down," he said. "When they trust you and start airing their dirty laundry."

Maggie swallowed and picked at the cabbage left on her plate. She knew that moment. She hated it.

Hated it even as that particular moment unfolded right now.

"I love watching people. Blending into a crowd and studying the human condition in all its raw glory."

"I like that, too," she said. "Watching people when they don't know they're being watched. Like at a mall," she added so he didn't think Margaret Warren was some kind of Peeping Tom. Or FBI.

"In those moments when people don't know they're being watched, when they're the most honest and real, that's when you find out the most about them. That's when you find out who they really are."

Those very same reasons were why she'd opted for undercover detail in the Bureau. It was as if he had read her mind.

She shrugged, knocked off balance by this strange trait they shared. "I wouldn't know," she lied.

"Do you want me to tell you who you really are?" he asked.

Her breath stalled in her chest. He was just making small talk, playing a game. *It's not as though he could really know,* but her food stuck in the back of her throat all the same.

"This should be good," she joked.

"You're less serious than you take yourself to be," he said. "You think there's no fun left in you."

Direct hit. She thought of her house. The cruise brochure. Her plans for a life that never seemed to happen. Her father's censorious gaze.

Her loneliness.

"I work hard," she said, the truth easily applicable to Margaret and Maggie.

"That you do," Caleb agreed.

"You figured all that out by watching me?"

"Yeah. That and you can hold your own in a fight."

She jerked startled eyes to his. "Excuse me?"

"You move like a woman who's taken a self-defense class or two."

"Well," she said. "Long Beach kind of required a woman to know how to take care of herself."

Maggie picked up the startled pieces of herself and forced herself back into line.

"What about when you go undercover and it's dangerous?" she asked. "Don't you get scared?"

"Sure," he said.

"So, why do you do that?"

"I like finding what makes bad guys tick. Finding what they want and then using it to bring them down. It's like watching the fall of the Roman Empire every time. They're so surprised, like they never knew that wanting that much money or power would one day get them in trouble."

"You should be a cop," she said.

He made the sign of a cross. "God forbid. All guts no glory. I like a little fanfare at the end of the job."

"The FBI then. You could be on—"

He smiled, a thin glacial curve to his lips. "I think the FBI are about one step away from Orwell these days. Illegal wiretaps, entrapment, the U.S.A. Patriot Act—"

"How is that different than what you do?" she asked, feeling her temper build in her belly. *What about Patrick? What about Lita Delgado?* she wanted to ask. "You trick people and spy on them. At least when the FBI are done people go to jail."

"Bad guys." He held up a finger. "I do it to bad guys. And my stories result in arrests, too. Probably more than the FBI. They do it to people just—"

"After you get your precious story. How much information do you have in that office right now that could help an investigation?"

A red stain flooded his cheeks and she felt vindicated.

"I've done good work in my time," he said. "And it wasn't just about the story. I believe in justice, too."

"You keep telling yourself that if it makes you feel better."

"It does," he protested. "It makes me feel great. Bad guys go down, people get informed and I have a job. What's wrong with that?"

Nothing. Except where their lives and lies intersected—at her brother's death. But she couldn't say that. She'd already said far too much, so she studied her hands, balled into helpless fists.

She looked up, shocked when he started to laugh.

"What's so funny?" she asked, still feeling hot under the collar at his aspersions on the Bureau. Yeah, they messed up sometimes, but they also got it right sometimes.

"Nothing," he said, still laughing. "But it's been months since someone stood up to me. Really gave me a good argument."

"I find that hard to believe," she groused.

"Trust me." He rolled his eyes. "People get a little nervous about upsetting me, like I might burst into flames again." He grinned, part little boy, part devil. "That was fun."

She stared at him, incredulous until she realized he meant it. He argued for sport's sake. He didn't have the Fitzgerald go-for-the-jugular instinct wherein every fight became personal and added to each other's long list of grudges.

Fighting for fun? For sport?

She smiled and shook her head. "You got a crazy idea of a good time."

"You don't know the half of it, sister," he joked. The atmosphere between them was no longer charged with animosity and she reached out cautiously to the common ground between them. Between Caleb Gomez and Maggie Fitzgerald. She'd regret doing so, but wanted to prolong this intimacy.

"Don't you get tired of it? The deceit and lies?"

"Sure." She could tell that he didn't tire of it the way she did. "But it is...*was* my job. You don't approve?"

She shook her head. "A few years ago I would have agreed with everything you've said."

He looked at her quizzically, as though wondering where her opinions on these things came from. Feelings that were so forbidden she shouldn't even be considering them swelled in her. Grew to dangerous proportions.

"Margaret, is there something—"

"More tacos?" she asked, cheerful and enigmatic Margaret Warren once more.

"Sure." He smiled, tactfully backing off. "Any more guacamole?"

She nodded and nearly ran into the kitchen where she ran cool water from the tap and splashed it onto her face.

"How about the nightmares?" she called out to him once she got herself under control.

"What nightmares?"

She entered the room so she could watch his

expression. "The one you were having when I woke you up."

He frowned. "I didn't think I had them anymore. I guess I don't remember them."

"You were telling me not to touch you. That you were an American citizen."

He twisted a paper napkin around his damaged hand like a bandage. "That fact didn't do me a whole lot of good."

She piled the plates, scattering the food everywhere in her haste. "Are you talking to anyone about what happened?" She thought of his father and could feel the man's pain. As bad as the physical scars were, the ones left on his psyche had to be worse.

"I talk to Bear."

"Caleb," she whispered, approaching him.

"Margaret, I do not want to ruin my fish tacos with this discussion." He looked at her, his wicked half-grin in place. "Okay?"

"We could argue about it," she suggested. "Wouldn't that be fun?"

He laughed, but shook his head. "Not today."

"Okay." Her head knew a brick wall when she continually rammed it.

"I know you just moved here but have you had breakfast down at El Sol?" he asked.

"That gas station across from The Pour House?"

"Yep."

"No." She laughed. "I can't say I've had breakfast at the gas station."

"Well, in front is a lowly gas station but in back, Guillermo makes the best *huevos* you've ever had."

She eyed him. "I sincerely doubt that. I've had some pretty amazing *huevos* and they didn't come from a gas station."

"And that is why they are not the best," Caleb said.

She felt warmed by his teasing, by the regard in his eyes, the easy smile. He didn't realize how potent his charm could be.

And at the same time, she knew an opening when she saw one.

"Meet me there tomorrow morning for breakfast."

The words hit the air and exploded. Caleb's smile faded. His eyes shifted away.

"I'm not—"

"If you can't drive, I'll come get you."

"I can drive," he said, his expression hot and cross. She remembered that bike in his garage and sincerely hoped he didn't mean he could drive that.

"Good, then you can meet me there."

And Gordon could break in after Caleb left.

Copy the computer files and tapes and be out before Caleb even got a chance to order his *huevos*.

This whole affair could be over. Done. She could be out of his life.

The muscles in his jaw worked hard. His eyelids twitched and Maggie waited. She forced herself to remain calm, to not push the issue. As time stretched she forced herself not to rescind the offer to end the tension in the room.

Caleb didn't leave this house, hadn't in the week she'd been here. Was she stupid to think the lure of breakfast with her would be enough for him to fight back whatever demons kept him locked up?

She itched with the sudden desire to stroke her hand down those tense muscles in his jaw. She wanted to cup his face, force him to look at her.

"Never mind," she said, cracking under the pressure in the room. "It was a—"

"You're making a mess of me, Margaret." His low, deep voice stroked the nape of her neck and slid down her spine in a warm caress. She fought to keep her eyelids open.

"This morning you gave me the impression that kissing me was a mistake."

She nearly flinched, but inhaled deeply instead, wishing she'd been smarter and not fallen for the man.

"If this invitation is as a friend," he said, "I'm going to have to say no."

Her eyes darted to his, surprised. "Why?"

"I don't want to be your friend." He shrugged and the unscarred part of his mouth tilted upward. "And I've not had an easy go of things lately, what with the kidnapping and nearly dying."

His humor slew her. "Caleb—"

He held up a hand and like a child she stopped talking.

"I like you, Margaret, and I'm attracted to you. Believe me, I fully understand if you aren't attracted to me…." He laughed but it didn't sound right or funny. "But if this is pity or an attempt to get the poor recluse out of the house—"

"It's not." The words were quiet when she wanted to yell. She forced herself to stay seated, to not go to his side and kiss that beautiful mouth. She couldn't kiss him and lie to him at the same time.

Oh, God, this hurts so much.

"Then what is it, Margaret?" His blue eyes pinned her, laid her open and stripped her bare. The lies, the stories and the reasons she had—the good reasons, her family and Patrick and Delgado—they all burned to ash under that gaze.

"You're my boss," she said. It wasn't the whole truth, but in the parameters of the lies she constructed it was the closest she could come to the truth.

His eyes went wide. "You want to have breakfast with me because I'm your boss? It won't get you a raise or—"

"No." She cleared her throat. "You're my boss here. There—" she gestured to the closed door "—we're just people."

She watched his doubt shift to belief.

Don't believe me! The words knocked at her teeth, screamed to get out. *Don't trust me. I will only hurt you.*

"Just people?" he asked.

"Eating eggs." She forced herself to smile.

"Oh."

She waited for him to say more, but he remained silent, his eyes fixed on the coffee table.

"That's it?" She felt embarrassed and slightly angry. He wanted to go. Clearly. He'd told her he was attracted to her, the stubborn cuss. *"Oh?"*

"Well—" he cocked his head to the side "—I might be busy."

Maggie wondered how far he could be pushed. Just how much she could say without chasing him into his office.

This maneuver was a bust. Gomez wasn't about to leave his house for Margaret Warren. Probably smart, anyway. She couldn't seem to keep herself removed from the situation. Sharing brunch with him at his favorite restaurant was probably too intimate a move.

The smart thing would be to drop this pursuit. Leave. Come back on Monday and begin the careful extraction fresh. That's what a good FBI agent would do. Play it smart. Safe. Let the skirmish go to win the battle.

"You're a coward," she said, abandoning the smart path. "It's hard to believe that Caleb Gomez, fearless journalist, is actually scared to leave his house."

He became a stone statue perched on the edge of his sofa. His jaw flexed hard.

She waited a split second for him to deny the charge. For him to jump to his feet and tell her she was nuts, didn't know what she was talking about.

But he didn't. He simply sat.

Which gave her hope.

"I'll be there at nine," she said. "I'll wait for one hour."

She walked past him and grabbed her purse. She looked over her shoulder as she headed for the door. Still he sat, not moving, watching the floor with fixed eyes, looking for all the world like a man at a crossroads.

As she left, Maggie smiled in satisfaction even as she knew the danger of this path she'd stepped onto.

DRIVING DOWN THE HILL Maggie called Gordon and told him to be prepared in case Gomez left in the morning.

"Why?" he asked. "What happened? You didn't replace the bug. I've got no idea what's going on!"

"I didn't get a chance," she lied again. Everywhere she turned, she boxed herself in with half-truths and white lies. Her head spun and her heart hurt. The lies that had never bothered her before now hammered at her. She wanted to walk away. Leave it all—her feelings, Caleb's blue eyes, her father's expectations.

Except Caleb, the part of her that suddenly insisted on honesty piped up. *You want Caleb. You need him to feel better about what you are. What you've done.*

Maggie bit her tongue, hard, tasted blood and forced herself to do her job.

"I invited him to brunch tomorrow morning and he might come." She thought of him stone still on his couch. "Or not. If he does leave, you should be able to get in and copy those files."

"What about the dog?"

"Bring ham. Lots of it," she said, then hung up.

LATER THAT NIGHT Maggie booted her computer then took a long drink of water from her bottle. She'd logged some serious mileage in the foothills during her daily run and had been able to get herself focused again. A task so much easier to do when she was out of Gomez's house.

She opened her e-mail, paged through the daily memos from head office, deleting them without much of a glance—PR, minor policy changes, personnel reports. She might be bored here in her apartment, but she wasn't that bored.

At the bottom was an e-mail from her sister. The subject line read YAHOOO! Maggie smiled and opened it.

Had it out with Dan last night. You were right. When I asked him if all these late-night meetings and his crappy dismissive attitude and outrageous stress level were about Patrick, he said they were. And he's apologizing by taking me to Santa Barbara for the weekend. Hello breakfast in bed! Hello sex! Thanks sis, for talking me off the ledge…again.
Thanks!
Love, Liz.
P.S.—I borrowed your Hugh Grant collection and loaned *About a Boy* to a friend at

work. She claims to be a huge Hugh Grant fan but has never seen it!!!

"Well, there goes that DVD," Maggie groused.

She deleted the message and leaned back in her chair, finishing her water.

Sex.

Over the years she'd said goodbye to it without ever intending to.

It had been three years since she'd had a lover she cared enough about to go away for a weekend. And a year since she'd cared about any man enough to get naked.

She closed her eyes and tried to imagine the men she'd been with, many of whom left when her job got in the way.

She'd tried to explain to them that being an agent wasn't something she could turn off. She couldn't live that separately from her job.

Well, you'd better, one had told her, *or it will be all you've got.*

Considering the number of conversations with the cruise brochure she'd had, she realized he might be right.

I am lonely.

She thought of Caleb in that empty house on the hill. His beautiful ruined face. His long sexy feet.

The integrity and bravery and strength of character that hadn't been taken away from him.

She thought of the eagerness with which she hoped he'd show up tomorrow. And not just so Gordon could get into the house and they would wrap up this case.

I'm lonely.

I am lonely for him, the small voices said. *I've been lonely for him all my life.*

CHAPTER ELEVEN

THE COFFEE at the gas station tasted delicious with condensed milk, but was strong like tar. She'd had two cups already and her ulcers were screaming for mercy.

But no Caleb.

Maggie checked her watch for about the hundredth time. 9:30 a.m. She'd told him she'd wait one hour, but with each passing minute she figured the chances of him showing significantly decreased.

She sighed and stretched out her legs, propping them up on the Formica bench opposite her.

"Breakfast?" A short, round-faced man with a giant smile—Guillermo, she assumed—asked.

She shook her head. "Not yet." She lifted her cup. *"Café por favor."*

Guillermo nodded, wiped his hands on the white apron that stretched across his belly and left. Maggie tilted her head so she could see around the giant cactus wrapped in blinking Christmas-tree lights—very festive against turquoise walls adorned with dusty fake evergreen wreaths, poised for the holidays—and watched the door. She was a fool, and not just because Gordon sat outside Caleb's house ready to break and enter, but because she wanted Caleb here.

Idiot, she told herself and took a sip of the creamy hot coffee Guillermo set at her elbow.

"IDIOT," Caleb told his reflection. He wiped the steam off the bathroom mirror to get a better look at his cowardly self. "There is a beautiful woman waiting for you."

He tipped his watch, which rested on the edge of the sink. 9:30 a.m.

"Idiot!"

The shower had not helped with the shame and the jittery feeling that exploded in him every time he looked at the door.

She waited, sure. But so did the rest of the world with their mouths agape and their watchful eyes and unasked questions. No doubt the restaurant would be filled with children who would stare at him unabashedly until their parents forced them to avert their eyes so they wouldn't burn out their retinas or have nightmares.

But she's waiting!

He braced his hands against the sink and hung his head. He couldn't believe this irrational fear that came out of nowhere. He couldn't believe it and he couldn't fight it. He let it run rampant in his head like an unruly dog.

"Come on," he muttered. *You are the man who worked the floor at a slaughter house and lived to write about it. You spent a week in a prison. You infiltrated the home of gang leader. For Christ's sake, Caleb, you went to war!*

He looked up into his eyes, seeing past the scars.

"I went to war," he said aloud.

And the man who came back had nothing to do with the man he had been. He hardly recognized himself in his memories. Wondered what recklessness he'd been sickened with, what callous disregard for his own human frailty.

Now, in these dark days, he was obsessed with his frailty. Consumed by his limitations.

"And I'm sick of it," he muttered. "She's waiting, Gomez."

He opened the medicine cabinet and stared down the amber vials of Vicodin, lined up like little soldiers on the shelf.

Margaret had cleaned those shelves, moved those bottles, probably counted them, probably wondered what kind of addict he was. And yet, she still waited for him.

Trouble was, he couldn't leave the house, battle those unasked questions and sideways looks, without a little help.

He strapped his watch on. Popped a pill and left the bathroom.

He had just enough time to drive into town before the pill kicked in.

MAGGIE GAVE IN and ordered the eggs. Caleb was right. They were the best eggs she'd ever had. The best eggs that ever stuck to the roof of her mouth like paste and sat in her stomach like lead.

9:50 a.m.

She sighed and pushed the half-eaten eggs, ham and tortillas away.

"More *café?*" Guillermo asked. He'd been watching her like an owl for fifty minutes, his gaze growing more sympathetic with every moment that passed, confirming her stood-up status.

"No, thanks." She drained the last of her water and wondered what point there would be in waiting out the last ten minutes.

So she could rub it in his face on Monday? Work the guilt factor?

She pinched the bridge of her nose.

Gordon was going to be pissed. The guy had spent an hour cuddled with a ham waiting for Gomez to leave. She smiled just thinking about it. Gordon had probably eaten it himself by now.

Resigned to seeing this through to the bitter end, she picked up the newspaper she'd been staring at blindly for the past fifteen minutes.

"Mags?"

Her name, here in a place where she was only known as Margaret, wasn't what made her jerk the paper down. It was her sister's voice that sent a cold shiver down her back.

"What are you doing here?" Liz asked, her face alight with surprise and happiness.

Maggie blinked, her heart thudded. She glanced past her sister to where Dan talked to the woman at the cash register and then back at Liz.

"What are you doing here?" Maggie asked, stunned to say the very least. "You're supposed to be in Santa Barbara."

"We're on our way." Liz stepped up to the table and dropped her purse on the cracked red plastic table. She looked like a catalogue come to life. "Are you working?" she asked in a horrible stage whisper. Maggie shot her a venomous look.

Liz winced. "Sorry."

"You have got to get out of here," Maggie said,

keeping one eye on the door. Now, would be the time when Caleb would show up. She didn't need further mishaps on this case and Liz and Dan, lovely though they may be, could ruin everything.

"Dan's got his mind set on the scenic route to Santa Barbara," Liz said, ignoring her completely. "We've stopped at every single little town along the coast. Look—" she pulled up her coat sleeve and a beautiful turquoise and red coral bracelet slid down her thin wrist "—look what he got me in Malibu."

"That's beautiful." Maggie looked her sister in the eye. "Get the hell out of here."

Liz blinked. "That's not very nice." Liz turned and both she and Maggie watched Dan pull a photograph out of the pocket in his jeans to show it to the cashier.

"What the hell is he doing?" Maggie asked.

"He's on a case. They're looking for a girl. Dan says she probably ran away, but when the chief heard he was heading north he asked Dan to take a picture."

"What's she look like?"

Liz shrugged, looking mutinous. "I haven't seen the picture. I'm supposed to be on vacation."

"Do that."

"Fine. You must be undercover as a hostile, humorless woman." Liz grabbed her bag but before she could turn Dan was behind her. The sun through the dingy windows showered the two with golden light. Golden light for a golden couple. Dan was tall and wide, with blond hair and a grin that even Maggie found herself sighing over. Like Liz, he managed to look like a million dollars.

"Hiya, Mag—" Liz gave him a small shot to his stomach with her elbow and leaned up to whisper in his ear. He angled his head slightly and rested his hand on the nape of Liz's neck and the touch seemed so sweet, so intimate that Maggie forced her eyes away.

Sometimes it wasn't just sex she missed. It was those kind of touches, the confident ones that spoke of mutual ownership.

"Okay." Dan put his hand under Liz's elbow and grinned at Maggie who, despite the nerves and surprise at seeing them here, grinned back. "Good to see you." He winked, Liz waved over her shoulder and then they were gone.

And she—a glance at her watch said the hour was up—was a woman stood up by a man too scared to leave his house.

Of course, she told herself, shoving the newspaper in her purse with too much force, tearing the front section. Of course she would nearly blow this case, her whole career, over highly inappropriate feelings for a man so damaged he couldn't meet her for eggs.

Of course, after a year of physical celibacy and years of emotional celibacy, he would be her type.

"Of course." She stood, threw some money on the table to pay for her meal and swung her purse over her shoulder.

It hit Caleb Gomez square in the chest.

He wore dark sunglasses, no doubt thinking they hid him, that people would not watch him if they couldn't see the worst of his face. But she could tell him he was terribly wrong.

He looked dangerous in a black leather jacket with a motorcycle helmet under his arm. He looked like a man people would watch no matter what. Her heart thudded against her chest as though she'd never undergone training to control such bodily reactions.

But Caleb circumvented all those lessons. If she let him, Caleb could circumvent everything.

She swallowed, speechless.

"Hi," he finally said into the vast silence between them.

"Hi." Her voice came out as a croak.

"You waited."

She nodded, unsure of what to say. He was here,

he smelled like gum and Irish Spring soap. Her fingers ached with the need to pull those glasses off his face so he couldn't hide. Not anymore.

"*Huevos Mexicana* and *patats,*" he said, smiling at Guillermo who approached the table with a cup of coffee. "*Dos* orange juice." Guillermo pointed to her and the cup in his hand, eagerly asking her if she wanted more.

"*No más,*" she muttered, clutching her stomach as a joke.

Guillermo headed back to his kitchen and Maggie eyed Caleb, still angry at herself, at him. At Liz and Dan for being so happy. She was angry at the world and was more than ready to take it out on Caleb.

"You were going for drama?" she asked, crossing her arms over her chest. "Making an entrance?"

"Something like that." He slid into the booth, set his helmet stuffed with leather gloves beside him, then gestured that she should join him.

"I've already eaten. While I was waiting."

He inhaled through his nose. "I'm sorry," he said. "I didn't know what to wear."

"That's a dumb thing to say to woman who waited over an hour for you."

His mouth gaped open for a second.

"And take off those sunglasses," she said. "They make you more conspicuous."

He faced the table and carefully pulled the dark aviator glasses from his face. His burn stood out along the jaw he had clamped so hard she was surprised he didn't break teeth. "Maybe I should go," he said, his voice low. His humor gone.

"No," she said, sitting opposite him. "Maybe you should be on time." He darted a quick look at her. She grinned, just enough to let him know that she wouldn't be angry much longer.

"It was harder than I thought," he said, playing with the earpieces of his glasses. "I can't believe it, but walking out my door was the hardest thing I've done in about a month."

Her anger left.

"But it was worth it." He grinned at her, watching her from beneath his incredibly long eyelashes. "You're pretty when you're in a snit."

"*Snit?*" She laughed, they both leaned back to let Guillermo put down a small pot of coffee for Caleb and two glasses of freshly squeezed orange juice.

"Mood?"

"Keep going, buddy, and you'll be enjoying those *huevos* all by your lonesome."

He sighed and stretched his arms out along the back of the booth. "Feels good to be out of my house."

"I'm sure." She took a sip of juice, pleased that

Caleb had ordered it for them. "Maybe now that you've handled this hurtle you can get back to work—"

"Let's not go overboard," he said. "It's going to take me about a week of FreeCell to recover from this." He leaned forward suddenly and she was awash in his scent. In this small room, out of his natural habitat, she was reminded of what a big man Caleb was. Larger than the average man, his intensity surrounded him like a physical aura, adding to him. Tall and broad through the shoulders, he was so physical, so striking. Not just because of his wounds, though they added to his character. If Caleb could ever see himself for what he really was rather than the monster he saw in his head, he'd know that.

"And you know something else," he said, waving his hands in front of his face. "I'm tired of talking about me. I want to talk about you."

His gaze lasered in on her and she felt like an insect about to be dissected. "Are you high?" she asked.

"A little bit," he said with a grin. "I am here today with the help of Vicodin."

Who could blame him really? "Some day we'll talk about all those pills in your bathroom and whether they are really necessary."

"Oh, they are. But that's a conversation for another day. Today—" he sat back and Guillermo slid a plate mounded with ham, chilies, eggs and potatoes in front of him "—today is about you." He glanced down at his plate and grabbed Guillermo's hand. "Guillermo, you've outdone yourself."

"It is good to have you here," Guillermo said in broken English. "I missed my biggest customer."

When he walked over to the cash register, Maggie wanted to point out that he didn't seem to behave differently toward Caleb. But the woman at the register couldn't stop staring at Caleb, so much so that Maggie felt the need to say something to her. The opportunity passed as she pulled Guillermo into the kitchen.

"So?" Caleb dug in with relish. "Margaret Warren, tell me."

"What?"

"Everything."

She laughed, uncomfortable. "You're going to have to—"

"Tell me why you don't like your Dubliner father."

She swallowed and searched madly for composure. "What gives you that idea?" She tried to laugh again, but she was so caught off guard that it sounded more like a cough.

"I see things. I see all. So? What's the story?"

"There is no story." She hedged and took another sip of juice. "He's a good man, just a little…disapproving." To put it mildly. Thomas Fitzgerald could teach judgment to the supreme court.

"Of you?"

She nodded. "Of me, my brother, everyone."

"You have a brother?"

She nodded, she was cutting it a bit close here, mixing her life with that of Margaret Warren's but it wasn't as if Caleb would ever know.

"Had. He died."

He set his fork down, all merriment wiped from his face. "I'm sorry."

"I told you," she said back on script. "Crime in Long Beach is getting worse."

His eyebrows knit together. "Was he in a gang?"

She should have made something up. Gomez was too good, too quick.

"Innocent bystander," she said.

"Well, if it makes you feel any better, once I get this story done, I should have enough to put one of the gang leaders away for a good long time."

"If you have information, why don't you give it to the police?"

"Didn't we go over this last night? I'm already talking to the LAPD. Well, I'm waiting for a return call from a detective. I will give him everything I've got once my research is done. Doesn't that make you happy?"

"Yes," she said with a grim smile, her heart chugging, her blood rushing through her veins. She flexed and clenched her hands, the only outward sign of her sudden exhilaration. "It makes me feel much better. How long do you think it will take?"

He sighed. "Not sure." He waved his fork again. "But back on subject. We're talking about you."

"This shouldn't take long."

"Why not go to law school?" he asked. "I mean, I heard you when you said it was difficult with a son. But if he's in school and his father has him on weekends, what's to keep you from doing that?"

"Who's to say I want to?" she asked, defensive. Good God, was she that damn transparent?

"You're pretty transparent, Margaret Warren. To me, anyway."

She feared that was the case. He had the ability to read her like an eye chart, no matter what she did to muddy the waters between them.

"It's complicated." She took another sip of OJ.

"Well, I don—"

"It's complicated and it's not something I want to talk about." He sat back and she met his level gaze. "I don't like being investigated," she said.

He winced. "I thought I was flirting."

She laughed, she couldn't help it. "You need some help if you think that's flirting."

He didn't laugh with her, instead he watched her carefully as if she were something worth studying and she grew uncomfortable with his scrutiny. "What?" she asked, tucking her hair behind her ears. "Is there something—"

He brushed her lips with his fingers and all her words scattered at his touch. He grazed the corner of her mouth and she could taste chili and salt and Caleb. He stroked her cheek, her jaw. Her lips, of their own accord, fell open. Her brain was nowhere to be found. She felt full—thick and warm and clumsy with this sudden desire.

He leaned forward, his intentions written in the air around them. Even though she knew it was wrong—more than wrong—she leaned forward too, helpless against his delicate touch. And there, in the back room of a gas station, they kissed.

It was a sweetheart of a kiss. Warm, but dry, with a hint of something more, of something restrained but not for long.

He eased back a mere inch and when she should have jerked away, she didn't. She let her eyes open to soak him in.

So handsome. So real.

"Life is too short, Margaret," he whispered and she could taste his breath on her tongue, "to not do exactly what you want."

"Is that what you're doing?" she asked, flirting in equal parts with Caleb and disaster.

He grinned and she could see in that heart-breaker grin all the women he'd loved and left in his life. "Not…exactly…" His eyes were hot and this time when he pressed his mouth to hers, he licked her lip and she opened her mouth to him. To his tongue and his heat and his taste. To the ir-resistible danger.

Finally, she pulled herself together and sat back, his lips clinging to hers in an unbearably sexy way.

"Well," she said, searching for composure and humor when it felt like everything in her shook and trembled. "That was worth waiting for."

AN HOUR LATER they stepped into the sunshine outside of the gas station. She lifted a hand to shield her eyes and Caleb slid on his sunglasses.

"Nice day," she said.

"There are some advantages to California."

"Well, Caleb." She turned to say goodbye and at the same time slid her hand into the pocket of her light coat. She had a text message on her phone dialed into Gordon. All she had to do was press Send and he'd know Gomez was headed home and that he had to get out of the house if he was still in it.

"You know," Caleb sighed. "Seems like a waste to go back inside. You want to go for a ride?"

"On that?" She pointed to the Ducati.

"No, on my magic carpet. Yes, on that."

She grinned, practically feeling the bike beneath her. It would be an obscene pleasure to take a ride on that bike. And a risk if Caleb wasn't up to snuff. A delicious risk.

"You won't kill me?" she asked, though the decision had already been made. She'd take her chances of a little wipeout, if it meant getting on that ride.

"I will do my best."

He smiled and again she went warm and gooey inside. He was potent stuff, and she was susceptible.

It will give Gordon more time, she rationalized, but in truth she was so sick of lying, especially to herself that she stopped.

I want to spend more time with him.

It was that simple. He was the most interesting and attractive man she'd spent time with…ever.

And this might be my last chance.

If Gordon did his job and those files got copied, this was the end of the road for Margaret Warren.

"Where would we go?"

"It's a surprise. A very good one."

She nodded and withdrew her hand from her pocket. "Works for me."

He pulled a helmet from the seat locker. She took it, shook back her hair and slid it on, like the old hand she was.

"You've done this before?" he asked, watching her.

"My brother and I used to race Nighthawks. We did some longer trips up the coast when I graduated high school." The truth came harder than the lies. She hadn't talked about herself so easily in eons.

"You are full of surprises, Margaret Warren. I knew there was more to you than met the eye."

You don't know the half of it.

"Well, then, maybe you'll let me drive us home." She flirted, dangerously, carelessly and it felt as good as racing on a motorcycle.

His smile was wicked. He straddled his bike and she sat behind him, hugging herself to his back.

She pressed her head to that sweet spot between his shoulder blades and forgave herself for her feelings for this man.

She crossed her hands over his chest and felt his heartbeat beneath her palm, smelled the spicy clean scent of him and reveled in it. She gave in to her body, shut off her mind and let herself experience Caleb.

Regrets could come later, when he hated her and her feelings for him remained the same as they were in this moment. But for now, the sun hot on her back and Caleb warm in her arms, she was going to let it all happen.

"Hold on tight," he said over his shoulder and kickstarted the bike, which roared to life under her seat. She tilted her hips forward, slid up in inches until her thighs cradled Caleb's.

She shut out everything, until there was only her, him and the road beneath them.

THE SURPRISE was a point overlooking the green, brown and gray foothills undulating to the asphalt river of Highway 1. Beyond that, the magnificent endless blue of the Pacific Ocean beckoned. They climbed off the bike and stepped to the rocky edge of nothing in silence.

The sky was clear, the sunshine bright. The wind smelled of sage and asphalt. It was one of the best moments of her life. She turned and looked at him and realized how much of himself he had given Margaret Warren. He was going to feel like such a fool when the truth was revealed. Which, really, could be any moment.

Suddenly, she was shaken, consumed by the wish to give something of herself to him. The real her, not the fiction of Margaret Warren and not the parts of herself revealed by accident because he affected her so deeply. She wanted to *give* him a piece of her truth. A piece that would let him know that not everything was lie.

"This is one of the best moments of my life," she said. He faced her and she did not blink or look away. She met his blue eyes right on.

This is me, she thought. *This is the real me.*

"I don't often live my life for myself," she said, the wind whipped her words away and he leaned closer to hear her. She felt his heat and she wanted to lay him bare on this mountaintop and do a whole litany of things to him. "My family has always come first."

And second to them was the FBI. A distant third was her.

"I feel like I take care of them until there's nothing left of me. I give myself away and try to fix everything until I'm the one who needs fixing."

She'd told him more than she'd told any man. Let him in to who she really was, who she really wanted to be. And yet she was lying to him. It seemed ludicrous. But, somehow, right.

She smiled. "We're a pair aren't we? I give

myself away and you—" She stopped. *Are selfish, by nature. Secretive and distant.*

"Don't?" he asked. He laughed and turned to watch the endless wave of the ocean. "That's one way to put it. I believe my last long-term girlfriend called me a selfish bastard with intimacy issues."

"Well." She shrugged, letting him know she didn't disagree with that assessment.

"I think maybe I've changed," he said. "Iraq, the accident, having to figure out who I am all over again. I feel like a different man."

They were so high up, she could see the earth's curve and it made her feel small. Insignificant, which was a nice change from feeling as though she had to control every variable in her life.

"You fix things and I'm a guy who could use some fixing." He grinned at her. "Seems like a pretty good match to me." He took a deep breath. "It's weird but I feel like I've known you forever."

It's because I'm deceiving you, she thought with the part of her mind that resisted these moments with him, that wanted her to flee and get herself back on track. *I'm manipulating everything I know about you so that you'll feel that way.*

That didn't explain her feelings, however.

"I feel the same way," she admitted.

She reached between them to touch his hand.

She slid her fingers through his until their palms pressed together. She could feel him watching her, his gaze as tangible as a touch along her cheek. Her neck.

The wind wailed like a voice, the voice of her better judgment, screaming no.

"Margaret—"

"Shut up," she said, hating that fake name on his lips. She grinned at him to take the sting from her words. "Let's not talk anymore."

"Okay."

She wondered what would happen if she told him right now. If she came right out and said, "I'm lying to you. I'm using you and lying to you." Could she convince him that her feelings at this moment—her attraction and gratitude and respect for him—were as real as the rocky soil beneath their feet.

"I like you, Margaret Warren," he said, his eyes fixed on the ocean.

"I like you, too," she whispered.

They stood there a long time, their palms touching, the wind buffeting them and spinning her hair into cyclones.

She gave herself this time on the top of this mountain, standing next to a man who captivated and attracted her. She sank into the moment. She breathed deep air that tasted like freedom and clung to Caleb's warm hand.

She wished they could stay here forever. But as she watched the white crests of waves roll against rocky banks she knew there was nothing that would change the outcome of what she'd started. She couldn't have it both ways. She couldn't live for her family and herself.

And, as usual, she picked her family first.

"I've got to go," she finally said, pulling her hand free from his.

"Okay," he said, still cheerful, having not caught onto her dour mood. "Want to drive?" he asked, holding out the keys.

"I'd love to," she said and she swung her leg over his bike. He stood watching her in such a way that she felt like a young girl again.

"You look good," he told her. "Minus a few clothes and you'd be one of my favorite fantasies." He kissed her, his lips cool and chapped against hers.

I'll finish this, she told herself, while memorizing the play of his fingers in the hair at the nape of her neck. She distanced herself from her body, so as to not fall victim to her long-ignored desires. *I'll put Caleb and Delgado and my brother's murder to bed, then I'll make choices for myself.*

Though she knew the choice she'd want to make at that point would be Caleb and he wouldn't choose her. Not then. Not ever again.

CALEB DROPPED HER OFF at her car in front of the gas station. He kissed her again and she let him. In fact, she kissed him back, wrapping herself around him, holding him as close as possible as if to soak him in through her clothes and skin. As if to take some of him with her.

"Uh," he said against her lips. He pulled back a millimeter so he could look into her eyes and she couldn't meet them. She just couldn't. Lies and want and desire choked her and she didn't know what he'd see there, he who saw her all too clearly. "Do you want to come home with me?" he asked, he practically stammered and her heart melted further. They were a pair all right. "I mean, normally I wouldn't ask but you seem…inclined."

She smiled, her eyes focused on his chin, the scar tissue that crept across that jutting feature. It was as if his words, his body, the man himself were a magnet and she was made of metal shavings. No flesh, no bone, no will or sense of right and wrong. There was only attraction and want.

"I wish I could," she said and meant it. "But I have some things I need to do." Her partner waited for her—her boss, the Bureau, her brother all insisted she deny herself a little longer.

She did, however, kiss him again. One last time before she stepped away and shaded her eyes with her hand so he couldn't see into them. Into her.

"Goodbye," she said, knowing that as they stood here her partner was collecting the evidence they needed to remove her from Caleb's life. "It was fun." She gestured to the bike so he wouldn't guess at her meaning, at the sadness that clawed up her throat.

"Okay," he sighed and revved the engine of his bike. She watched him drive away, her regrets and desire like ash on her tongue.

As she sent the text message warning Gordon, she hoped he'd gotten what they needed, because as of this moment her life was too short to work for the FBI any more.

MIGUEL DELGADO sat like a puppy in the corner of the leather couch.

"What did I say?" Benny asked. There was no rage burning holes in his gut anymore. Now it felt like a giant weight, a heavy sadness pressing down on him from the heavens. His mother would say God was punishing him, sending him doom in payment for hurting his sister.

"You said not to get involved, but *jefe*—"

"No *but jefe*," Benny said. His brother always had an excuse. A reason for why he did the drugs, slept with the wrong women, beat up the wrong men. His brother's reasons added to the heaviness in him, pounds of pressure in his head. His chest. He could barely breathe.

He turned, faced the wall and struggled to take a deep breath. Another.

Reyes was in town right now. The newspapers had been filled with photos of the ambassador shaking hands and meeting with the mayor and governor.

Immigration. The headlines said he was here for ten days to discuss immigration between Mexico and the United States with city and state politicians.

On the eleventh day he was here to talk drugs, with Benny.

But his brother, his stupid bungling brother, was ruining everything.

"Why were you there?" he asked, without looking at Miguel. He couldn't look at him, not without feeling torn. His life would be easier without Miguel, but even thinking that… He was a man resigned to his place in hell. But killing his brother—even if he was a jackass and threatened everything—would earn Benny terrible punishments. "You think you don't stand out in front of city hall?"

"He didn't see me," Miguel whined.

"You were on television!" Benny roared. "You were standing right behind him while the reporters asked him questions!"

"I was just watching. What if Munoz had sent some guy to shoot him or something. You think no one knows about your deal but everyone knows."

"Because you can't keep your mouth shut!" Benny whirled on his brother, only to find him on his feet, anger and courage turning his handsome young face into something darker, meaner. He really did look like their father.

Oh, no, Benny thought. *Not this.* Not Miguel angry and hurt. There were too many guns around and Miguel was too stupid to realize that if he shot Benny and killed him, he'd go to jail and die. If he shot Benny and didn't kill him, he'd die faster.

"When are you going to treat me like a man?" Miguel asked. "You won't let me help with the reporter. You won't let me help—"

"Fine." Benny sighed. "You can help with the reporter."

The dark cloud left his brother's face and Benny resigned himself to the fact that he could not protect him forever. Miguel wasn't bright enough or mean enough to survive the way Benny had, without protection. And he had known, though he didn't want to admit it, that some day Miguel would chafe under his protection. He was too stupid not to.

Chains of responsibility fell from around Benny's neck. He couldn't take care of his brother forever. If the idiot wanted to be killed, wanted to act the big shot and die like a punk in the street somewhere, fine.

Benny nearly smiled he felt so much better.

"How?" Miguel asked.

"I got a cop on this who owes me some favors. He's coming tonight to tell me what he's learned."

"And then I can go kill him—"

"I told you, Miguel!" Benny shouted, there still had to be rules. Rules to protect Benny from jail, or worse. "You aren't getting your hands bloody. If you go down, the whole family goes down with you. Is that what you want? To send Lita to jail? Me?"

Miguel looked down. "Of course not, *jefe*."

"Then promise me you won't do anything stupid. That's why I've got people who owe me favors. You can come with me to the meeting."

"Okay, *jefe*." Miguel smiled at him, once more a little boy. "Thank you."

"Get out of here," Benny said, cuffing his brother affectionately on the head.

I can't control everything, he thought, nearly giddy. *If my stupid brother gets himself in trouble… what can I do?*

Some things were better left to God or the devil to handle.

"Don't you have money to collect? You've been losing more than you've been bringing in down at The Rails."

Miguel blanched and Benny wanted to tell him that there was nothing about Miguel that he did not know. Nothing.

"It's okay," he told him, kindly. Patiently. "I've known for a long time. Just don't get yourself in trouble."

Miguel nodded and turned to the door. *"Jefe?"* he asked, pausing in the doorway, "what's this cop's name?"

"Dan," Benny said. "Detective Dan Meisner."

CHAPTER TWELVE

GORDON WAS SITTING on the stone stoop in front of her apartment when she pulled up. He did not look happy.

No, she thought, her heart plummeting to her feet. *No, we need to be done. We need to get out of there.*

"Hey, Gordo," she said, approaching him from the parking lot. "You don't look like a man who just cracked the biggest case of his career."

"Yeah, well, because I didn't." He kicked his feet out and sprawled backward on the cement.

He smelled like ham.

"Don't tell me you didn't get past the dog."

"The dog was fine. Ugly and vicious as all get out, but the ham worked."

"You couldn't break into a locked office?"

"I couldn't break his pass code. All his files are password protected about three different ways. I was about to break the code when I realized the whole thing was booby-trapped. The dude is paranoid."

A selfish man with intimacy issues. She almost smiled, Caleb thought he had changed, but his actions told the truth. He would never change. He was a suspicious man and when he found out about her it would only fuel his fears.

Maggie sat down next to Gordon, feeling nauseous from the sickening mix of emotions in her belly.

I shouldn't be happy, she told herself. *I shouldn't be glad.*

But she was and it felt as though she was betraying her brother, her family, to be so relieved that she'd see Caleb again.

It's a second last chance. One more time to see him.

Gordon sat up and wiped his face. "I did copy some of the tapes."

"Even if we get a court order to confiscate the originals, that won't hold up in court," she said, pleasure and panic warring in her.

"I know," Gordon groaned. "Worse, Curtis wants to see us in—" he looked down at his watch "—two hours."

Maggie nodded. She might talk a good game,

but quitting the FBI was nothing she'd ever made official.

Until right now.

"Good," she said. She sighed and looked up at the crystal-clear blue sky. Birds flew overhead, trees rustled and the constant mess of emotions in her belly finally quieted. Everything slowed down and went still. It was if the racing thoughts, the hammering heartbeats and the ulcer pain she'd lived with…vanished. She was motionless. Pain-free.

"I'm resigning, Gordon," she said and watched him spin toward her. "This is my last case."

"You're kidding."

She shook her head, feeling better than she had in…well, since that moment on the mountain with Caleb earlier. But previous to that she hadn't felt so good in years. Since she'd become an agent, since she'd listened to her father. "I'm out." She turned to face her partner who looked shattered at her news. "Life's too short, Gordon, to not do exactly what you want."

NONE OF THEIR NEWS went over well with Curtis. Not Gordon's failure to access the computer files and not Maggie's resignation.

"I'm not totally surprised," Curtis said, leaning back in his chair at the head of the conference table. "You're a good agent," he told her and she nodded, pleased to be complimented by a man she admired. "But your heart hasn't been in it for a while. Which is not to say I am pleased with your decision." He thumped the table with his fist. "I've invested a lot in you. Taken risks and gone out on branches, backing you when I realize now I would have been better off backing someone with more staying power."

Maggie blanched and swallowed the hard ball of guilt lodged in the back of her throat. Still, her relief at actually resigning was too great to be diminished by guilt. She could no longer live for other people. Not anymore. Caleb Gomez changed her life and she couldn't change it back, no matter who wanted it that way. "I'm sorry, sir."

He nodded, but didn't say anything and she knew he did not accept her apology. That hurt.

Just getting you ready, she told herself. *Just preparing you for Dad's disappointment and judgment.*

"You'll finish the Gomez case and then be done?"

She nodded.

"What's the revised time frame?"

"Two more days, sir," she said. She'd come to this conclusion driving to the field office. One more day, Sunday, to see if things came together without her having to reveal herself. She'd surprise him at home when he least expected her. If that didn't work, she'd tell Caleb who she was, what her stake in the Delgado case was and hope that was enough for him to do the right thing. "By Monday night we'll have the information we need. We know he's got it. It gives us one more day to make an airtight case for a court order to confiscate his property and, if that doesn't work, I think I can convince him to give me the tapes."

Curtis nodded, staring out the window to the mostly dark and silent lab. A few desk lamps were on, casting pools over solitary men and women working hard at trapping the bad guys with the clues they'd left behind.

I want out, she thought, uninspired by the sight of her colleagues working hard. *I just want out.*

"Two days," Curtis confirmed. "And then you're done." He didn't say it, but she read it in his body language, in his face in the way he talked to her. *You are done, because I don't trust you anymore. You are no longer one of us.*

She nodded, expecting to feel hurt, saddened, heavier, carrying the weight of Curtis's disappointment. Instead, she felt a thousand pounds lighter.

She stepped out of the Bureau into a gray day. The fog had rolled in, making everything ghostly, surreal.

"Well," Gordon said coming out behind her. He jangled his keys in his pocket. "I'm going to go wash the smell of meat off myself and get some sleep."

She nodded and clapped him on the shoulder, a decision coming up behind her like a wave, carrying her inevitably toward confrontation.

"I'm going to go talk to my dad," she sighed, and walked to her car like a woman facing a firing squad.

HER PARENTS lived in a little bungalow on a street north of Wilshire, so her drive wasn't far. She surprised herself by not marshaling her defenses. She didn't prepare a speech or justification.

She'd been doing all of that in order to talk to her father since she was eight.

And she was the favorite child.

She parked in front of the sand-colored house and stepped up the narrow cobblestone path, bracketed by impatiens that seemed to perpetually bloom in the sweet California air. Her mother's doing, of course. The little shamrock sign on the door proclaimed this to be the home of the Fitzgeralds.

Her father hated the shamrock and Maggie, out of her ridiculous loyalty and idolatry of her father, had hated it, too.

Mom was a second-generation Irish-American and Dad still called her watered-down Irish.

Maggie touched the faded green wood and, with new eyes and an independent heart, she decided it was kind of cute.

The door jerked open before she could knock. Her parents had a crazy sixth sense regarding the proximity of their children. Mom smiled. Dad scowled, his gray eyebrows the barometer of his mood.

"Sweetie!" Mom cried and hauled Maggie against her. Her mother was so thin it was like being hugged by a loving skeleton. Bones everywhere. And she'd lost more weight since Patrick. Maggie hoped quitting the Bureau wouldn't send her family further into a tailspin.

It doesn't matter, she told herself when she felt her resolve weakening. *I have to do this. For me. Right now.*

"What's the occasion?" Bridget asked.

"You off assignment?" Dad asked, his brogue worn away by so much time on the West Coast. He didn't hug her. He stood, arms by his side, an invincible force field around his solid, working-man frame. He hugged Liz, but never her. Patrick had been such a momma's boy, he'd never lacked for hugs from Mom. And Liz was such a girl, she had practically grown up perched on Dad's knee.

Maggie had never really thought about it, had taken it, stupidly, as a compliment that she and her father didn't hug. They shook hands. As though they were equals.

I don't want an equal, she thought, tears burning in her eyes for the years she'd lost trying to be something she wasn't, all for this man's approval.

I need a dad.

"Dad." She sighed and crossed the threshold, pushed through the magnetic force field that separated them and she wrapped her arms around his neck. "I have to talk to you."

"You're pregnant," Mom cried, managing to look horrified and delighted at the same time.

Maggie laughed and leaned over to kiss her mother's cheek without letting go of her dad.

"I'm not pregnant," she said and turned to smile into her father's eyes, hope a bubble in her chest. She patted his cheek, smelled his familiar smell and hoped that, in the end, he'd love her all the same.

"I'm going to law school."

His eyebrows rose, indicating a shift in his mood toward danger.

"What about the Bureau?" Mom asked.

"I just quit." She didn't look away from her

father even when his eyebrows crept ever upward. "I'm on my last assignment."

"You've put a lot of years into the Bureau," he said, the brogue creeping in and she braced herself. "Your brother wanted to go into the Bureau, you know. In honor of—"

She shook her head. "Patrick was happy with the police, Dad. He loved his job. Please don't bring him into this."

Her mother pressed a fist to her mouth, both at the mention of Patrick and at the brewing trouble in her living room.

"I can't keep doing this for you, Dad."

"Doing what for me?" he asked, pulling away from her, but she held tight, cupping his big shoulders in her hands. He was short, amazing how she'd never really noticed that before.

"Working for you," she said. "Living my life for you. In fear of you."

"I never laid a finger on you. You got no reason to be scared of me." His eyebrows nearly lifted right off his head. He didn't know the power he had, the way he could affect her with a look, a cold shoulder, a throwaway comment about always wanting to be in the FBI.

"It wasn't that kind of fear, Dad." She smiled, sadly. "I was so scared of disappointing you."

He blinked, his mouth opening and shutting.

"Well, that's the dumbest thing I ever heard," he said, finally.

"You have a way of filling a room with your disapproval, Dad. You're doing it right now."

He pulled himself free of her and stormed into the kitchen. "Well, I don't see why you gotta go leaving an organization like the FBI—" he cried over his shoulder.

Maggie stepped after him, preparing for battle.

"Sweetheart," Mom said, placing a hand on Maggie's shoulder, stopping her. She smiled sweetly, tears in her eyes. Maggie knew what her mother was going to say. *Would it kill you to stay at the Bureau? Would it kill you to make him happy?*

"Mom, I have to do this," she said, stopping her mother from trying to turn her against herself.

"I know you do, sweetie," she said instead and Maggie turned, astonished to face her mother. "I'm so proud of you." She sighed and Maggie felt the burn of hot emotion behind her eyes. "Your father is, too. You always worshipped him so much, neither one of us knew what to do about it." She shrugged. "So we just convinced ourselves that you wouldn't do anything you didn't want to."

Stupefied, Maggie rocked back on her heels.

"You're doing the right thing. He knows it. It's

just hard for him to hear that you weren't happy and he had something to do with it." She smiled again, cupping Maggie's face in her solid hands. "Give him some time by himself."

"Ma." She folded her mother into her arms, listening to her father clump downstairs to the basement.

"Stay for dinner," Mom said. "He'd like that."

Emotions, reality and fantasy and the inevitable conclusion to her relationship with Caleb spun and clicked within her. She couldn't waste anymore time doing things for her father.

"I have to go, Mom," she said. Hope was a butterfly with stone wings, but it gave a valiant effort to fly in her heart. "I'll come back in a few days." She almost told her mother that when she came back she'd be a heartbroken mess and she'd need some motherly TLC. But if she did that, she'd never get out of the house.

It was 7:00 p.m. and she wanted to make the most of this night.

SHE DROVE NORTH to Caleb, the sun setting electric pink and bright orange on her left. Heat built in her until she unrolled the window and let the breeze brush her cheeks. The warm scented air felt sensual.

Every part of her was alive, tuned to the physical.

I want to make love to him, she thought. *That's what I want. Before he hates me and this all falls apart. I want to touch him.*

She smiled and stepped on the gas.

IT WAS DARK by the time she pulled onto Caleb's street. She waved at the guys staked out at the entrance of the cul de sac. They'd wonder, she was sure, what she was doing here on a Saturday night, but she didn't care. Her career was over. They could think what they wanted.

The stars were obliterated by the clouds that rolled in from the ocean. It was a black night and the light in Caleb's window was a beacon calling her home.

She put her head to the door and sighed. Since she was no longer fighting her feelings, she tried to restrain the smile that trembled at the corners of her lips. She couldn't go giggling into the house.

Would he be surprised? Happy? Awkward?

How did one go from cleaning woman to lover?

But as she pushed open the door, it wasn't Margaret Warren stepping into that house. It was Maggie and Maggie had a mission.

"You're not the pizza delivery guy," Caleb said, his voice a quiet rumble from the couch. He paused for a second, his smile turning wicked, his eyes suddenly hot. "Are you?" His voice teased her and she realized the step to lover was going to be very easy indeed.

"I could be," she said, knowing him too well. She dropped her purse on the chair.

"I am a very good tipper."

She smiled, adoring him and his rusty humor. "You're a dirty man."

"You were thinking the same thing," he said. "I saw your face."

Caleb sighed, his arms behind his head like some sexy war hero on the cover of a book. "What are you doing here?" he asked. His grin was sly but sweet and hesitant, as though he could pass the words off as a joke should she say no.

But they both knew it wasn't a joke.

It took a moment for her mind to catch up to her body, which was growing soft and warm under his gaze.

Patrick would want me to be happy.

Life is too short.

Everything she needed to live this night for herself clicked into place with unheard of ease. She didn't need to plan or manipulate anything. The opportunity was here for her to take if she had the courage.

Courage was never something she'd been short on.

"You invited me," she said, toeing off one shoe and then the other. She channeled a little Mae West, her voice a purr. "Remember? You said I seemed... inclined."

"I remember." His playboy smile was still on his face, but when her hands went to the buttons of her shirt, the smile vanished and he looked as though he couldn't believe that after all the pressure he'd applied she was saying yes.

"What...what are you doing?" he asked, leaning up on his elbows. "Margaret...you don't—"

"Yes, Caleb." She undid the last button, letting the shirt hang open over her taut stomach and breasts. "I do. And call me Maggie."

Caleb swallowed. He resisted the urge to pinch himself, to rub his eyes as if this were a dream he could wake himself from. Not that he wanted to.

Margaret...Maggie—that suited her infinitely better—was here. Taking off her shirt.

His body roared to life.

"Okay, Maggie." He felt stupid. Thick with his nearly unmanageable lust. "Let's go." He sat up, ready to take her hand and lead her to the bedroom where there was space and utter darkness.

She'd seen the worst of him that day in the hallway but he didn't need the soft light from the lamp by his head shining on his imperfections.

"Let's stay here," she said. "Right here."

She shrugged off her shirt and came to stand in front of him. Her hands grazed his shoulders, working their way up to his neck, to the scars and then his cheeks until she cupped his face. He burned where she touched him, his skin suddenly hot, his blood on fire for her.

"I want to make love to you here," she said.

"Okay," he said. Should she want to make love on the roof of the garage he'd find them a ladder. He placed a trembling hand on her belly, felt the twitch of muscles and smiled, pleased with the understanding that she wasn't feeling in complete control herself.

He spanned her lean waist, felt the curve of her hips, the ridge of muscles along her spine.

He brushed her shoulders, muscled and tight, he cupped the lovely muscles on top of her toned arms.

"Wow," he said, taking her all in. "You…" He looked into her eyes, amazed at this body she hid beneath her clothes. "Wow."

She smiled. "Good genes," she said. "And I run."

He nodded. "You won't find anything quite so beautiful under my clothes," he said, joking as she lowered herself to her knees in front of him.

"Yes," she said, her eyes direct and earnest. "I will."

"Maggie," he breathed, stunned and embarrassed by the generosity in her gaze. "You don't have to say that."

"You're right," she whispered. "I don't. I don't have to do this either." She kissed him, the corner of his lips where the scars started and she followed them across his cheek, down his neck. She pulled at the hem of his brown T-shirt and he lifted his arms as much as he could so she could slide it off.

He felt more than naked. He felt naked and raw and…new. Each brush of her beautiful mouth destroyed him and rebuilt him in the same instant. She kissed his chest, licked the tangled mess of his skin. She pulled her warm beautiful body close to his and the heat between them eroded every misgiving and doubt.

"But I want to," she said. "I want to so much I can't sleep. I tell myself stupid lies that I don't believe. I—" Her eyes, when they met his, were baffled, confused. He knew exactly how she felt.

How could he want her this way?

How could he feel this way about a woman he barely knew?

"I know," he breathed and slid his fingers into her hair and cupped her small head in his big hands. She groaned and her eyes fluttered, her mouth opened and the knowledge that he could affect her with his touch the way she did him boosted his confidence.

He pressed his lips to hers. Touched his tongue to hers. Pulled her up between his legs, flush against his body. He swallowed her soft sigh as his fingers traced her spine. Her bra fell away under his clumsy hands and he felt the soft swell of her breasts, the hard press of her nipples against his chest and they both groaned.

He slid his hands down to the back of her jeans, curved his hands around her hips. She rocked forward against him. The mood changed.

A sense of urgency crept into their careful explorations. Her nails raked lightly over his skin; he used his teeth on the soft flesh of her neck. She hissed into his ear and nipped him back.

They fell onto the couch shifting until they were face-to-face. He leaned back and watched her. "You seem different," he said.

"It's because I have my shirt off." She moved to kiss him and he dodged.

"No." He wasn't in love. He wasn't the kind of guy who fell for a woman so fast. Well, he never used to be and he was mostly sure he still wasn't the kind of man who ran headfirst into an emotional relationship. But what he did feel for Margaret... Maggie was real. Solid. "You seem—"

"Has anyone ever told you talk too much?" she asked, her hands snaking down his back toward his hips.

He shook his head, speechless as her fingers popped free the top button of his jeans. And the next.

"Maggie—" He gasped when her hand slid into his jeans, between his legs.

"You do. Shut up. We're having sex."

He laughed into her mouth as joy tripped and rocketed through him. He slid his arms around her and pressed openmouthed kisses on her neck, along her collarbone, across the tops of her breasts.

He sucked on her skin, wanting to leave some kind of mark on her. Something visible and barbarian.

Her hand cupped his penis, her thumb ran up the length across the head and he shuddered with agonized delight. But he caught her hand.

"Um…if you want things to work out in your favor, you won't start there," he said. "It's been awhile."

"We've got all night," she said and kissed her way down his chest, across the scars and the hard muscles of his stomach. He knew what she was doing and could have stopped her. She didn't need to be so selfless.

But he didn't stop it and when she pulled his

jeans off and kissed his knees, the ravaged muscle of his thigh, the strange knot of scar tissue at his hip, he didn't even flinch, or shy away or distract her with his own selfless lovemaking.

He let her heal him in a way the doctors and the therapists never could.

Caleb pulled her hair free of the rubber band she always wore and the blond strands shimmered across his lap. He stroked the beautiful fall of hair, clenched it in his fists when she took him in her mouth and knew the changes in him were innumerable. Thanks to the accident. Thanks to Margaret.

He was a different man and, he was beginning to think, a better man.

"Maggie." He sighed, lost in the sensations she created. Lust and release coiled in his lower belly. He cupped her chin, pulled her from her excruciatingly tender and exciting ministrations. He smiled into her upturned face, her lips red and wet and so gorgeous he could die just kissing them.

She sat up, straddling him, half-clothed while he lay naked beneath her.

Gotta fix that, he thought through the haze of sensation her warmth built in his blood.

Their fingers fumbled with the button and zipper of her pants. She slid half off the couch and he reached for her, but her momentum pulled them both onto the floor.

"Are you okay?" she asked, concern pushing aside the hazy look of a woman steeped in pleasure.

"Great," he growled and crawled over her. He yanked off her pants, the pretty pink underwear she wore, until, finally…there she was, naked on his floor.

"You're so pretty," he said.

"You don't have to say that," she murmured, her hands stroking his arms.

He leaned down to kiss the soft concave muscle of her stomach between the delicate span of her rib cage. He licked her belly button. "It's ridiculous how pretty you are," he said. And she sighed.

He kissed the hard ridge of her hip bones. The muscles of her thigh where they met her torso. "Well," he said, re-kissing that area because it so clearly deserved it. "That's just amazing. And look…"

The curls between her legs were so tenderly feminine, so soft and sweet that he felt humbled before her. The secrets of her body, the secrets of her guarded and hidden behind clothes, distanced expressions and questions. It was all revealed now.

For him.

He made love to her like a man reborn. He kissed

and licked and cherished her. He adored every gasp, every soft mew of pleasure, the hiss of desire climbing. Her nails dug into his flesh and her legs, so strong and smooth, circled him. Her hands pulled at his hair attempting to direct his movements.

"Just a minute," he said, pausing. The taste of her hot and sweet and spicy on his tongue.

He loved her until she fell apart on his living room floor, shuddering and crying and clutching at him.

Sweat ran down his body, every muscle in his legs burned from the position he'd held. His arm had long since grown numb and useless so he rolled to his side.

Her fingers cupped his arm, slid over his stomach and he gasped, his erection jerking with the biting need to have her.

"Wow," she murmured.

He only nodded.

"You deserve a medal or something." She sighed and he laughed.

"A reward?" He turned his head, relishing the naughty talk. She purred and sat up to grab her purse, pulling out a condom.

Oh, thank you, he thought on behalf of his roaring libido.

Her smile was pure Eve and, like Adam, at this moment he'd do anything she wanted.

CHAPTER THIRTEEN

CALEB, AS A RULE, wasn't one to brag. But as he sprawled on the floor where the couch had been—he'd shoved it aside with Herculean strength because their heads kept banging into it—he knew the past hour and a half were really something to brag about.

Tombstone worthy, really.

Caleb Gomez, journalist, love god.

Not too shabby, he thought, looking over at Maggie's back as she lay on her side facing the windows. He leaned up on his elbow and brushed her hair from her face, revealing her closed eyes and smiling lips.

"Hey," she croaked.

He smiled and stroked the back of his fingers down the delicate curve of her stomach, the soft swell of her hip. She was something else. In truth, she was the love god, he was a mere mortal delighted to have attracted her notice.

"I don't suppose you have anything to eat, do you?" she asked.

"We could order a piz—"

Maggie sat up on one elbow, her body suddenly tense, vibrating. "Dan?" she whispered.

And then the whole world exploded.

With a loud *crack!* the patio door shattered in a waterfall of glass and, at the same time, the couch exploded.

"What the—" he cried, suddenly covered in glass. Time moved at hyper speed. Something—a man—stood framed by the gaping hole at the door and then vanished into the mists. Maggie was on her knees at her purse, pulling out a walkie-talkie and...a gun?

In the office, Bear went nuts.

"Stay down," Maggie yelled. "Get behind the couch."

"Maggie—"

There was another crack and something hot brushed his cheek. He scrambled over glass fragments to the relative protection of the couch. "Get down, Maggie."

He peered over the edge of the couch. She was running, naked, but wearing tennis shoes, out the door and into the black night after the man.

He reached around the edge of the sofa to grab his pants. A piece of glass bit deeper into his knee.

He dug it out, brushed off the worst of the shards, then pulled on his pants. He had to get Maggie. What the hell was she doing?

Someone out there had a gun and—

She reappeared at the doorway. "He's gone," she said. "Get dressed," she said, without looking at him and then took a deep breath before bringing the radio to her mouth.

"Shots fired. I repeat, shots fired. Alert drivers on street west. He's coming out of the ravine." She threw the walkie-talkie onto the chair and pulled on her clothes in record time.

He watched, knowledge like cement settled in his bones. His gut. His world-class gut that never saw this coming.

"I'm serious, Caleb, put your clothes on. We're going to have company in a few seconds." He didn't even recognize her. This wasn't Margaret Warren, the woman he'd just made love—

He closed his eyes as the cement surrounded his heart.

His clothes went on slow. He stood with the help of the couch, his limbs, so limber moments ago, were crippled again.

He turned for the bedroom.

"Where are you going?" she asked, her voice a dagger in his head.

"Shoes," he said. It was all he could say while a hundred words, questions and denials clamored in his throat.

He walked to his bedroom, his body, his heart, his head throbbing with pain and regret.

MAGGIE WATCHED HIM GO, his shoulders bent under the weight of what had just happened. She longed to follow him, but the front door crashed open and Gordon, accompanied by two police officers, weapons drawn, were in the house.

"Where's Gomez?" Gordon asked, his eyes focused beyond her head on the broken window and the mists outside.

"Bedroom," she said.

"Anyone hurt?" he asked.

"Cut up a little," she said, wiping blood that ran down her cheek on her T-shirt. "But okay. Anyone see the guy come out of the ravine?"

"No." Gordon shook his head. "We need CSI," he called over his shoulder and one of the uniformed men radioed it in. He crossed to the couch and pulled out a small flashlight and examined the bullet hole. "We've got some guys and dogs in the forest. Did you see him?" Gordon asked.

Maggie nodded. Grief and disbelief a bitter

storm in her stomach and head. She wiped a hand over her face and pressed hard on her eyeballs catching the tears she couldn't stop.

"Fitzgerald?" Gordon asked. She felt the brush of his hand on her shoulder and she shook it off. She'd been touched too much today. Her skin was gone and all she had left was bones and raw nerves.

"I need you to get my sister on the phone," she said.

"Why?"

"The shooter was Dan Meisner," she said. "My brother-in-law."

"You think this is still related? How—"

She shrugged. "How could it not be?" she asked. "I mean that's some kind of coincidence, isn't it? We don't know who Delgado has on this and then my brother-in-law—"

"Okay," Gordon said, trying to calm her down. "I agree. Too many coincidences. But do you think he saw you? I mean, would he bring your sister into it?"

"I'm not sure. But I saw him and I'm not taking any chances. This bastard isn't killing any more of my family."

"I'm with you," Gordon muttered and then turned away to speak into the radio wired to his shoulder.

"You've got some bad cuts," a medic said, approaching her with his kit and sterile gloves. "Let me look at you."

"Someone clean up this glass. And let's get some plywood to cover this window. We can't leave the door open for another attack," she snapped.

Two uniformed men hopped to; Maggie let the medic pull a piece of glass from her cheek and bandage the worst of her cuts, mostly on her arms since she'd covered her face with her hands. She didn't feel any of it. It was as if she were dying, slowly. From the outside in. All those places where she'd felt so alive, so flushed with blood, were now cold. And growing colder.

"Check on Gomez," she said as the medic cleaned up.

"Someone already is."

"Gordon!" she yelled.

"We're working on it," he yelled back. "So far no answer on her cell or at home. We've got men on their way there. Don't worry, Maggie. She's going to be okay."

"Let me get this straight." Caleb's voice sliced through her and she nearly doubled over in pain at his cold tone.

You knew it would come to this, she thought. *You knew all along.*

And she'd known it would hurt, she'd just never guessed how much.

"Your brother-in-law just tried to kill you?" Caleb asked.

She swallowed, gathered up what remained of Special Agent Fitzgerald and faced him. He was okay despite a red burn across his cheek where one of the bullets had gotten too close and a cut above his eye that had been stitched.

Thank God, I was here, she realized, relief and gratitude that he was alive nearly lifted her off her feet. He would have been shot. And while she knew he would no longer be in her life, she couldn't stand the thought that he wouldn't be in the world.

"Tried to kill *you,*" she corrected. Her eyes met his and the anger in those blue depths scalded her. She didn't look away, she soaked in his rage because she deserved it.

"Benny Delgado is after you. Has been since your release from the hospital."

Caleb nodded, his jaw granite hard. He swallowed audibly and she prepared herself for what was to come.

"Who are you?" he finally whispered.

"FBI," she murmured. Caleb sucked in a deep breath and she could feel his disbelief and pain.

He pursed his lips and nodded, his eyes bright with suppressed anguish.

"Caleb." Her voice was a whisper. There were too many people in the room, her job beckoned. "I'm so—"

He laughed and the bitterness sliced her to ribbons. He turned away from her without a second glance. Her spine, ramrod straight in front of her colleagues, quivered under the weight of her own pain.

She called on all of her training to keep herself from showing her own emotion. From grabbing him and pouring out her apologies and rationale. Her excuses.

She could tell as he walked away from her, it wouldn't matter anyway.

"Mr. Gomez, I'm going to need a statement." One of the officers approached Caleb and she bit her tongue. It was too late to ask him not to say anything about what they had been doing. Perhaps he'd like to hurt her that way anyway, muddy her name, tarnish her professionalism. Let everyone know how much she'd screwed up.

"What were you doing when the shots were fired?" the officer asked.

Caleb glanced over his shoulder. She didn't know what he saw, what shattered portion of herself that she hid from everyone in the room but him. He turned back to the officer and said, "Reading the newspaper on the couch."

"Agent Fitzgerald?" the officer asked her and she saw Caleb digest her name. Irish, just as he'd suspected. "Do you want to add anything?"

It seemed to her the whole room waited for her answer. No matter what Caleb had said, she knew that smart men could see the truth on their faces. Their bodies.

The room smelled like gunfire and sex.

She couldn't look at Caleb without wanting to hold him, touch him, assure herself that he was okay. And his rage toward her was so primal, so personal, it went beyond a journalist being infiltrated by the FBI, it was about a man being lied to by a woman.

"Nothing," she said and she could see some of the men smirk.

"Okay." The officer made some notes and Maggie turned away to grab her cell phone.

She had work to do.

FORENSICS HAD LEFT and only Maggie, Gordon, Curtis and Caleb remained in the house. The window was boarded up and secured. Shades were drawn, curtains closed. They'd put the furniture and blast shields against the patio doors, so if someone stood on the patio and sprayed the house with machine-gun fire, they'd be safe.

Well…more safe.

There were undercover agents all over the neighborhood. Dan wouldn't get past them. Not without being seen by someone.

Even Bear was staked out in the yard by the trail in the ravine.

But Maggie's ulcers were spitting acid through her body.

She still had not heard from her sister.

"We need to get you out of here," she said to Caleb who had not looked at her since she'd told him she was FBI.

He shook his head. "No way."

She rolled her eyes. "The man wants you dead, Caleb. This isn't a joke."

"If he wants me dead," he said, his tone scathing, "he can come back and try again. You guys can get him, and this will all be over."

"We can't guarantee your safety," Curtis said.

Caleb laughed, his feelings about the FBI were in full view. "You couldn't guarantee my safety if I was a witness in a safe house or a cop about…" He trailed off and finally his eyes lifted to hers. A question was buried there.

The cop was your brother?

She nodded, imperceptibly and looked away. She didn't want to see the pity or the blame or whatever emotion was in his eyes.

Truth. Lies. It was all such a mess.

"You were comfortable enough using me as a trap before. What's different now?"

"It wasn't a trap," Maggie said. "We were hoping to find your files on Delgado before it came to this."

"You couldn't ask?" Caleb asked with an incredulous laugh. "You had to break into my home and…spy on me?"

"You don't have a record of cooperation with the FBI," Maggie said and his angry gaze swung her way.

"I wonder why?"

"Don't pretend like you would have handed over the files," she snapped. "You've sat on that information for years without handing—"

"I got a little distracted in the desert, Maggie, or Margaret, or whatever the hell your name is," he nearly shouted.

"Don't hide behind what happened to you, Caleb. You've done enough of that."

The words were out, flying around the room and all the emotion on Caleb's face dried up as he turned to marble right in front of her.

She didn't retreat in the face of his anger. It was the truth and she'd stand by it.

"In any case—" Gordon cleared his throat, breaking into the heated battle between them "—we were hoping to find the files before Delgado found you."

"And did you?" Caleb asked, his words shot from his mouth like bullets. "Did you sneak into my office and find my files?"

She nodded, kept her voice strong. Sturdy. "We did."

"But we couldn't break your code," Gordon said, but Caleb didn't seem to be listening to him. His blue eyes were locked on Maggie and she couldn't look away.

"When?" he asked. And she nearly cringed. He wanted the map of her betrayal.

"It doesn't matter," she said. "What matters—"

"When?" His voice was steel-plated, iron hard.

"Mr. Gomez." Curtis stepped in.

Caleb's gaze slid through Curtis. Caleb was the man he'd once been, tough, hard, smart and ready for a fight. Eager for it. She'd seen all of this in him, hidden and buried under his experiences overseas. Her betrayal had set him free.

Caleb Gomez was back.

"I have a few questions that need to be

answered," Caleb said. "And it would behoove the FBI to answer those questions." Curtis's eyes dropped and Caleb looked as though he would attack at the sign of weakness.

"Wednesday," she finally said, to end the standoff. "While you were in the shower."

He nodded, his jaw clenched tight, but remained silent.

"I need you to understand the risks you're taking in wanting to stay here," Curtis said. "We expect Delgado to try again in a matter of hours. We've got men in the neighborhood."

"Dan came from the ravine—" Maggie started and Curtis nodded.

"We've got two guys at the trailhead and another two on the street." Curtis shook his head. "I doubt they'll come in the same way. We've got more men stationed at the top of this street."

"Great," Caleb snapped. "Let's get this over with."

"We could remove you from the house," Curtis offered. "Use a decoy in your place."

"I went to war, Agent Curtis," Caleb said, bracing himself against the couch. He didn't look at them anymore, as if they were beneath his notice. "I'm not scared."

"No," Curtis said, watching Gomez walk to the

bathroom. "I don't guess much scares you any-more."

Except leaving the house and talking to his parents and not taking painkillers. Everyday life scares him.

The shrill electronic ring of her cell phone shattered the quiet of the house. She checked the caller ID and nearly laughed with relief to see her sister's cell number on the screen.

"It's Liz," she said to the men and turned away into the kitchen for a little privacy in order to tell her sister that her husband was wanted by the FBI for attempted murder.

BENNY HELD THE GUN to the woman's head while she dialed her cell phone. Her fingers trembled and she kept hitting the wrong numbers.

"Sorry," she whispered, over and over again. "Sorry."

Benny wasn't sure if she was talking to him or the sister she was about to betray.

"This isn't necessary," Dan said, watching his pretty wife cry. "We don't have to involve her. I can go back tonight and take care of this."

It was touching how much Benny's dirty cop was sweating over his wife, but it was useless.

Meisner had screwed up. It was his fault his

wife was here in this dirty rat-trap hotel along the highway. It was his fault that she was going to have to die with him.

He could see Meisner knew that, so he didn't belabor the point.

"Let her go," Meisner begged, tears welling in his eyes. "Please."

Jesus, Benny thought, *what is the deal with all the crying men in my life.*

Benny cocked his 9 mm and let that be answer enough for him.

"Shut up!" Miguel cried and lifted his own gun to smack the cop. Benny nearly rolled his eyes in exasperation. This situation was only more complicated by Miguel who was a tad overeager.

"Sit down, Miguel," he said in quiet tones.

"I…got…it," the woman stammered and held the cell phone to her ear. Benny leaned into her pretty face, streaked with mascara and red and swollen from her tears and the few necessary cuffs he'd given her across her smart mouth.

He stroked the gun along her smooth cheek.

She shook and wept.

"Be smart," he told her. "Get it together. If you let your sister know what's happening, I will let my brother beat your husband to death."

She choked on a sob and Meisner hung his head, rubbing his face with his hands.

Love, Benny thought, *this is what it comes to.*

He arched an eyebrow at Liz and she took a deep breath. "Hey, Mags," she said into the phone, her voice bright and casual despite the tears running down her face. "What's the emergency?"

Nice job, he thought, nodding at her. *She's as good an actress as Caleb Gomez. And soon to be just as dead.*

"Liz," Maggie said, relief and love a brick in her throat. "Are you okay?"

"I'm fine, except I have about thirty phone calls from you on my cell."

Maggie laughed and braced herself against the wall, her knees suddenly weak. "Sorry. Where are you?"

"I'm at Gwen's. We went to see a movie and now we're going to have some wine and pizza. What's going on?"

"Have you seen Dan?"

There was a pause.

"Liz?" Maggie asked, worry chewing at her. Was something wrong?

"Sorry, no. Dan…" She cleared her throat. "Dan took off earlier. It's why I'm with Gwen."

Maggie made a quick decision against telling her sister about Dan on the phone. This was the sort of thing a woman needed to hear face-to-face. "Liz, promise me you'll spend the night there tonight. And that if Dan calls you, you won't tell him where you are, but you'll call me right away."

"Okay. Where are you?"

Maggie pressed her head to the wall near the phone in the kitchen. "I'm finishing things up."

"Are you in L.A.?"

"No, I'm still in Summerland. We're really close to catching the guy that had Patrick killed. It's almost over. I think things will be done tonight."

"What are you doing? Are you in danger?"

She smiled. "Always. Look, there's something I need to tell you, but I don't want to do it now."

Again there was a long pause and Maggie lifted her head.

"When this is over?" Liz said, her voice thick with emotion. Maggie didn't blame her. Liz was smart. She knew her husband was into something bad. Had known all along and Maggie had been the person to talk her out of worry. She should have worried. They all should have.

"Yes," Maggie said. "When this is all over we've got some stuff to talk about."

"Oh…okay," Liz said and took a deep breath. "I love you, Mags," she said.

Maggie's eyes burned with sudden tears. Her sister was safe. She'd get a car outside Gwen's house and Liz would be protected. She wasn't going to die. Not like Patrick.

"I love you, too, Liz," Maggie said and waited until her sister disconnected before hanging up.

She walked into the living room where Gordon and Curtis were talking strategy.

"She's okay," Maggie said, answering their questioning expressions. "We need to put a car outside of the house she's at. But she's safe and she doesn't know anything."

"That's good," Gordon said, patting her shoulder awkwardly.

"What's the plan?" she asked Curtis.

"Well," he said, brushing the edges of his coat from his hips. "The man is right, this will be fast and if he knows the risks, I say we finish it. Right now. We get Dan or whoever Delgado sends and maybe he'll roll on Delgado."

"What if he doesn't?" Gordon asked.

"I'm staying." Maggie said. "I'll wait it out with Gomez and maybe he'll give me those files."

Gordon smirked. "Looks to me all that dude wants to give you is a punch in the face."

Curtis smiled. "The cost of doing your job right."

She nodded and chewed her tongue, distracting herself with that ache so she wouldn't howl from the pain in her chest.

"What if no one comes tonight?" Gordon asked. "He's got to know the cops have been brought in."

"It hasn't stopped Delgado before," Maggie said. "Nothing stops this guy."

They were all silent, counting the bodies they'd taken to the morgue because Delgado was smart and insane and nothing scared him. Not cops. Not agents. Nothing.

"All right, we got men on the perimeter so he shouldn't get past us, but be smart anyway," Curtis said. "Keep yourself sharp."

She nodded. Wearing her gun and her badge gave her a sense of strength. She felt armored in some way and she knew, once Curtis and Gordon left, she'd need that armor. Because Caleb would come out swinging.

CHAPTER FOURTEEN

CALEB TOOK THE LAST PAGE from his printer and then ejected the CD he'd burned all of his Delgado files onto. He slipped it into a plastic CD case and tossed it into the green box with the original tapes and notebooks. He stapled the printouts together and laid them down on top of the CD.

There, he thought with grim satisfaction, *that's everything she used me for.*

He wished he could keep it simple and believe that he was handing his files to Maggie to get her out of his life, to prove his moral superiority. But that would have been untrue.

Giving her the files was the right thing to do.

He wasn't unfamiliar with the right thing to do—he was simply used to doing it at his discretion. Not having his hand forced by his lying cleaning woman-government agent-lover.

He expected to be lit up, on fire with his injured civil rights, his sense of injustice and betrayal.

But he wasn't. He was hollow. Empty.

He rubbed a hand over his face and counted his losses: no Delgado story, front page, top of the fold; no shot at a second Pulitzer, no more storm of ego or the desire to get the story out.

No Margaret Warren—only an impostor using him for information.

He sighed and sat back in his chair. The curtains were drawn at his back, blocking out the night and keeping what little light emanated from his monitor from leaking out into the darkness, giving Delgado, or whatever madman he sent, a better chance to put a bullet in his brain.

"Not a good night, old man." *And it started so well.*

He knew the house was empty but for the two of them. He could almost smell her through the walls, in the draft that slipped under the door.

He could feel her, like a beating heart in the other room.

He'd been wrong. He wasn't empty. He was filled, choking on his feelings for her. Anger, disbelief and a sadness he couldn't believe swirled through him like winds gathering for a storm.

The bottle of pills on the corner of his desk beckoned. A little oblivion, a little sweet who-the-hell-cares-that-she-used-me-like-toilet-paper.

Not a great idea considering there were lunatics outside his house aiming guns at him.

Without even thinking about it, he swept the pills into the garbage can.

No more pills. Ever.

The fog of painlessness had allowed him to be stupid about her. Perhaps if he'd been sober the whole time, all of his faculties intact, he'd have been able to see her coming.

I was falling in love and she was playing me for a fool. He sat in his dark office and replayed the week. Every second. Her first kiss. That moment in the hallway when he'd come out of the shower, she'd probably just left his office. And then later when she scrubbed at the bottom of the…

His eyes flew open.

My damn house is bugged.

Of course, that's why she'd scrubbed the underside of the table and that's why she wanted to make love in the living room.

He grabbed the box and lurched around the desk. He threw open the office door and stormed into the living room where she paced, cracking her knuckles in the dim light from the kitchen. The rest of the room was dark.

Intimate.

I had her on the floor, he thought crudely, trying

to stem the tide of emotion that swept through him at the sight of her.

"Here's your prize," he said and dumped the box carelessly on the floor. Neither of them jumped at the clatter it made. "All you need to put Delgado away."

She looked at the box then at him.

"Go on," he urged. "It's all there. I even printed out my notes on the story. Should help your case."

"Caleb, if we had thought you'd hand over the files we never would have done this." She was subdued, apologetic. Sad. And he hated that.

"Don't hide behind the FBI, Maggie...it is Maggie, isn't it?"

She nodded and he continued his attack, wanting to hurt her the way he'd been hurt. "*You* did this. *You* lied to me. *You* came into my home and used me. You."

"I had to, Caleb," she said, her voice strong, but her eyes melancholy. "My brother—"

"Right, the dead cop. Vengeance is as good a motive as any, Maggie. I just don't care." He balled up her reasons, all the noble and fine rationalizations she had for treating him the way she had and threw them in her face.

"But, you're right. I wouldn't have given you

the files before. I am now. I didn't lie when I said I was a different man. I never lied."

He watched the anger gather in her face and he liked that better. The hurt he'd seen there earlier mirrored his own too much, called for softer emotions like forgiveness.

I will never forgive her. Ever.

"You don't lie now, but you have. You're not that different than me, Caleb," she snapped. "Remember? You said it yourself, you love that moment when the subject lets down his guard and tells you his secrets."

He stepped in close, the old Caleb back in charge of his new body. "Did you enjoy it, Maggie?" he asked, his double entendre both enticing and insulting. Crazy, but he wanted her again. Maybe more now that he knew she wasn't mild-mannered Margaret.

"Did you like it when I let my guard down?" His voice was a purr and he watched her fight it, fight him.

"No," she finally said. Her skin taut and flushed against the fine bones of her face. "I hated it. I hated lying to you."

He shook his head, his lips curled with distaste, for her, for him, for the whole damn situation. "I don't believe you, Agent Fitzgerald."

"It's true, Caleb," she cried. "I swear, once I—" She stepped forward again, reached out a hand as if to touch him and he stepped back, stopping her. He put up his own hand telling her in no uncertain terms that she would not be touching him again. Ever.

"Come on, Caleb," she said and ignored him, pushing closer to him, tempting him and tormenting him all at once. "You love to fight. So—" she shrugged, threw out her hands "—let's fight. Let's have it out."

"There's nothing to fight about," he said. "Not anymore."

"Of course there is. Do you want to pretend that we didn't have sex? That you didn't tell me—"

"Yes!" he hissed, stopping her before she threw his foolish words, his sentimental longings back in his face. His anger, no longer manageable, boiled over and spewed like black tar. "Yes, I want to pretend like I never touched you. Like I never knew you. That you don't exist."

He watched her digest his hate, the color fading from her face.

"Caleb." She practically moaned his name. "Please, it wasn't all—"

He knew what she was going to say—that it wasn't all lies. That she'd meant what she said on that point overlooking the ocean. That when she'd touched him it hadn't been for the FBI. It had been for her. That she'd told the truth when she said she liked him. And he, stupidly, would want to believe her.

So, he couldn't let those words be uttered. He couldn't give himself that temptation.

"You bugged my house, right? Surveillance mics? Cameras?" he asked. She was silent, her face so composed, her eyes so pleading. "Where are they?" he asked, cold as ice.

She didn't say anything, as though she was waiting for him to see reason. To see her side. To understand that what had happened between them couldn't have been faked.

"Tell me!" he yelled.

She sucked in a deep breath. "Okay," she said, her tone brittle. The woman he'd known this past week, the woman he'd made love to disappearing, obliterated by the icy control of Agent Fitzgerald.

She walked to the kitchen. "There was one in the kitchen phone so we could listen to you order pizza. Oh." She turned. "Call your parents. They're worried about you."

"When did you talk to my parents?"

"The night after the therapist was here. You were in a drug coma on the couch so I talked to your father."

His chest hurt, all the emotions tumbling through him were jagged and sharp.

"What did you say to him?"

She shrugged. "Not much. That you were eating. Taking too many pills. That you don't leave the house."

Everything. She'd told his father everything. Every secret he tried to spare his parents in the hopes they wouldn't worry, that they would believe him when he said he was fine.

"Was there anything you didn't touch?" He bit the words out. "Any part of my life you didn't get dirty?"

"No, Caleb," she said. "I'm very good at my job. I got into everything."

The air between them seethed with all that they repressed. Emotion, barely contained, crackled around them like Fourth of July sparklers.

"The phone line itself was tapped so we heard your conversation with your editor. Too bad you don't have the guts to go down there and have lunch with him," she sneered.

She tore the receiver off the wall, popped the cap off the mouthpiece and pulled out a small black electronic. He stared at it in her palm, until suddenly she smashed the bug against the wall.

The violence was startling.

"We also heard you call Lita Delgado." Her eyes were hard. Her body tense. "A stupid move."

Well, he couldn't argue with that.

She whirled past him. "There was one here," she said, pointing to the end table by the couch. "But I removed it the morning after I kissed you, because I was scared that you were going to say something about the kiss and I would lose my job. Which—" bitterness coated her laugh "—is hardly something I need to worry about now."

She turned toward the hallway and he went after her, his hip feeling stronger, better than it had in a long time. He barely limped. Anger seemed to heal him.

"Why?" he asked. "Did you lose your job anyway? For sleeping with me? I'd imagine that's a no-no."

She stopped and spun and he brought himself up short, but still they stood too close.

"No," she said, quietly. "I quit my job. Life's too short to not do exactly what you want," she repeated his words. Her eyes fell to his lips and his blood churned hot and needy in his body.

"What are you saying?" he asked. His hands tingled with the desire to stroke her again, to hold her open, to touch every part of her.

"I quit to go to law school. I want to be an eagle-eyed, no-nonsense prosecutor."

"Well, I'm glad I could give you some career direction."

"No." She shook her head. "I've always wanted to be a lawyer. I'd been accepted into law school but deferred enrollment when my brother was killed. I'm very good at my job," she said and he could attest to that—the most suspicious journalist on the planet had never suspected a thing. "But you saw right through me. To the secrets I'd kept from my parents, my boss. Just about everyone."

"You think that proves something?" he asked.

She lifted one shoulder, her Mona Lisa smile enigmatic and beguiling. "You tell me."

He leaned in close. "It proves nothing."

Their eyes clung, the temperature in the hallway escalated until she turned toward the bedroom. "There is one in here. On the bedside table." She grabbed a Leatherman tool from the holder on her belt and scraped off the bug. "I saw your dirty magazine, Caleb. And I copied all the files on your iPod. So, you're right. There's nothing of yours I didn't touch."

And again, she mashed the surveillance equipment on the wall. The violence was exciting. He wanted to smash something, too. "The dog licked this one off one morning. I tell you that threw me into a tailspin."

"What morning?"

"The day of the fire in the oven."

"Was that real?"

"Nope." She faced him. The room was pitch black but for the diluted light from the front room. She was all shadows, her hair and body in darkness, her profile illuminated like a pearl. "That wasn't real. My marriage, my son, all fake."

"Your father?"

Stop it! he warned himself. *Just stop it. It doesn't matter. You don't care.*

But he did. And it did matter, more than he'd like.

"Real. I told him last night that I quit the Bureau and I'm sure he's still angry with me."

"The family you put first?" he asked.

"Real. Delgado killed my brother, I'm sure of it. And I've put my life on hold. I've…denied my life so I can get revenge."

He knew what she implied, but forced his heart to be uncaring. "You don't have to lie," he said. "I've given you what you want. The box is yours. I'll testify, I'll do whatever."

"You're right. I don't have to lie," she whispered, stepping closer again. "So why would I? Caleb—"

"I suppose you have a file on me?"

She nodded again.

"Photos?"

"Before and after the accident."

He laughed. "Too bad you were assigned to me after Iraq, huh?"

She shook her head. "I like you now. How you are now."

He would *not* believe her.

"My stories?"

"I read them all."

"Well, I'm glad they made a greatest hits—"

"I read them when they were published. I've admired your work for years."

"Flattery will get you nowhere." He scowled and she laughed.

"You've got to be kidding me," she said. "Flattery got me into your pants."

"The debrief? From the hospital?"

"I read it."

He swallowed, he'd told Sergeant Drury everything. Every horror. Things he'd never told the press. And she knew them all. He felt scourged all over again.

"You had no right," he said, his eyes blazing. He meant all of it. Reading his file, being in his home, making him feel things for her that he didn't want to feel anymore.

"I know," she whispered as he walked out of the room.

SPEECHLESS, she watched him leave. Fighting with her must make him forget his other pain because he barely limped.

But even as she knew the futility of what she wanted she felt compelled to make him understand. She could see in him the desire to believe her, the desire for her, and that had to mean something.

"Caleb," she said, following him into the hallway. He was about to close his office door and lock her out, but she got in the way of the door shutting.

At the expression in his eyes she wondered if maybe things weren't so futile.

She put her hand on the door, close enough to his to feel the heat between them.

"Maggie." He sighed, sadness overshadowing anger. "Nothing you say can change what's happened. You lied to me. You used me to get information."

"I know, but—"

He shook his head and Maggie felt hope plummet. "There are no buts. I don't trust you. I don't know you. I—I don't want to know you."

She stumbled out of the doorway. Pain bloomed in her chest, making her limbs heavy, her heart sore.

She turned away, forcing hope and worry and sadness aside. There was nothing left for her here now but to finish the job. Finish the job and move on.

Caleb, it seemed, already had.

Maggie sat on the floor next to the box of Delgado evidence. She put her back to the couch, flipped the top off and dug in to all that she'd been seeking for six months.

THE WOMAN FAINTED at the first sign of blood. Well, Delgado amended, wiping the bloodied knife on the dead cop's uniform, she *puked* at the first sign of blood.

When he slit the neck of the first cop, she'd lost her dinner all over Miguel, which had caused a bit of an incident, but Benny managed to calm Miguel down before he beat the woman to death.

Liz, that was her name. Liz Meisner.

Granted, slit throats were gruesome, but they were the only way to get the job done and ensure there would be no cries for help.

These beat cops had been watching for him. Liz's sister had all but told him that with her unguarded conversation. Things wouldn't be *done tonight* unless they were setting a trap for him.

But he knew his way around traps. They'd been

walking for miles, came over the mountain instead of up from the ocean. So, they'd avoided any cops stationed on the streets. And he never used a gun. That was like trying to kill someone with a marching band.

"Is this necessary?" Dan asked, his face was white, his hands, tied in front of him, fisted with rage. But he was a pretty cowed puppy since his wife kept taking the beatings.

"Yes" was all Benny said and he put his knife back in the small of Dan's back. His shirt bled red from where Benny had nicked him, sliced him a little when he got jumpy.

They stepped onto the trail and down into the ravine, on their way to Gomez. He could see the dark outline of the house, but no light from inside. No sniper could pick Gomez off.

But Delgado wasn't interested in long-range killing. He wanted to look into Gomez's eyes, the way he had the two beat cops.

He'd forgotten how much he liked the dirty work.

The blood on his hands smelled like copper, like fresh money, sex and power. He'd gotten too important to put steel blade to vulnerable flesh. That was too bad; killing felt good.

He could see the bloodlust in Miguel's eyes as

he dragged the woman with him and Benny didn't know whether to be sickened or proud.

Miguel was doing a good job with the woman—a little too ready to smack the daylights out of her—but, so far, he'd managed to keep himself under control.

Benny figured the FBI agent wouldn't get trigger happy with her sister in the room. Dan was expendable once he finished being a good decoy.

They made their way single file through the brush. Dan led the way. When the ugly mutt, chained in the backyard, caught sight of them, Benny leaned into Dan. "Make a noise and I'll kill your wife." He shoved Dan toward the beast.

The dog did its job, snarling and fighting like a good soldier.

The dog barked like mad before sinking his teeth deep into Dan's left thigh. Dan bit his lips against the scream and the dog only whimpered when Benny smashed the butt of his knife against the canine's head.

CHAPTER FIFTEEN

BEAR BARKED, then it was silent. Really silent. Scary silent.

Caleb pulled open the bottom drawer of his desk and took out the little pug-nosed revolver he'd kept around since starting his life undercover. The *Los Angles Times* had even paid for the marksmanship lessons.

At the time, he'd laughed about it. Called it his company life insurance policy. But he was very very glad to have this gun now.

He checked to make sure it was loaded and then tucked it into the back of his jeans before going out to the living room to see what Maggie was doing about the creepy silence.

He found her on her feet, weapon drawn, body tense and alert, looking every inch an Amazon warrior.

"Attention, all units," she whispered into her walkie-talkie. "Look alive out there."

"You heard Bear?" he asked and she nodded, putting her finger to her lips as she crept toward the narrow slit of night visible between the plywood and the empty frame of the sliding glass door.

The knock on the door was cannon fire in the tense silence. He jumped, but not Maggie. Maggie was as cold as ice.

"Who's there?" she asked, her gun, cocked and ready in her hand.

Silence.

Another knock.

She looked back at him, her eyes unreadable. "Get out of sight," she mouthed and waved him to a safer place behind the couch, out of the line of sight from the door.

He wasn't stupid. He wasn't FBI or a police officer trained for these situations. He was a journalist who wanted to get out with the story.

So he moved but he didn't get down.

He'd had enough of hiding.

She shot him a deadly look but he ignored it. If they got out of this, she could be pissed. Until then, he wasn't moving.

"Who is it?" she called out. She put her hand to the doorknob and he saw all the muscles in her arm tense, ready to rip the door open.

"Ma-Mags?" The voice from the other side of the door was subdued. At the sound of it Maggie's face went white then red. Her hands spasmed on her gun.

"Careful, Maggie," he said, able to see that something had shifted in her. Agent Fitzgerald had left the building and Maggie—his Maggie—was standing there, wounded in some deep way. "Don't—"

But she was in motion and she threw open the door to a nightmare.

Liz! Maggie's heart cried as her sister was shoved into the room in front of a man who looked like a rabid version of Benny Delgado. She trained her weapon on Delgado and ignored the presence of her sister.

A hostage, she told herself, keeping her heart rate low, her mind clear. *Like any other.*

But she could feel the explosive element in the room get infinitely less predictable.

Maintain until backup arrives. Maintain. Don't be stupid.

Dan followed Benny and Liz, bent over his co-piously bleeding leg. Finally a young, handsome Hispanic man with a gun pulled shut the door behind him.

She immediately recognized him from surveillance photos as Miguel Delgado, Benny's younger brother.

"Miguel, keep an eye outside," Benny said, his eyes trained on Maggie. "Shoot anything that moves."

Miguel broke the glass of the small window in the door and peered out into the night.

"Put down your weapon," Benny said to Maggie, his voice so quiet she had to strain to hear it. It was a sick contradiction, his calm voice and his rabid appearance. Chills clawed at her back.

They were locked in a standoff. She had her gun pointed at his head and he had a knife to Liz's throat.

"Not a chance, Benny," she said, her voice cold steel.

She spared a quick glance for her sister who was in a very bad way. Her eye was swollen shut, her lip split, blood ran down her face from a cut at her hairline. Her skin looked like raw meat.

"Let her go," she said and Benny laughed.

The stakes in the room skyrocketed.

Benny tightened his fist in Liz's hair, the tip of the knife bit into the tender skin behind her ear and she whimpered. "Please, Mags…"

"Delgado, I am an FBI Agent," Maggie said, keeping her weapon aimed at Benny. "This house is surrounded…"

"By dead cops," Benny said. "And an unconscious dog."

"There are dozens of agents out there, Delgado."

"And none of them saw us coming. Please, Agent Fitzgerald, put down your weapon. I would hate to kill your sister because you can't follow instructions."

Maggie could still take him, it wasn't a great shot but it was a good one.

She blinked hard. If it were any other hostage she would have pulled the trigger without a problem, which is why Benny had brought Liz.

He was smart.

From the corner of her eye she saw Caleb step forward, like some kind of misguided hero.

Too much at stake. Too many lives at risk.

She put down the gun. Benny smiled and she immediately slid right two feet and got between Benny and Caleb. Not that she thought he wouldn't shoot her to get to Caleb, but she felt better knowing Benny would have to go through her to get to him.

I can still keep them all safe, she told herself, trying to figure out the angles. Benny she could incapacitate, but Miguel with the gun and jumpy eyes was an unknown factor.

"*Hola, amigo,*" Benny said to Caleb.

"Benny." Caleb nodded once. "You sure have changed."

"And you, *amigo*. Not for the better, may I say."

Dan fell against the wall, his hands bound in front of him, his face ashen. His lips blue. "Benny," he pleaded. "I need…help. A bandage."

"Please," Liz said, her voice a rough whimper. Her eyes trained on Maggie. "Help him."

"Delgado," Maggie said, reluctant to give Dan anything, willing to let him bleed to death on the floor for what he'd done. But Liz looked like a woman about to lose grip on reality and Maggie would do anything to prevent that. "Let me get—"

"He's fine," Delgado said. "Dirty cops are expendable." His smile was a razor. "You should know that firsthand, Agent Fitzgerald. Your brother wasn't—"

"Patrick was clean, Maggie. He was always clean. I set him up." Dan gasped, blood seeping from between his fingers to fall to the floor.

Maggie didn't look directly at Dan, kept her eyes fixed on Benny. If she looked at Dan—her brother-in-law, Patrick's best friend—she'd kill him herself.

"It seems the good detective's wife was used to the finer things," Benny cooed, stroking Liz's cheek with his knife. "The extra money came in handy."

Liz's eyes shut and she groaned, deep in her chest.

"None of this is your fault, Liz," Maggie said. "Don't listen to him."

"Liz," Dan gasped. "Baby, I'm so—"

There was no warning. No chance to change the course of events.

Delgado leaned backward, lowered the long lethal blade he held on Liz and jerked it across Dan's neck.

Blood gurgled from the wound. Words, too quiet to hear, trembled from his lips and Liz sagged in Delgado's arms. Her eyes shut tightly against the horrors, her mouth open in a silent scream.

Blood spread across the floor in an ever-widening pool and Liz fainted dead away. At the door Miguel got jumpier, shifting his weight from foot to foot, unable to keep his eyes off Dan's corpse.

"Now," Benny said, "I have business with Gomez."

"No," Maggie said swallowing bile and shock. Things were escalating at a deadly pace. She'd have to get to Benny and take her chances with Miguel. "This is between us."

BENNY'S BLACK EYES shifted back to Maggie and every muscle in Caleb's body went berserk with the need to pull her behind him. To save her in some way. But the only way to do that was to get Benny out of the house before he killed everyone.

And the only way to do that was to go with the monster.

His gut said it would be worth it if Maggie lived. If she got her chance at law school, at changing the world.

"Your heroics are wasted on a lying bastard, Agent Fitzgerald," Benny said. "You should step out of the way."

"Not on your life, Delgado."

"Get out of the way, bitch!" Miguel shouted.

"Maggie," Caleb said and her back went ramrod straight. "It's okay. Get out of the way."

"No."

"Maggie," he breathed. "Please, for your sister, get out of the way."

Years seemed to pass, he could feel himself aging, dying inside while waiting for her to be smart. He didn't think she would listen to him, but finally she moved aside.

Her eyes, trained on that knife at her sister's neck, flickered to his and he winked at her. Hidden by the couch he showed her the gun in his hand.

It's okay, he tried to convey to her. *This is okay.*

Maggie showed no reaction, but he could tell

something in her relaxed slightly. Tension dissipated.

She trusted him. They were in this together.

"You inspire great loyalty in women, Caleb," Benny said. "I nearly had to kill Lita for bringing you into our lives. Do you know how that felt? To hurt my sister because of you?"

"I didn't make you do anything, Benny."

Staring into Benny's eyes burned away the mess of pride and lies and ego. Caleb knew that what Maggie had said to him—about her feelings, about how not everything was false—had been real. He could sense her feelings for him rolling off her in waves.

"Let the women go," Caleb insisted.

"That, I'm afraid, is impossible. I will need them to get out of here." Benny smiled and it was more terrifying than the violence had been. All the madness Caleb had suspected lurked deep in Benny's brain had wormed its way to the surface.

"If you let them go, I'll go anywhere with you. I've got a motorcycle in the garage. We could outrun all the cops."

Benny seemed to consider the suggestion; Caleb's hope that Maggie and her sister would get out of this alive surged.

"That is very appealing," Benny said. "Perhaps I could pick up where the Iraqis left off."

Caleb swallowed. "Then let's go. I'll let you know how you rank."

"But, *jefe?*" Miguel asked, a muscle at his mouth twitching. "What about me?"

"What about you?" Benny snapped. "Isn't this what you want? To murder people? To be a gangster? An *hombre?*"

"Yes, but—"

Maggie shifted, drawing one arm behind her back, while Benny was locked in some brotherly dispute.

But he saw her from the corner of his eye. He dug the blade into Liz's throat and Maggie turned to stone, her arms at her side.

"Don't move," he cried, spittle showering Liz. "My brother will kill you. And then your sister will have no protection."

Miguel cocked his gun and pressed the barrel to Maggie's head, bloodlust in his eyes. "I'll kill you, bitch. I'll kill you if you even look at me."

"Enough of this talk." Benny shook his head. "I need to know about the story. Your story on me."

"There's no story," Caleb said. "I've got nothing on you. I never did."

"No more lies," Benny screamed, jerking Liz

and she cried out in sudden pain. "No more games! I want the story!"

Caleb clenched the gun in his hand, hidden by the couch.

Time was running out.

"I trusted you," Benny cried. "I let you into my home. I thought you were a friend."

Caleb said nothing, watching as Delgado dropped Liz's hair, but kept his knife at her throat. She weaved, unsteady on her feet.

"*Jefe!*" Miguel was distracted. His eyes focused out the window. "I think I heard something."

Benny ignored him. Adrenaline flooded Caleb's body and he waited for the right moment. He hoped that whatever mysterious connection that held he and Maggie together wouldn't fail them now.

"*Jefe?*" Miguel insisted, his gun dropping from Maggie's temple.

"I can't have you ruin everything. My family counts on me. They need me to provide for them." Benny reached into the back of his black jeans and Liz pitched forward. Maggie lunged, pushing her sister to the floor and dove to cover her.

Caleb lifted the gun and before Benny could clear his weapon Caleb fired. The first shot hit Benny in the arm and spun him sideways. The knife clattered to the floor.

Benny's eyes were incredulous. Angry. Miguel's mouth hung open, his gun at his side in surprise.

"Stop, Benny," Caleb said. "I don't want to kill you."

Benny smiled, lifted his own gun. "You're going to have to."

The room exploded and something hot sliced open Caleb's arm, but his aim stayed true and his second shot laid Benny out against the wall. Benny dropped the gun, lifted his hands to his chest as if to stop the blood that poured out too fast.

"*Jefe!*"

"Caleb!" Maggie cried and Caleb turned to look at her, but caught Miguel out of the corner of his eye.

"Don't," he cried, but it was too late. The barrel of the gun Miguel had trained on Caleb blazed white and he couldn't duck or save himself in any way.

But Maggie tackled him, forcing him to the floor. He landed hard, brought his gun up and put two right in Miguel's heart.

The silence was deafening. It hurt, it was so quiet. But Maggie's weight, warm and solid against him, felt good.

"Maggie," he breathed, against her hair. "We did it."

She didn't move.

His body went still. He couldn't feel her breathe.

The front door burst open and a stream of men entered, weapons drawn shouting things at him and Liz that might as well have been Greek for all he could understand.

There was a swarm around him. A swarm in his head. His chest.

"Maggie," he whispered into her hair, a desperate disbelief clawing up his throat, through his brain.

No! No, it can't be. It can't.

"Maggie."

Shaking, he rolled sideways, gently lowering her to the floor. Across her chest gaped a black wound, a hole from which a crimson flood flowed.

CHAPTER SIXTEEN

THE PARAMEDICS WERE FAST. She was in his arms and then gone before he knew what had happened. The scream of the ambulance siren burned through the night.

"Protect her," he prayed through dry cracked lips. "Take care of her."

His eyes burned. His hands ached from the force with which he had clenched them, the force with which he had clenched Maggie's body to his chest. They'd had to pry her from him.

The other bodies were taken away. Liz had been given a heavy sedative of some kind and they'd offered the same to him, but he waved them away.

"No," he said. "No drugs."

"We need to take you to the hospital," the medic who treated him earlier said. "We need to check you out."

"I'm fine," Caleb mumbled, his eyes trained to the door where he'd last seen the bright flag of her hair, splayed out across the white cover of the stretcher.

Maggie, his body sighed.

Caleb let the guy check his pulse and his pupils. He bandaged his arm in white gauze.

"Dizzy? Sick to your stomach?"

Yes, he wanted to say. *Yes. Yes. Yes.* But instead, knowing what the guy was asking, he trained his eyes on him.

"I know the limitations of my body. I know what shock feels like." *I know what having my fingernails pulled out feels like, I know what it means to be branded and now I know what it feels like to have my heart torn from my body and taken away on a stretcher.*

He watched the medic's eyes drop to the scars across his neck and chin. "Trust me," he said, belying the horrific sight of himself. "I'm fine."

The medic looked skeptical but there was little he could do to force Caleb to go to a hospital.

He watched Gordon, Maggie's partner, approach. "You did a good job here," he said. "We didn't know you knew guns."

"Believe it or not, she didn't find out everything," Caleb said. And he regretted every minute of the last week that he hadn't spent with her.

He'd have traded all his ghosts and skeletons

willingly for ten more minutes in her bright-eyed company.

The activity around them slowed until all that remained were a few uniformed officers and blood. Everywhere.

"It's straightforward," one of the police officers said. "The evidence backs up Gomez's statement."

As if I could lie about what happened here, he thought incredulously.

Gordon nodded. "Let's clean this up and get out of here, then."

Caleb flexed his hands and watched the dried blood crack and flake from his fingertips.

"She's tough," Gordon said. "If anyone could survive that chest wound, it's her."

Caleb nodded, but his gut—his world-renowned gut that had been witness to far too much carnage and death in this world—disagreed.

"Can we take you someplace?" Gordon asked. "I mean you probably don't want to stay here."

"Where's my dog?" Caleb asked.

"Sleeping. The doc checked him, he'll be fine."

Caleb could only nod, emotion for the dog thick in his throat.

"But," Gordon said, "perhaps if you have friends nearby and—"

"Where will they take Agent—" He stopped. Who the hell was he kidding? "Maggie."

"Mount Sinai."

He nodded and finally stood, his leg sore and trembling under his weight. "Thank you, I'd like a ride there."

"There's nothing you can do for her tonight. She's in surgery. Probably will be for hours," Gordon said. Caleb trained his burning eyes on the man who clearly had no idea that Maggie was dying and Caleb needed to be there, with her.

"Would you like to shower? Change?" Gordon asked after a moment.

"No. I'd like to go now."

THERE WAS PAIN and then there wasn't. She was floating and then she was deep under water. For a while there were voices.

Her father.

Her mother.

She heard Patrick laughing.

And then there was nothing.

SOMETHING BEEPED. Something else burned in her veins. Pain exploded through her chest.

"Nurse!" her father cried.

And then there was nothing.

SOMEONE WAS CRYING. Her hand hurt. Something big sat on her chest.

"Mags…"

Her sister? Her sister sat on her chest? Crying? That was weird.

"Liz?" The hoarse whisper ravaged her throat.

"Mags! Mags! Can you hear me? Can you open your eyes?"

Her eyes were open, right? It was just night-time. Middle of the night. "Get off my chest, Liz."

People were laughing.

God, she was tired.

"Thirsty," she managed to croak and then there was nothing.

"SHE'S GOING TO PULL THROUGH," her mother said. "You can go home. Get a change of clothes."

"I'm okay, the scrubs are fine." A voice…Caleb. Caleb! Maggie was so far under water. She tried to push her way to the surface. She tried to force her eyes to open, though they weighed a million pounds. Everything weighed a million pounds— air, the sheets against her body.

But suddenly her eyes were open and there was Caleb.

He pitched himself forward in his chair.

"Hi," he said, his face alight with emotion and she felt an answering emotion flood her body.

The memory of what happened filtered through the haze and she tried to smile.

"You're a good shot," she managed to croak.

"You're a good tackle," Caleb whispered, his red-rimmed eyes the most beautiful thing she'd ever seen. "We're a good team."

Oh. That was a nice thing to say.

"Liz?" she whispered.

"She's okay. Or will be okay. She's pretty rattled."

"Benny—"

"Dead. Miguel and Dan, too." He squeezed her hand.

Sadness lanced through her. She hurt. She was sad. And she wanted him next to her. This man she barely knew.

As if he'd read her mind, which after the events in the house she wouldn't doubt, he leaned forward, through tubes and wires and all the questions they had for each other, and pressed his damaged lips to hers.

Her eyes fluttered and the world swam. "Go to sleep," he whispered against her skin. "I'll be right here when you wake up."

"Get in bed with me," she sighed.

Caleb looked startled and then embarrassed, his eyes flicking to the foot of her bed.

"I don't think that's a good idea, sweetie," her mom said. Maggie tried to roll her head, but the darkness was coming back, a giant wave of nothing welled up in her and she wanted to turn and embrace it.

"It's okay," her dad said. "I'll help you, Caleb."

The bed dipped and Caleb was warm and solid and right there next to her.

Then there was nothing.

THE SMELL OF FOOD was a powerful incentive to open her eyes. The weight was gone from her chest and her eyelids. Instead her whole body ached with a dull throb. Thirst was an uncontrollable burn in her throat.

Sunlight flooded the room. The smell of bacon and eggs wafted from the tray by her table.

Bacon and eggs that were already half-eaten.

She turned her head and found the culprit sipping from a plastic container of orange juice at the window.

Her orange juice.

He was here. Had always been here, from the looks of him—scruff covered his cheeks and his hair looked like something was living in it. She remembered him in bed with her at one point. She remembered the solid warm weight of his hand on hers.

Hope, foolish and unstoppable, rained down on her. Hope that he understood, that he'd forgiven her for her lies. Hope that they could move on from this, together.

Because she didn't know what she'd do if he was here out of guilt and gratitude.

"Stealing a sick woman's breakfast? You should be ashamed," she said in a weak whisper.

He jerked away from the window.

"Save some of that juice for me."

He stepped over to her tray, slid a straw into the juice and held it so she could drink from it.

Her eyes burned with sudden tears. *Please don't be here out of guilt. Don't look at me with gratitude.*

"How are you feeling?" he asked, his voice a low rumble that settled in the deep parts of her belly, her chest and heart.

"Like I was shot in the chest," she said around the straw.

He humphed a little laugh and smiled.

"Where is my family?"

"They went home to shower and change."

She couldn't meet his eyes. She was too vulnerable. Too much in need of him. "How long—"

"Four days."

Courage. Maggie. Courage.

She lifted her eyes to his and what she saw there galvanized her. "How long have you been here?"

He nodded. "Four days."

She took a deep breath. This was the moment. "Why?"

He stroked her hair, the side of her face. "You saved my life, Maggie."

She pulled away, shut her eyes against the biting pain. But he cupped her chin and forced her to look at him. The beauty of him, the untouchable strength of him. His integrity, which was as much a part of him as the scars, was like a punch in the stomach.

"Caleb, don't—" she whispered. "It's okay. I was doing my job. You don't have to—"

"Shut up, Maggie." His voice was tender. "You saved my life when you walked in my house," he said, tilting her chin up. She was mortified that tears she couldn't control ran over his fingers.

"Benny—" She shut her eyes.

"It has nothing to do with Benny," he whispered and she stilled. "When you asked me what I was hiding from, when you made me dinner and looked at me with your level, no-bullshit eyes. When you forced me out of my house. When you made me embarrassed about the pain medication

I was taking. When you kissed me. When you touched me." He paused and she opened her eyes and met his, saw the truth of what he said, the truth of what he was—the man for her. "That's when you saved my life."

She smiled and the tears fell faster. "We barely know each other."

"I don't know." He laughed his wry man-of-the-world laugh. "Your mom's been giving me the *Cliff's Notes* version. We're up to your senior prom and we're both wondering what you saw in that Mike guy when you could have gone with that nice Palmer kid next door."

She laughed and then moaned when pain radiated through her chest. "Oh, don't do anything funny, it hurts."

He jumped up, concerned. "Do you need the doctor?"

She smiled. "No. I need you."

He sat back down, wrapped her hand in both of his and kissed her fingers. "I could get used to this."

As much as she wanted to relish these moments, there was a reality outside of this hospital room that she needed to deal with.

"My family—"

"Seems to like me." He shrugged. "Your mother has barely left my side."

"Yeah, she's the easy one. My dad—"

"Has not stopped crying since you came in. Are you trying to scare me off?"

"No, I'm just letting you know that I come with baggage."

He howled with laughter. "Right. And I'm just a former recluse kicking a drug habit with occasional unpleasant dreams about torture and fire. I'm a peach."

"I like you like that." She tried to be stern. "I'll tell you every day if you want me to. But it would just be easier if you'd believe me right now."

"Your family is right, you are like your father. He's the one who bullied the nurses into letting me stay here as long as I have."

To say she was shocked would hardly have covered it. She felt like her morphine had been bumped up.

"Okay." She nodded, pushing forward. "I'm going to law school. I quit my job."

"That's okay. I'm going back to work."

"Writing?"

He nodded. "I've got the Delgado story and… teaching."

She jerked back, startled.

"I'm going to take up a friend's offer and accept an adjunct position at the University of Califor-

nia, Santa Barbara. Give some students a thrill."
He winked at her and then was quiet. They sat
staring at each other, while the reality she was so
intent on reminding them of, changed, morphed
into the present. The here and now.

"How is this possible?" she whispered.

He shrugged, his eyes bright with hope and
love and a future.

"I don't know," he sighed, stroking her hair.
"But we've got years to figure it out."

EPILOGUE

Five years later

"Is this redundant?" Caleb asked his wife.

"What?" Maggie shifted in the small doorway so they could both comfortably stand at the threshold of the closet. "Naming all the dogs Bear?"

"Yeah." Caleb shrugged. The five pups all slept cheerfully in a heap next to the heaving belly of Girl Bear. Bear number one was curled around her, licking the top of her head.

"Well, it keeps things simple."

"I like simple."

Maggie—*my wife*, he never tired of that—smiled at him and backed out of the doorway. "We can worry about that later. We're going to be late."

He groaned and rolled his eyes, but followed her from the closet, where his second beloved dog had given birth on his favorite shoes.

He followed her into the living room. They'd had the glass replaced and the blood scoured from the walls and floors. They'd briefly discussed moving, but they loved this house on the hilltop. He'd fallen in love with an amazing woman, twice, in this house. His dogs had dug holes in the backyard. His favorite pizza place was on speed dial.

It had been a decent location right between his job at the University of California, Santa Barbara, and Pepperdine University, down in Malibu.

"Let's not go," he suggested, already hating the suit coat, but certainly appreciating his wife's legs in the high heels she wore more often since starting her internship in the attorney general's office. "Let's order pizza, instead."

"We can't. You are the guest of honor."

"Yeah, but—"

Maggie shot him one of her eagle-eyed looks and he resigned himself to his fate.

She strolled over to him, her eyes bright, her shoulders back. He could never get his head around the fact that she thought she was plain. Was she nuts?

She'd always been gorgeous, even as Margaret Warren. And now doing exactly what she wanted with her life certainly suited Maggie.

"Teacher of the year is a big deal, babe," she said, fixing his collar and stroking his shoulders. "They don't just give those things away. And your folks are meeting us there."

"What about your sister?" he asked, knowing

the depth of pain Maggie felt over Liz leaving California.

"She sends her congratulations but couldn't get a flight from South Carolina today." Her smile was brave but sad, so he kissed her.

"Okay," he finally said, "but we're only going if we take the bike."

"One step ahead of you. I gassed it up this morning."

He sighed. Had there ever been a better partnership? He doubted it. In fact, more and more he'd been thinking about expanding their little team of two.

"You know," he said, catching her hand as she turned away. He stroked her palm, the strong but fragile bones of her wrist. "I've been thinking." He inclined his head toward the closet door, where the young family slumbered on.

She smiled that amazing smile, like sun coming up over the desert, like a sunset over the ocean. "One step ahead of you, babe," she whispered and leaned in to kiss his gaping, astonished mouth.

* * * * *

Look for the next book by Molly O'Keefe
coming December 2007
from Harlequin Superromance.

Every Life Has More
Than One Chapter™

Award-winning author Stevi Mittman delivers another hysterical mystery, featuring Teddi Bayer, an irrepressible heroine, and her to-die-for hero, Detective Drew Scoones. After all, life on Long Island can be murder!

Turn the page for a sneak peek
at the warm and funny fourth book,
WHOSE NUMBER IS UP, ANYWAY?
in the Teddi Bayer series,
by STEVI MITTMAN.
On sale August 7

"Before redecorating a room, I always advise my clients to empty it of everything but one chair. Then I suggest they move that chair from place to place, sitting in it, until the placement feels right. Trust your instincts when deciding on furniture placement. Your room should 'feel right.'"

—TipsFromTeddi.com

Gut feelings. You know, that gnawing in the pit of your stomach that warns you that you are about to do the absolute stupidest thing you could do? Something that will ruin life as you know it?

I've got one now, standing at the butcher counter in King Kullen, the grocery store in the same strip mall as L.I. Lanes, the bowling alley cum billiard parlor I'm in the process of redecorating for its "Grand Opening."

I realize being in the wrong supermarket

probably doesn't sound exactly dire to you, but you aren't the one buying your father a brisket at a store your mother will somehow know isn't Waldbaum's.

And then, June Bayer isn't your mother.

The woman behind the counter has agreed to go into the freezer to find a brisket for me, since there aren't any in the case. There are packages of pork tenderloin, piles of spare ribs and rolls of sausage, but no briskets.

Warning Number Two, right? I should be so out of here.

But no, I'm still in the same spot when she comes back out, brisketless, her face ashen. She opens her mouth as if she is going to scream, but only a gurgle comes out.

And then she pinballs out from behind the counter, knocking bottles of Peter Luger Steak Sauce to the floor on her way, now hitting the tower of cans at the end of the prepared foods aisle and sending them sprawling, now making her way down the aisle, careening from side to side as she goes.

Finally, from a distance, I hear her shout, "He's deeeeeeaaaad! Joey's deeeeeeaaaad."

My first thought is *You should always trust your gut.*

My second thought is that now, somehow, my mother will know I was in King Kullen. For weeks I will have to hear "What did you expect?" as though whenever you go to King Kullen someone turns up dead. And if the detective investigating the case turns out to be Detective Drew Scoones… well, I'll never hear the end of that from her, either.

She still suspects I murdered the guy who was found dead on my doorstep last Halloween just to get Drew back into my life.

Several people head for the butcher's freezer and I position myself to block them. If there's one thing I've learned from finding people dead—and the guy on my doorstep wasn't the first one—it's that the police get very testy when you mess with their murder scenes.

"You can't go in there until the police get here," I say, stationing myself at the end of the butcher's counter and in front of the Employees Only door, acting as if I'm some sort of authority. "You'll contaminate the evidence if it turns out to be murder."

Shouts and chaos. You'd think I'd know better than to throw the word *murder* around. Cell phones are flipping open and tongues are wagging.

I amend my statement quickly. "Which, of course, it probably isn't. Murder, I mean. People die all the time, and it's not always in hospitals or their own beds, or…" I babble when I'm nervous, and the idea of someone dead on the other side of the freezer door makes me very nervous.

So does the idea of seeing Drew Scoones again. Drew and I have this on-again, off-again sort of thing…that I kind of turned off.

Who knew he'd take it so personally when he tried to get serious and I responded by saying we could talk about *us* tomorrow—and then caught a plane to my parents' condo in Boca the next day? In July. In the middle of a job.

For some crazy reason, he took that to mean that I was avoiding him and the subject of *us*.

That was three months ago. I haven't seen him since.

The manager, who identifies himself and points to his nameplate in case I don't believe him, says he has to go into *his cooler*. "Maybe Joey's not dead," he says. "Maybe he can be saved, and you're letting him die in there. Did you ever think of that?"

In fact, I hadn't. But I had thought that the murderer might try to go back in to make sure his tracks were covered, so I say that I will go in and check.

Which means that the manager and I couple up and go in together while everyone pushes against the doorway to peer in, erasing any chance of finding clean prints on that Employees Only door.

I expect to find carcasses of dead animals hanging from hooks, and maybe Joey hanging from one, too. I think it's going to be very creepy and I steel myself, only to find a rather benign series of shelves with large slabs of meat laid out carefully on them, along with boxes and boxes marked simply Chicken.

Nothing scary here, unless you count the body of a middle-aged man with graying hair sprawled faceup on the floor. His eyes are wide open and unblinking. His shirt is stiff. His pants are stiff. His body is stiff. And his expression, you should forgive the pun—is frozen. Bill-the-manager crosses himself and stands mute while I pronounce the guy dead in a sort of *happy now?* tone.

"We should not be in here," I say, and he nods his head emphatically and helps me push people out of the doorway just in time to hear the police sirens and see the cop cars pull up outside the big store windows.

Bobbie Lyons, my partner in Teddi Bayer Interior Designs (and also my neighbor, my best friend and my private fashion police), and Mark, our carpenter (and my dogsitter, confidant, and ego booster), rush in from next door. They beat the cops by a half step and shout out my name. People point in my direction.

After all the publicity that followed the unfortunate incident during which I shot my ex-husband, Rio Gallo, and then the subsequent murder of my first client—which I solved, I might add—it seems like the whole world, or at least all of Long Island, knows who I am.

Mark asks if I'm all right. (Did I remember to mention that the man is drop-dead-gorgeous-but-a-decade-too-young-for-me-yet-too-old-for-my-daughter-thank-God?) I don't get a chance to answer him because the police are quickly closing in on the store manager and me.

"The woman—" I begin telling the police. Then I have to pause for the manager to fill in her name, which he does: *Fran.*

I continue. "Right. Fran. Fran went into the freezer to get a brisket. A moment later she came out and screamed that Joey was dead. So I'd say she was the one who discovered the body."

"And you are…?" the cop asks me. It comes out a bit like who do I *think* I am, rather than who am I really?

"An innocent bystander," Bobbie, hair perfect, makeup just right, says, carefully placing her body between the cop and me.

"And she was just leaving," Mark adds. They each take one of my arms.

Fran comes into the inner circle surrounding the cops. In case it isn't obvious from the hairnet and bloodstained white apron with Fran embroidered on it, I explain that she was the butcher who was going for the brisket. Mark and Bobbie take that as a signal that I've done my job and they can now get me out of there. They twist around, with me in the middle, as if we're a Rockettes line, until we are facing away from the butcher counter. They've managed to propel me a few steps toward the exit when disaster—in the form of a Mazda RX7 pulling up at the loading curb—strikes.

Mark's grip on my arm tightens like a vise. "Too late," he says.

Bobbie's expletive is unprintable. "Maybe there's a back door," she suggests, but Mark is right. It's too late.

I've laid my eyes on Detective Scoones. And while my gut is trying to warn me that my heart shouldn't go there, regions farther south are melting at just the sight of him.

"Walk," Bobbie orders me.

And I try to. Really.

Walk, I tell my feet. *Just put one foot in front of the other.*

I can do this because I know, in my heart of hearts, that if Drew Scoones was still interested in me, he'd have gotten in touch with me after I returned from Boca. And he didn't.

Since he's a detective, Drew doesn't have to wear one of those dark blue Nassau County Police uniforms. Instead, he's got on jeans, a tight-fitting T-shirt and a tweedy sports jacket. If you think that sounds good, you should see him. Chiseled features, cleft chin, brown hair that's naturally a little sandy in the front, a smile that…well, that doesn't matter. He isn't smiling now.

He walks up to me, tucks his sunglasses into his breast pocket and looks me over from head to toe.

"Well, if it isn't Miss Cut and Run," he says. "Aren't you supposed to be somewhere in Florida or something?" He looks at Mark accusingly, as if he was covering for me when he told Drew I was gone.

"Detective Scoones?" one of the uniforms says. "The stiff's in the cooler and the woman who found him is over there." He jerks his head in Fran's direction.

Drew continues to stare at me.

You know how when you were young, your mother always told you to wear clean underwear in case you were in an accident? And how, a little farther on, she told you not to go out in hair rollers because you never knew who you might see—or who might see you? And how now your best friend says she wouldn't be caught dead without makeup and suggests you shouldn't either?

Okay, today, *finally,* in my overalls and Converse sneakers, I get it.

I brush my hair out of my eyes. "Well, I'm back," I say. As if he hasn't known my exact whereabouts. The man is a detective, for heaven's sake. "Been back awhile."

Bobbie has watched the exchange and apparently decided she's given Drew all the time he deserves. "And we've got work to do, so…" she says, grabbing my arm and giving Drew a little two-fingered wave goodbye.

As I back up a foot or two, the store manager sees his chance and places himself in front of Drew, trying to get his attention. Maybe what makes Drew such a good detective is his ability to focus.

Only what he's focusing on is me.

"Phone broken? Carrier pigeon died?" he asks me, taking in Fran, the manager, the meat counter and that Employees Only door, all without taking his eyes off me.

Mark tries to break the spell. "We've got work to do there, you've got work to do here, Scoones,"

Mark says to him, gesturing toward next door. "So it's back to the alley for us."

Drew's lip twitches. "You working the alley now?" he says.

"If you'd like to follow me," Bill-the-manager, clearly exasperated, says to Drew—who doesn't respond. It's as if waiting for my answer is all he has to do.

So, fine. "You knew I was back," I say.

The man has known my whereabouts every hour of the day for as long as I've known him. And my mother's not the only one who won't buy that he "just happened" to answer this particular call. In fact, I'm willing to bet my children's lunch money that he's taken every call within ten miles of my home since the day I got back.

And now he's gotten lucky.

"*You* could have called *me*," I say.

"You're the one who said *tomorrow* for our talk and then flew the coop, chickie," he says. "I figured the ball was in your court."

"Detective?" the uniform says. "There's something you ought to see in here."

Drew gives me a look that amounts to *in or out?*

He could be talking about the investigation, or about our relationship.

Bobbie tries to steer me away. Mark's fists are

balled. Drew waits me out, knowing I won't be able to resist what might be a murder investigation.

Finally he turns and heads for the cooler.

And, like a puppy dog, I follow.

Bobbie grabs the back of my shirt and pulls me to a halt.

"I'm just going to show him something," I say, yanking away.

"Yeah," Bobbie says, pointedly looking at the buttons on my blouse. The two at breast level have popped. "That's what I'm afraid of."

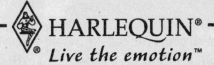

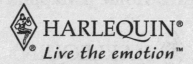

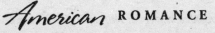
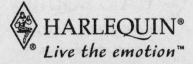

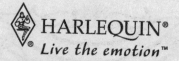

Harlequin® Historical
Historical Romantic Adventure!

Imagine a time of chivalrous knights and unconventional ladies, roguish rakes and impetuous heiresses, rugged cowboys and spirited frontierswomen— these rich and vivid tales will capture your imagination!

*Harlequin Historical...
they're too good to miss!*

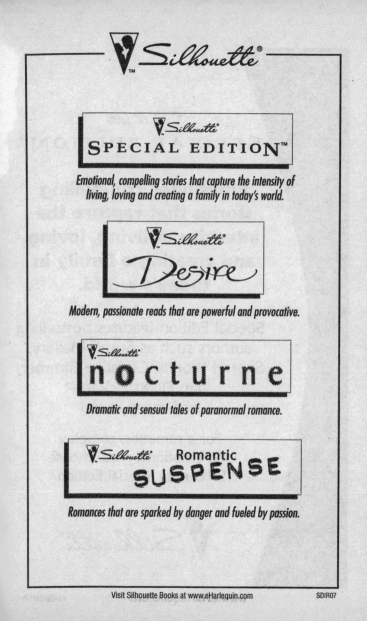

Silhouette®

Silhouette® SPECIAL EDITION™

Emotional, compelling stories that capture the intensity of living, loving and creating a family in today's world.

Silhouette® Desire

Modern, passionate reads that are powerful and provocative.

Silhouette® nocturne

Dramatic and sensual tales of paranormal romance.

Silhouette® Romantic SUSPENSE

Romances that are sparked by danger and fueled by passion.